SPECIAL MESSAGE TO READERS

This book is published under the auspices of

THE ULVERSCROFT FOUNDATION

(registered charity No. 264873 UK)

Established in 1972 to provide funds for research, diagnosis and treatment of eye diseases. Examples of contributions made are: —

A Children's Assessment Unit at Moorfield's Hospital, London.

•

Twin operating theatres at the Western Ophthalmic Hospital, London.

•

A Chair of Ophthalmology at the Royal Australian College of Ophthalmologists.

•

The Ulverscroft Children's Eye Unit at the Great Ormond Street Hospital For Sick Children, London.

You can help further the work of the Foundation by making a donation or leaving a legacy. Every contribution, no matter how small, is received with gratitude. Please write for details to:

THE ULVERSCROFT FOUNDATION,
The Green, Bradgate Road, Anstey,
Leicester LE7 7FU, England.
Telephone: (0116) 236 4325

In Australia write to:

THE ULVERSCROFT FOUNDATION,
c/o The Royal Australian College of Ophthalmologists,
27, Commonwealth Street, Sydney,
N.S.W. 2010.

June Barraclough was born and brought up in Brighouse, West Yorkshire, and now lives in Blackheath, London. *Emma Eliza* is her twenty-first novel.

EMMA ELIZA

Little Emma Eliza Saunders, the eldest child of a poor cottage family in rural south-west Norfolk, grows up in the 1860s with the memory of a boy who befriended her as a toddler but who then vanished from her life. When she is thirteen, Emma goes as a servant to Breckles Hall. Four years later she meets a young man called Jabez Smith, whom she believes is the friend of her earliest days. When the wife of the Hall coachman, George Starling, dies, Emma has to decide whether to accept his proposal of marriage. In the 1920s, Emma recounts some of her life to her granddaughter, Lily, who writes it all down. Lily's daughter then puts together the family history . . .

Books by June Barraclough
Published by The House of Ulverscroft:

TIME WILL TELL
FAMILY SNAPSHOTS
THE VILLA VIOLETTA
NO TIME LIKE THE PRESENT
ANOTHER SUMMER
LOVING AND LEARNING
THE FAMILY FACE

JUNE BARRACLOUGH

EMMA ELIZA

A Family Saga

Complete and Unabridged

ULVERSCROFT
Leicester

First published in Great Britain in 2002 by
Robert Hale Limited
London

First Large Print Edition
published 2003
by arrangement with
Robert Hale Limited
London

British Library CIP Data

Barraclough, June
Emma Eliza.—Large print ed.—
Ulverscroft large print series: family saga
1. Norfolk (England)—Social conditions—19th century—Fiction
2. Domestic fiction
3. Large type books
I. Title
823.9′14 [F]

ISBN 0–7089–4783–2

Published by
F. A. Thorpe (Publishing)
Anstey, Leicestershire

Set by Words & Graphics Ltd.
Anstey, Leicestershire
Printed and bound in Great Britain by
T. J. International Ltd., Padstow, Cornwall

This book is printed on acid-free paper

Dedication

For all my 'mitochondrial mothers', especially Elizabeth Dixon, Ann Tooke, Eliza Banham, Emma Eliza Saunders, 'Beattie Starling', and 'Lily Dyson', and for my daughter, Frances Benn Nestor.

Preface
by Jane Chapman

Emma Eliza Starling was born Emma Eliza Saunders in 1851 in a small village in Norfolk. She was my great-grandmother and I can just remember her, a tiny figure in black, a black ribbon at her throat, and black boots at the end of legs that dangled in the air, as they were not quite long enough to reach the floor.

In her childhood, my mother, Lily Dyson, Emma Eliza's first granddaughter if not her first grandchild, saw a good deal of her. Later, sometime in the nineteen twenties, Emma went to live with her eldest daughter Beattie, my grandmother. Sitting in her Windsor chair before the fire, the old lady seemed to go back more and more to the old days. Lily was still living at home and used to listen to her grandmother reminiscing about those early days in Norfolk, her marriage, and the move from Norfolk to our Yorkshire town in 1872.

My mother and my grandmother would read, or Beattie would do some tatting, or crocheting, or just chat during the long evenings, and listen to Emma Eliza talking about the first twenty-two years of her life at home in a Norfolk village. All old people recall the distant past better than the years of their maturity. When Mother knew her as a child her grandmother had already become quite redoubtable, what people called a 'real tartar'. She had had to be fairly strict with herself and others after her husband died and she had perforce to keep afloat. No pensions then. Later, as an old woman she mellowed somewhat.

Mother was fascinated by the way her grandmother spoke, and wrote down what she had said in Emma Eliza's own words. She had always kept the rich Norfolk accent and intonation of her childhood, and Mother noted down some of the Norfolk dialect she used.

In summer Emma Eliza talked less, for then she would take a chair to the front door that looked out upon gardens and allotments owned in common by the householders of the terrace. She loved seeing flowers and breathing in fresh air.

One day, long after the old lady's death, Mother began to make a story out of all she had heard, but the account stopped just after her grandparents settled in Yorkshire. I found all this among Mother's papers after she died, and decided I would finish the story as well as I could. I had been told quite a lot about my maternal great-grandparents, and about my grandmother's childhood, and as I was interested in family history I did a bit of further research.

One thing always puzzled Mother. Her grandmother had occasionally spoken about the young man she called 'Baz', whom she thought she had known as a child and had met later, but she would always hesitate or go silent when she found herself alluding to him. Once, though, she said 'Look it up in Chronicles, in the Bible'. Beattie had not been there when this was said, and Mother had still wondered who 'Baz' was. Beattie, when consulted later, was vague, except to say she might once have met a sort of uncle with the name Jabez, not Baz. There might be an old photograph somewhere but the album may have been given to her son John.

Here then is some of Emma Eliza's life story. Her early years are recounted in her own words just as she described them to my mother.

I gathered together more details about the family, and in books of local history came upon descriptions of the life they all used to lead in Calderbrigg at the end of the nineteenth century and in the first quarter of the twentieth. From all I have discovered after much consultation of early births and marriages at the Family Records Centre, and putting two and two together, I believe I have succeeded in piecing together the truth about some ancient family history, as well as continuing the story of Emma Eliza's life after 1873. How I wish, though, that I could hear my great-grandmother's voice in my own ears as my mother did!

J.C.

PART ONE

Norfolk

1851 – 1873

EMMA ELIZA'S OWN STORY

1

Mam, Eliza Saunders, that was once Eliza Banham, allus told folk she was born 'three years after Waterloo'.

Mam's youngest brother, my Uncle Isaac, said most people didn't know the date of Waterloo, so why not just say 1818? But Mam liked to make little dramas out of life, and anyway there was a Waterloo Cottage in Caston, Mam's village. Uncle Isaac told us that in fact his sister Eliza arrived in the family the same year as the Wesleyan chapel was built in the village.

I don't expect Mam knew many dates. Her eldest brother, my Uncle George, would most likely have once told her the date of Waterloo. He'd had a bit more schooling than the rest. Mam could just about read, and she could sign her name, which was more than many folk could manage. She was good at adding up numbers too. Mayhap her dad had taught her to count when he was a-countin' his sheep.

The family name Banham, was the same as the name of a village some miles away. Folk from Banham must have travelled all over the shop, for there were — still are — hundreds with Mam's family name in Norfolk, lots in what they call 'Breckland'.

Mam's mother was called Ann and her father was William Banham the Shepherd. Mam was baptized Elizabeth but they always called her Eliza. She didn't have an easy life, being the middle child of nine. One baby died before her and one died after her, and then her mother died not long after having her last baby, Isaac. Mam's sister Mary Ann was only fourteen, and Mam was eleven, but they brought up the three youngest children — Matilda, Frances, and Baby Isaac.

Her big brother George was a clever man. He got apprenticed when he was fourteen to a carpenter and wheelwright, and then to a gig-builder in the village. Six years after his mother died he wed a girl he'd courted for ages. I mustn't get forward with my story but it was not so many years after this that George became a gig-builder hisself and started his own business with premises on 'the Green'. Brother Robert married not long afterwards, and worked for his elder brother for a time. I had plenty of Banham uncles and aunts and cousins when I was a child, though I didn't see a great deal on 'em unless they walked over, or George gave them a lift in his trap to Bedon, where we were living at that time, in the next village to Caston.

Mam didn't marry till she was thirty, and her sister Mary Ann never did. When I was a little girl Mam told me about her sisters and brothers bit by bit, but she wasn't never to know that William, her father, lived till he was eighty-seven. I was always Grandpa Banham's favourite, I think. They buried him just afore I left Norfolk for ever.

Mam took us all to Caston to be christened in the church she was married in — Dad said the Bedon parson were a 'complainin' critter'. Caston Church was the Church of the Holy Cross, and in those days, Mam told me once, it had a thatched roof. Later, I discovered that the church bells were three hundred and fifty years old, the font where I was christened even older. At that time, St Botolph's, the church in Dad's village, my childhood village, Stow Bedon, was nearly falling down and its thatch needed a good overhaul. They decided to start building a new church when I was one year old. It wasn't finished for some time, so that was another reason my brothers and sister all got christened in Caston too.

When I was a-growin' up, the next generation of Banhams in Caston, along with a neighbour family, the Starlings, were known in the village as bell-ringers and handbell-ringers. You had to have a good sense of rhythm for the handbells, and all the Banhams had that, including Mam, though girls didn't ring bells. But she loved to dance and sing. I liked singing too and we both sang at home when we were busy working. I still did when I had my own family, took the habit from Mam, I suppose. We often sang hymns in those days. Almost to the end of her life Mam could sing beautifully, though she stopped when she was a-dying.

Mam told me that Banhams and Starlings had known each other for years; it was the bell-ringing that had brought them together generations before. I didn't know any of the Starlings right well before I went to work at Breckles Hall, but I knew they were a big family. I liked thinking about families and I used to name my pretend dolls, that Mam made out of plaited knotgrass, with all the names of the families I knew. I knew all the names of my own families of course, both Mam's and Dad's. Some of them had the same names as the Starling family did.

Dad's mother was Elizabeth and his Dad had been called Benjamin when he was alive. The Starling father was James and the mother Rebecca and they had a son called James Valentine along with a Mary Ann like Mam's sister, exactly the same age as Uncle Isaac, my favourite Banham uncle. The Starlings had a George too. He wasn't a gig-builder though, but a groom and coachman. What Mam told me was that he had the name 'Christmas' as well, because he was born on Christmas Eve! Like Mam's family there were lots of other children, younger brothers and sisters — William and Henry and David and Emma, and another Eliza. Like in Mam's family, two had died as babes.

Mam was eleven years older than the eldest little Starling, Mary Ann, like she was eleven years older than her brother Isaac, but she knew 'em all as they grew up, like she knew other Caston — and Bedon and Griston and Breckles and Carbrooke — families. They were often all related, young men finding their wives in the next village, or the next but one, as I discovered later.

* * *

Mam married my father in Caston church, as I have said. Dad wasn't Caston born but came from the next village, Stow Bedon, that was a mile and a half away south, where I was born and brought up. All the little villages were only a mile or two one from another, and all the countryside around there were little 'meres'. Bedon had a mere, and a common where you could gather firewood and cut turf; some families still used to grow little patches of barley there. But when Caston or Bedon folk needed to buy something special — not that in my childhood there was ever much money for extras — they'd go to Watton, our market town. The farmers went to the market to sell their butter and cheeses and sometimes the rabbits they'd snared, but they sold their sheep in Swaffham or further away in Thetford. The better-off farmers' wives went to Thetford too to buy muslin or gingham, or even silk for their best dresses. Many villagers though had never been to Thetford, twelve miles away, though there were coaches that went there from Watton, even coaches from Watton to London till the railways came and they went to London as well, but not directly.

About three miles to the north of Caston was Wayland Wood that was famous for the tale of the Babes in the Wood. It was all true, had really happened. Mam told me the story, and at first it made me frightened of woods. Later, I once went there bluebell-picking with my brothers.

Long after I was grown up and married, clever people who didn't live in Norfolk used to ask me about another place that was about as far from Caston as Caston was from Thetford. It was called Grimes Graves and was already thousands of years old when Jesus was in Palestine. They found flints there used by folk umpteen thousands of years before. But when I was a child I hadn't even heard of it!

When I was little I liked stories about Jesus who always seemed to be on our side against the wicked rich. I heard these tales at the Methodist chapel. I knew some rich families. One lived at Breckles Hall, not far from Bedon where, when I was about nine years old, I went along with Mam for a few weeks, to help as a servant. That time was the first but not the last.

There were meadows on each side of the hall, some with mares and foals, and the house, Mam said, was very old, built in the reign of Henry the Eighth and said to be haunted by ghosts. I never saw any myself, but Mam told me as we walked back that first time that the place was haunted by the sound of wheels and horses' hoofs. Folk said there was a ghostly coachman too, but now one of the coachmen was George Starling from Caston. She seemed to know a lot about the place — she had worked there before she was married, she said. There were many stories about the family who used to live there years and years ago. They had been Roman Catholics and there was still a priest's hole behind some panelling. None of the servants had ever been in it. The entrance behind part of the fireplace had been stopped up years before, but they all knew it was there and could be opened up if Mrs Upcraft felt like it. It led, Mam said, to a tunnel that went to the little church we passed at the hall gates. I had seen the church many times of course — it did not seem to be used now and the entrance to the tunnel was bricked up.

There were other cupboards inside the fireplace, I discovered later. Mam said one of them had held the family wigs. There must have been lots of Roman Catholics in our part of the world, because folk said there was an underground passage that linked the manor house of a rich Caston family both with Caston church and with the village cross on the green. We were told it was on account of that family too having been Catholics, before Caston church and Bedon church became Church of England. The manor house was just an ordinary farmhouse when I saw it, not like the hall, which was enormous. Some of the downstairs floors were built of ships' timbers and there was panelling on the walls as well. The fireplaces were like rooms, they were so big! I got to know it all much better later. But that first time stands out in my memory because Mam seemed so happy to be there and she was really keen to tell me all about it.

My Dad's family was not Church of England, but all the village folk from Caston and Bedon had to get christened in the church, and then the rector wrote down their names in his big parish book. My dad's family, the Saunders, belonged to the Wesleyan Methodists, who had built that bran' new chapel in Caston when Mam was little.

If I speak more of Caston than of Bedon it's on account of I always liked going there, and felt I really belonged there. It was a prettier village than Dad's, and Mam always belonged to Caston. There was even a turnpike road that went by the village, and a school for the poor, and you always saw flocks of ducks waddling around. My Granddad Banham said his ancestors, like the Starlings, had lived in Caston from the beginning of time. The Starlings were better off than any of the Banhams except for Uncle George. They still owned a plot of land in Caston, north of the village, which they had worked for years and years. Uncle told me that before the 'henclosures', our family had owned our own bits of land, but almost all of them now were poor and went on being poor. The common had been bigger then as well, and barley had been grown there, like it still was in Bedon.

* * *

When my mother was eighteen she told her father she wanted to emigrate to America. I found out later that lots of Norfolk people did leave, mostly those who had no money. But Mam's father would not let her.

'I was that furious,' she told me, as I sat shelling peas with her one sunny morning when I was about twelve. 'You don't realize when you're young that they don't want you to go away because they love you. I thought Father didn't care about what I wanted.'

I suppose she spoke those words to me with a purpose.

Well, when *I* was eighteen they built that railway line in Stow Bedon and the Bedon folk was very chuffed.

'There ain't no railway in Caston!' they said.

It linked with all the big cities as well as London: Cambridge and Norwich, and if you kept changing trains you could get to the north of England. But when I was little I didn't think about getting away. I might have done a bit later, when I was always kep' so busy.

I remember the great celebrations we had in the rectory grounds when the Crimean War ended and we were given plum pudden and tea and bread and butter. And when I was twelve there was a feast in Caston to celebrate the Queen's son marrying that Alexandra of Denmark that was a very beautiful woman. Later, folk said she was very deaf. But by that time Mam was very ill.

I must go back a bit.

As I said, Mam married my dad in Caston church. She was thirty, which was old to be wed. Dad was called Robert Saunders, and he laboured on the land in Bedon for a farmer called Osborn, a man who was related in some way to his mother, my Granny Saunders who had once been called Osborn. 'Osborn's Piece', the name of part of the farm, must have shown that at one time they were not as poor as Dad later became. I worked that out for myself later. Granny was now a widow since my grandfather Ben Saunders had died a few years before.

Mam and Dad went to live in a little cottage Dad rented from a farmer; that home was cold and damp in winter, but most cottages were. Ours was cleaner than most, and Dad would bring in wood for our fire when we couldn't afford coal. There was a coal-club in the village but you had to put pennies aside for it and we couldn't always manage that.

My parents didn't have me straight away. Mam was thirty-three when I was born and forty-two when her last child arrived. As I told you, I was baptized in Caston church and given the name Emma Eliza. Emma was Mam's favourite name and Elizabeth was after her, so I got two names, which was more than most girls did, apart from the Mary Anns. Mam always liked to be a bit different.

After me there was Percy, then Bob, and lastly Myra. There were three years between each of us. I was closest to Percy, I suppose, since he was the next to me. We called him 'Botty', I can't remember why. Perhaps it was because his little breeches were allus falling down. Or he went around with his pants off once he was breached. I can remember when he came out of long clothes and stopped being a baby. I can also remember the day my next brother, Robert, was born. He was called after Dad, though usually we called him Bob. The last baby, Myra, nine years after me, was the beauty of the family with her big eyes and curly hair.

I went to school in Bedon off and on from the age of four. The church erected a new building for it whilst I was there and it was called the National School. I'm afraid I didn't learn much. I'll tell you more about that in a minute. We went now and again to chapel, not every Sunday, and they had books there too.

What I liked best was hand-sewing and making things, and helping Mam with the cooking. Sometimes we had right tasty meals of rabbit pie and rabbit stew — there was plenty of rabbits in our neighbourhood! Now and then we had sheep's kidneys — a neighbour asked Mam to cook them for him and let us have some of the stew. The gentry had pheasants and partridges and woodcock, and some of the village folk would shoot pigeons or snipe, and even blackbirds, but I never had any of those except once we ate a hare that had died in the field off Green Lane — that was our name for the road that ran from Stow Bedon to Caston. Mam taught me to use the vegetables we grew behind our cottage, taters and cabbage and onions and carrots and turnips, in with the rabbit or the mutton in slow-cooking stews. She also knew all about herbs for cooking and for healing and taught me about them. But often at the end of the week we just had dumplings that was made only from flour and water and a snitch of baking powder. The best times was in the autumn when folks gave you apples from their trees, Norfolk Biffens, Pearmains and Blenheim Oranges. We just ate 'em as they came from the tree. If we got given cooking-apples Mam made apple pies from them.

I haven't told you what Mam and Dad looked like. Mam had lovely thick goldy-brown hair with a curl in it, and big grey eyes. I wished I'd inherited the curl in her hair. Mine was not completely straight and it frizzed in the damp, but it was thinner than Mam's and more of a mousy shade. Mam used to cut all our hair, even Dad's, and she'd keep mine quite short as it was easier to manage than the hair of girls with long locks. We were all a-feared of getting nits. Not that we minded missing school but they were horrible itchy things.

Mam was a medium-sized woman though I thought she was very tall when I was a little lass. Dad wasn't much taller and quite young-looking. He was younger than our mother by about four years though they never let on to us about that and I didn't find it out till he died. He was quite thin with a long nose and hazel eyes and his hair was straight and ordinary-coloured. He worked hard all day for the farmer doing most everything — hedging and ditching mainly. Above all he liked to plough and could make a good furrow, though he wasn't chief ploughman but would help out when they were getting ready for barley sowing. He knew all about animals and flowers from having worked in the fields for so long but he wasn't really interested in 'em. It was my Grandmother Osborn who liked flowers. When Dad had a minute to himself, which was not often, he'd sit out the door and whittle a piece of wood and whistle, or just shut his eyes if it were a sunny day.

There was one public house in the village at that time and he'd go once a week Sat'day evening to meet his brothers and friends over a pint of small beer. I never saw him worse for drink. He hadn't the money for it and even if he'd had some he'd have given it Mam, I'm sure of that, though he was not what you might call a provident man. His mother had brought him up a Methodist and they was not supposed to drink at all.

* * *

As I grew up I seemed to remember that when I was very small — I don't know exactly how old — someone else used to live with Dad and Mam and me in the Bedon cottage. I don't mean Dad's younger brother Ben, who did live with us later or 'stayed over' in the cottage from time to time. No, it was before the time our Percy was born so I couldn't have been quite three years old — and it was most likely a year earlier than that. This lodger, or whatever he was, had red hair and blue eyes. To myself I called him My Friend because he was always kind to me. I seemed to remember too that the others called him Baz. He made pipes out of hollow reeds from the mere and he used to play tunes on them, or he would sing to me, and he took me with him hazelnutting and blackberrying. Then he wasn't there any more.

I didn't realize at first that he had gone because he had only been now and then in the cottage, had usually been out in the fields. I think he must have slept on the settle downstairs.

One day I said to Mam, 'Where's Baz?'

She looked surprised, but all she said was, 'Oh he's gone away to work.'

I was heartbroken. Why hadn't he told me he was going away? I went on remembering him, and I looked all round the cottage for him. I even looked for him in the fields if I was out with the older village children.

All these very early memories got buried somehow, I suppose, and I was busy helping

Mam with the new babby, so I surprised myself when, much later, after Percy could walk — I remember that he was pulling at Mam's skirts and I was helping her doing the ironing — I found myself suddenly thinking about My Friend again.

I asked Mam once more, and she said, 'Who?'

'My friend!' I said, 'They called him Baz.'

'Fancy you remembering!' she said. But later she pretended she didn't know who I meant.

Even later, when My Friend would only appear if I was asleep and dreaming, I would wonder if I had made him up. It was clear I would get no more out of my mother. When I came across the word 'dead', I used to think the boy must be dead, and buried in the churchyard. But I wasn't sure.

I must have been eight or nine when I asked my father about 'Baz'. I'm not sure why I'd never asked Dad before — probably my father did not have much time for listening to me. I hadn't mentioned him for years.

Dad said, 'Oh, we did have lodgers, your Mam and I, after we were wed — but you wouldn't remember any on them.'

'I do! I do!' I shouted, and Dad said, 'You've too lively an imagination, Emmie.'

'But he was My Friend!' I said, and Dad

looked nonplussed.

'You'd better forget him, Em,' he said finally, and I had the feeling he didn't want me to mention him again.

As I grew up, my earliest memories of My Friend and his red hair and blue eyes and his grin and the tunes he played on his pipe got mixed up with asking my parents about him and remembering the times I'd remembered him. By the time I was about thirteen he was only one of my recollections of having once been a very little child. But what made him stand out in my dreams — I did dream a lot, sometimes of him — was a feeling of losing something and being very sad, as well as knowing I'd once been very happy. I had no recollection of his ever saying goodbye to me, but I knew in my heart of hearts that he had enjoyed playing with me and talking to me.

I puzzled over it all, off and on, for a good while.

2

Mostly my remembrances of myself and Mam and Dad and Percy and Bob are connected with our cottage, and with the fields around, and the lanes, and with feeling very cold — and often hungry. That cottage of ours wasn't very comfortable, but it was clean, 'cept when Dad brought muck on his shoes into the house-room, and Mam had to 'mamuck' everything up — make it all nice again. I knew lots of words then that I've never heard since 'cept from Norfolkers. If it had been frosty and the plants were thawing out we called them 'limpsy-leaved'.

At noon, we took the men working in the fields their 'fourses', just a few slices of bread-and-scrape. I liked going into the fields, specially at harvest time though winnowing was hard work. I enjoyed going to chapel services where they had a harmonium for folk to sing hymns to. Dad liked the preacher there better'n than the vicar. He thought the parsons at the parish church as well the rector of Caston were uppity folk.

I also enjoyed my visits to Dad's mother, Grandma Saunders. She kept a tidy house in the Lane, across from ours, and her fire burned brighter than ours. Every time I visited I'd complain 'bout my chilblains and the cold and the wet, and how I wished it was always summer, and she used to tell me that God had made the 'sasons', and we just had to put up with 'em. 'Don't forget, gal, God made the sasons,' — I can hear her saying it now. But I hated 'fog month' and 'winter month' and 'snow month' and 'rain month' and 'wind month' and looked forward to 'bud month' — April — and then all the summer months, till October came round, and then it would be fog month again.

⋆ ⋆ ⋆

Grandma had a garden with marigolds and columbines and lilac and roses, and mignonette and sweet peas, and there were gooseberry- and currant-bushes and a gage tree. Indoors she had a cupboard with a few pieces of fine chaney, two chairs and a sofy, and in the backyard she still kept fowl. I didn't know why Grandma, a widow, should have been a lot better off than us. I guess now that she'd inherited a little sum when her own father died. I know Mam envied her and they didn't get on all that well. I think my dad, her eldest son, was a disappointment to his mother, who had once been Elizabeth Osborn from a 'good' family. But Dad always said 'bout everything: 'I bain't a-complainin'.' I think Mam wished he'd complain a bit more!

Once or twice we ate Sunday dinner at Gran Osborn's — cold baked pork if Neighbour Turner's pig had been killed, a basin of hot potatoes and a wedge of cheese or sometimes a big rice pudden in a yellow pie dish.

When I was cold I'd imagine Grandma's fire, and that the warmth was going right up my legs and arms. At these times I was often very wet as well. If it was rainin' we walked to school in clothes that got soaked on the way and there was usually no space in the schoolroom to dry our boots and jackets, if we possessed jackets, which most of us children did not. If there were a lot of 'absences', there might be a bit more chance of getting near the stove. But we often sat in our wet clothes. If we were lucky and the man had brought kindling to the schoolhouse, or even a shovelful of coal, they'd light the stove, though it smoked a good deal. All us children suffered something terrible from chilblains.

If it were summer we'd munch 'bread and cheese' on our way to school. That wasn't no real bread or cheese but big hawthorn-buds and the young leaves from the hedges. We ate primrose petals and cowslips too, and sorrel that cooled your mouth if you were thirsty on a boiling summer day. They were our 'spice', as they say in Yorkshire. There were lots of wild flowers in our midders: poppies and scabious and speedwells and violets and white dead-nettle — but you couldn't eat *all* of them. As for trees and animals, not far away there were a few spruce and larches planted by folk at the hall, but nothing like they planted years later, that I saw when I went back. We had beeches in our lanes, and sweet-briar bushes, and furze bushes on the common, and we often saw red squorls and heard the nightingales.

Right at the beginning when I first went to school it was just one half of a cottage occupied by Miss Gooch at the back and I only had to walk half a mile to get there if we used the short cut across the fields. The fields though were very muddy in winter.

I was usually joined in my walk by Matty Cozens and Hannah Tooke who were both my best friends. At least, I knew I was Matty's best friend, and I wanted to be Hannah's. Matty was tiny with black 'corkscrew' curls — natural ones. Mam had no time in those days to have my hair 'put up' in rags at night unless it was for something real special like the Whit church treat, or a wedding.

Hannah Tooke had long fair hair and brown eyes and was taller than either me or Matty. Her dad worked for the hall so she had reach-me-downs from them up there. Her boots fitted her better than ours did and were mended more often.

Once I told Hannah about that friend of my earliest time, but I could see she didn't believe me, specially when I told her about the tunes he played on the pipe.

In another bid for her friendship I said to her one day — we were about eight and it was summer, so for once I wasn't cold:

'I'll tell you a secret if I can be your best friend.'

She stopped and pursed up her lips. 'You can't bribe me, Emmie Saunders, but tell me your secret and I'll see.'

I suddenly realized I didn't want to tell her any secrets and so I said, 'Oh, I've changed my mind.'

She marched off ahead of me but I could tell she was interested. Matty caught me up just as I was thinking, *I could tell Matty!*

The secret was that one day I was going to marry My Friend. It had come to me suddenly one day that if I couldn't marry Baz, I wouldn't ever marry nobody. But if I told even Matty it would make it all ordinary and unexciting.

I never told nobody, kept it to myself, and ended up deciding I'd keep *all* my secrets to myself. I went on feeling sad now and again for all sorts of reasons and I suppose when I felt like this it all got mixed up with other sadnesses.

⋆ ⋆ ⋆

I'd stayed away from school to help Mam when Bob was born until Mam's big sister, my Aunt Mary Ann, came and took over.

'I'm surprised at you, Liza gal,' she says, 'I thought you'd bring *that* infant up proper!'

I realized she was talking 'bout me when she went on: 'She,' pointing to me, 'must go to school — and take your Percy with her!'

'They won't have Botty yet,' said Mam. 'They'll take 'em when they're four and he'll go then.'

I don't suppose I really disliked school, and I'd miss Matty and Hannah if I stopped going, but Mam seemed to think they weren't learnin' me much. I could say my alphabet and read easy words but no real books. I could write my name and a few other words, and I could figger well — I knew my tables up to twelve times twelve. At first we was all crowded in that one small smoky room till the new National School was finished and then it was better. Even then, though, I'd rather have been out doing something. I liked the new building — I must have been in my ninth year then when the church took over from Miss Gooch and there came a new teacher who they all said was cleverer than her. Some other children came over from Rocklands, the other side of Bedon, that didn't have a school in their village and we didn't know any of them.

The new teacher, Miss Castle, kep' going on and on about clean calico pinnies and darned stockings and we girls were all fed up. There was a man teacher too with a beard and he took the boys for some things. The boys were in the next room and they were allowed to get dirty. The boys didn't care about muck. One or two still wore their dads' or granddads' cut-down smocks but usually it was cut-down cord suits.

The boys were given a plot to grow stuff on for the teacher; we were all amazed at that. But the girls weren't given nothing, and as I've said, we weren't allowed to get dirty. I enjoyed the sewing we did instead of outdoor work, but I'd have liked to have some seeds to plant. The schoolmistress had one of the new treadle sewing-machines. It was the first time

I'd ever heard of them and I longed for her to teach me how to use hers — then I'd be able to make clothes for everybody on it.

I began to stay at home more and more. I could sew at home and help Mam, and even dig at the back of the cottage when Dad didn't have the time. It wasn't necessary to go to school every day. Then when I was nine I went that summer along with Mam on some days to Breckles Hall to help in the kitchen. Funny I can't remember more about the work we did, but I suppose it was only for a few weeks, because Mam needed the money.

Then that work stopped, and then Mam was expecting Myra, though we didn't know it was Myra then, and now I was staying at home most of the time. In those days lots of girls did and they couldn't really make you go to school like they can now.

One afternoon Aunt Mary Ann had come over again and was talking to Mam. Myra had been born a week before and she was in the old wood cradle. I was peeling 'taters for dinner and I heard Mary Ann says:

'Old James was asking after you — said he could find Emmie work.'

'I don't want our Emmie found work alongside him!' Mam said.

'No — he didn't mean over in Caston. It's at Breckles again — they want to train up a maid of all work, starting at ten. She'd get her dinner and they'd pay her a wage at twelve.'

'That's where their George is, isn't it?' said Mam, taking the baby up and unbuttoning her blouse.

'That's right, sister. Think it over.'

Mam had enough to do with the new babby but if they wouldn't have her at the hall with Myra, she decided she could earn a bit of extra money mending folk's lamps. She was good at that sort of thing, which always surprised me, for you wouldn't have thought she'd be a 'handy' person. She could even mend old umbrellas and charged sixpence for each repair. But she hated cleaning and washing and always suffered from backache. I've inherited her hand skills but I was always a tidy cleaner and washer too, and this stood me in good stead when I did go to Breckles Hall without Mam.

But this was much later.

⋆ ⋆ ⋆

Mam had always said she wanted me to 'marry well'. Dad was a decent man, easy-going, no pusher or thruster, but he was very poor. 'Course, as I have said, most people were poor in Bedon and in Caston except them up at Caston Hall, and Stow

Bedon Hall and Breckles Hall — and the rector of Caston, and the vicar of Breckles, and a few of the bigger farmers. We all lived from hand to mouth. When you'd put your pence into the village coal-fund and the oil-fund and put more pence by for tallow candles and the boots-and-shoes club and the school-clothing clubs, there wasn't much left for food. We went rosehip gathering in autumn, and we used every morsel of nuts and berries we could find outside.

Although it was hard work bringing it to the surface, we always had enough water to drink and wash ourselves with. Most families in our village had a well in their gardens. Lots of places didn't, I found out later, and folk to had to get water from anywhere they could find it. Often it was dirty and, I was told, made children ill. But even if we hadn't had our wells there was always the mere. Stow Bedon mere wasn't as big as Thompson Water about three miles away but so far I had never known it dry out.

As I've told you, I helped my mother a lot. I don't know what she'd have done without me after Myra was born. Myra cried a lot. It was when she had begun to crape — you call it 'crawling' — before she could walk, that her hair suddenly grew, and it was red hair. I was looking at her one day as she sat on my lap and I knew she reminded me of someone.

That red hair. I looked again at her big blue eyes, and realized what a bright blue they were. I seemed to have known her long ago, and I was puzzled. I suppose that was why Myra was always my favourite though. Sometimes I had to stay away from school to look after her when Mam went to help out at Breckles Hall again. That was before she fell ill. She worked there for two years or so because money was so tight at home, mostly helping clean the silver and repairing their lamps.

* * *

Myra was four when Mam died, and I was thirteen. During her last year Mam told me again about wanting to emigrate, and more about when she was young, and how young girls were 'flighty' and I mustn't be like that. I'd be found work at Breckles Hall. But when she got too weak to work, Mam had to leave her work at the hall and I still had to stay home and miss school. The year before she died — but we weren't to know that then — there was that big feast on the green at Caston for the wedding of the Prince of Wales and Alexandra of Denmark. Mam had so looked forward to it and so wanted to go but her cough was very bad at that time and she had to give up the idea. She let me go, with the boys, so I could tell her all that went on. We joined Aunt Mary Ann there and other Banhams and their children but I didn't really enjoy myself. It was all wrong, Mam not being there.

I'd attended school on and off again before Mam got too ill to work, but after the feast I went there rarely. I was needed at home. If Mam hadn't been ill I'd have gone to work before this, would have worked in my first 'petty place' for a year, before the rector's daughter or the schoolmistress found me a job in service, perhaps in a distant household. Because of Mam I didn't work before I was thirteen except for the time I went with her to help out at the hall. I suppose I could have 'bettered myself' earlier, but when I did go out to work as a servant it was not like some girls who went to work in London in some nobleman's household found by the rector's daughter, but starting off at the bottom at Breckles Hall.

3

Breckles Hall

The year Mam died was the year the Caston brick windmill was built. They said it was fifty-five feet high and they were all very proud of it. It was what they called a tower mill. We hadn't a windmill in Bedon and I only saw the Caston windmill after Mam's funeral, when Uncle George came over in his gig and took me and the others over to see our cousins. I hadn't seen them for ages. Mam seemed to have been a-dying for so long and I had had all the housework and the cooking to do, and the little ones to look after. I'd almost forgotten the pink houses and the flocks of ducks and the farms and fields. It was still Mam's country, though she'd been buried over at Bedon.

A relative of Dad's sold ropes in Caston and he had another cousin there with the same name as himself but they hadn't kept in touch. Anyway, Dad couldn't come with us, he was too busy working. First we went to the shoemaker's because Uncle George said we needed our boots mended. If we stayed the night at Uncle's, the cobbler would do his best to patch up our boots and have them ready the next afternoon. Uncle was very kind though he had childer of his own to see to. I know Dad was ashamed, but what could he do? We just had to struggle on as best we could. We went to Uncle's house on the green where his workshop was. Our Aunt Elizabeth, who was, I suppose in her early fifties but who looked a lot younger than Mam had done, though Mam had been younger than our aunt when she died, had tea and bread-and-jam ready for us. Our cousins Sarah, William, and Alfred were waiting for us. Isaac, Sarah, and William were grown up, though none was married. Isaac the eldest was at work. The youngest boy, Alfred, was much younger than the others, only a year older than me, and very shy. There was Granfer too, in the chimbley corner, but soon he went out with his pipe, accompanied by Cousin William. Lambing was over but my grandfather was still working, though now he had a helper and was also training up William who had been a very sickly child, not expected to live.

Usually Granfer would wink at me but today he didn't. I knew he was very sad about Mam. I was making a big effort trying not to think about her. Granfer had already lost his wife, my Banham grandma. Sarah said that Isaac would see us later on that day. 'He works for Dad at the foundry,' she said.

After tea, my brothers and myself wanted to look round the village but our boots were at the cobbler's! Aunt Elizabeth said:

'I've got some old worn boots of Alfred's I kep' — if you don't mind 'em you can borrow 'em!'

I was delighted, though the boots didn't fit any of us very well. Cousin Sarah came with us, but Alfred soon disappeared.

'Shall I show you the windmill?' asked Sarah.

We said we'd like to see that. Bob and Percy ran on ahead and Elizabeth told us all about the houses we passed. We were on The Street. That was the main road leading down from the green but soon we came out into another lane that ran across the fields.

'That's Wood Farm House,' she said, pointing to a house at the side of the meadow, 'And over there's where my dad and your mam used to live — your Granfer still lives there — as long as he can work. They call it the Shepherd's House. He only came along to our house this afternoon in your honour!'

I saw a little cottage at the bend in the field. I didn't remember Mam ever showing us where she used to live. We walked round the field and came back to The Street. Then we walked up to the church where I was christened and all around the church were cottages. I did wish I lived here!

'Where's the hall? and the rectory?' I asked.

'Over the back — a bit further on — in their own grounds. Do you still want to see the windmill?'

'Oh yes,' said I, though my feet were hurting.

I don't remember seeing Bridge Farm that time or Church Farm or The Chase or the tollgate. I liked the place. I knew however that I was not at present destined to live here in Caston but in Bedon, and to work at Breckles Hall which was nearer to Bedon.

Much later, I would get to know Caston better. One day I might walk on the Green Lane along the Pilgrim Way to Walsingham, or by the little stream that drained on to the River Wissey; one day I'd stand in the sun and look at the soft pink brickwork of the village houses, and get to know the rectory and the manor house and Waterloo Cottage and Caston Hall and The Ark and Chase Farm and the Laurels and the Vines — all the local houses — but at the time I'm telling you about I wasn't yet a regular visitor there. I knew the church and the old rectory, and Uncle George's house, and the thatched cottages, and sometimes now it all gets mixed up in my mind, but I didn't know it right well at the time Mam died, only as a place she used to take me to. I'd always been talking to her or listening to her, not really looking at the place.

Now we could see the windmill against the sky. Sarah said knowledgeably, 'It's got a cap, and sail-frames, Dad says.'

We went across another meadow to get closer. It was built of pinky-red brick and was the tallest building I'd ever seen. It was beautiful.

'I'd get dizzy climbing up to build that!' I said.

'The lad who built it was a clever lad. Dad was furious though — they only paid him tuppence an hour — all that brickwork. Still, it took him plenty hours.'

'If he worked ten hours a day,' said Bob, chipping in, 'he'd earn one and eight pence — and six days would make ten shilling, two weeks a pound. Two pounds a month! How long did he take?'

My brother Bob loved adding up and making calculations with figgers.

'Oh, he could have slowed up if he'd wanted, I 'spect,' said Sarah. 'But he warn't that kind of lad and he finished within six month.'

'Twelve pound!' said Bob admiringly.

'I hope he didn't spend it all on beer,' I said, talking like Mam.

'Nay, he's saved it, I'm sure, and now they say he's to do some repairing down at Breckles Hall. There weren't no bricks left so they'll use ones from that broken mill over by the mere.'

'*I'm* off to Breckles Hall to work,' I said, and I expect I sounded proud, 'They want me, now that . . . now that Mam's . . . gone.'

'Yes, I know they've found you work,' replied Sarah. But she obviously wanted to get off the subject of Mam, her Aunt Eliza, not wanting me to burst into tears. She said, 'Did your mother ever mention the young bricklayer who built our windmill? He built it all by himself.'

'No, Mam were too poorly to talk much,' I said. 'She wouldn't know 'bout windmills,'

Sarah said, 'Aye, well, Jabez Smith was a marvel!'

'Did you say Jabez?' I enquired in a shaky voice.

'Aye, Jabez.'

I didn't ask her then. I durs'n't. But I was thinking, could Jabez be the same as Baz?'

Baz . . .

But then we came up to the mill and after having admired it, Sarah said,

'They even came and took a photograph! Have you ever seen one? Some man from Norwich came with a shawl over his head. They wanted to get young Mr Smith on the picture — but he'd disappeared.'

When we got back to Uncle's I thought and thought about what she'd said. I even woke in the night. I must ask Uncle George 'bout Jabez. But at breakfast he'd already gone out to work.

'Our Isaac's sorry he hasn't seen you,' said our Aunt Elizabeth. 'He was back late last night and had to be up at daybreak with our dad. But you can all go and see your other uncle — my brother-in-law Isaac,' said Aunt Elizabeth. 'He'll be in the smithy. He wants you to go over.'

Uncle Isaac, called after his great-grandfather, as was our cousin, had been at Mam's funeral, tears running down his cheeks. He had come with our Aunt Mary Ann, who never cried but who looked as white as a sheet. There were several other people there that I didn't know and I resented that they thought they had known Mam, when to my way of thinking I was the only person — along with Dad and the boys and Myra — who had really known her. Myra was too young to understand and had been looked after so long by me and our Grandma Saunders that I thought she did not really miss her mother.

I remember seeing Uncle Isaac and Aunt Mary Ann before they brought the coffin in, but afterwards my own eyes were so sodden with weeping that I remember nothing more that went on, only my own feelings. I was angry that Mam had gone, as well as grieving and feeling sorry for both her and myself. I did not want to remember the funeral now, so I was a bit reluctant to go over with Bob and Percy to the smithy. Then I thought, perhaps he'd know about this Jabez.

Uncle Isaac was shoeing a horse and gestured to us to keep well away. There was a smell of burning hoof as we stood at a distance and watched him. Of all Mam's sisters and brothers he looked most like her, I thought, even though he was a man.

I wasn't going to get much opportunity to ask him anything. He came out and said 'Good-day.'

He looked tired. Then, after we'd stood a bit tongue-tied, Perce and Bob shuffling their feet, I said:

'I'm to go back to Breckles as a proper servant, Uncle Isaac!'

'Is that what our Eliza — what your mam

— wanted for you?'

'Oh yes. They liked her there, I think, so they've said they'll have me.'

'It's a good post,' he said. 'I know fellows who've worked for old Upcraft. The new housekeeper Mrs Foster's got a tongue on her, but she's all right. See you behave yourself though!'

I was cross. 'Of course I will! Mam knew Mrs Upcraft. She promised Mam I'd be found work.'

'Well, I reckon she'll find out she's got a good bargain. She'll learn you up, or Mrs Foster will. Your mother wouldn't have known *her*.'

'Uncle Isaac,' I began tentatively, 'do you know anyone called Jabez Smith who works there too? He built the windmill.'

I thought he looked at me then in an odd way.

'Aye, I know who built the windmill,' he replied after a pause. 'But he's not at the hall no more, I don't believe. He moves around a lot they say, doing jobs for who wants 'em done'.

And he would say no more.

I dare not ask him if this Jabez had red hair.

In the afternoon, we said goodbye to everyone. Uncle George was ready waiting with the old trap to take us home to Bedon.

It was with a heavy heart that I went back home. No Mam, and everything to do in the house. But I'd soon be away. I hoped they'd let me stay over and live at the hall eventually if I proved satisfactory. I didn't want to stay at home. Grandma Saunders could look after Myra, I thought selfishly. I didn't want to think about Mam, I wanted to get away to where she wouldn't be, or the memory of her, I suppose. Even though I had worked those few weeks long ago with Mam at the hall, it was Mam when she came home to die that I remembered best. I may have been ruthless, but I was very young.

I was still, however, curious about the windmill builder.

Perhaps I'd meet him one day at Breckles if they needed a job done.

* * *

As I was a hard worker, what Uncle Isaac had said was true: in my small self the hall would get a good bargain. I'd been very young when I'd worked there the first time, and it hadn't been for long, so I expected they'd only given me easy things like peeling 'taters and helping the upper kitchen-maid. I did remember Mam had been under Cook, who took her orders from the housekeeper, Mrs Pearson, who saw the mistress every morning to receive her own orders. But Mrs P. had now left and Mistress Upcraft had found this new housekeeper, Mrs Foster. Mam had always found Mistress Upcraft a kind woman and I remembered she had once said the servants were lucky in this, for the gentry was often 'snaisty' — that was our word for it — thinking you was the lowest of the low.

In spite of still being on the school register and expected by the schoolmistress to turn up, Botty and Bob were actually out a lot of the time doing little jobs in the fields. Now that spring had suddenly come it was more pleasant. When Mam died it had still seemed to be winter — a cold early April. By haymaking and corn-harvest our boys, like most boys, would never see the inside of the school at all.

Grandma Saunders had taken Myra for the time being and this relieved me, for my sister too reminded me just then of Mam. The morning I left for work, two weeks after our visit to Caston, Dad was going round very quiet with a nasty cough, so to tell the truth, though I was sorry for him, I was glad to go out. I knew that if they ever mentioned my 'living in' at the hall I'd seize the chance.

Being nearly May Day it was quite light

when I set off very early to walk to the hall down the old familiar paths. I always enjoyed an early morning walk, the best time of the day, I thought. When I arrived at the hall, standing in its red brick, with its moat and gardens in front, I paused a moment to take it all in. The birds were singing, if not quite so loudly as they had an hour earlier around our cottage. Apart from them, the place seemed deserted. I decided to walk round to the back courtyard to see if I recognized anyone going about their business, and also to ask where I should make my way to see whoever wanted to see *me*.

I saw nobody at first, never mind anyone I knew. Everything seemed strange and I felt sort of not 'belonging' to myself — because I didn't seem to belong here either. I had felt this even at home too. But Mam would never come back to us; there was no putting the clock back. Now there was only work for me to look forward to — and I did look forward to it.

I looked round again by the servants' entrance in the back courtyard to see who might turn up. When nobody did, I knocked at the big door which was half open. The new Mrs Foster was nowhere to be seen. Perhaps *everything* had changed, from the housekeeper downwards.

* * *

Waiting in the corridor that led away inside the house from the courtyard door was a shortish man in a snuff-coloured coat. He had thick light-brown hair that stood on end at the back like a cockscomb. 'Good-morning,' he said to me.

I curtsied.

'Nay,' he said, 'I'm not your maister. I'm only the coachman. At your service!' And he bowed. I knew straight away who the coachman was.

I discovered later that Mr George Christmas Starling had only just taken up this post at the hall. He must have been in his late twenties when I first got to know him. I mean, at work, apart from knowing about his family from Mam. He had wed a woman called Elizabeth Ann, who came from Saham Toney, a village nearer than we were to the market town of Watton. George must have met her on some 'narrand' or other for the rector of Caston, for he had been trusted with doing business for him and for the families at Stow Bedon rectory, and the vicar of Breckles, and Caston Hall, and Mrs Gooch at Stow Bedon Hall, as well as the grander folk at Breckles Hall now. It didn't take me long to discover all this.

George Starling, whom I got to know for the first time that morning, was always to show me kindness. In this he was like my Uncle George. It was soon clear to me that this 'George Christmas' took a great interest in all Mam's family, all the Banhams. He said his family had always known Mam's, but they didn't know any of the Saunders family of Bedon.

I found out bit by bit that being one of a large family, George knew about being careful with money. Never to my knowledge or to that of the other servants did he drink too much or misbehave. George could read right well, and sometimes he would read the paper to the other servants. On that first morning though, as I stood listening to him, and was about to pluck up my courage and ask him whether he played the pipes or rang the bells, a little scullery maid came up and summoned me to see Mrs Foster.

I followed her reluctantly down the corridor. I'd have preferred to talk to Mr George. My depression had however lifted for the time being.

Mrs Foster was a middle-aged woman, quite tall with iron-grey hair and big hands. I noticed the hands especially because she was sitting at a table in one of the kitchens with her arms stretched out in front of her, her hands quite still. She asked me my age, and when I had last worked for the family, and what I could do. I said I was willing to do anything required. I thought it strange she should ask me what I could do. Did she expect me to tell her I wanted only light work? Whatever she thought of my answers, she said,

'Well, you will have to start off in the kitchens, but this morning as a favour you can help Amelia, a housemaid, with the dusting. I will inspect your work before you leave tonight. Tomorrow, you will be expected to begin to learn the duties of a scullery maid. Which are,' she said, fixing me with heavy-lidded brown eyes, and then looking down to her hands again and repeating her words as if she was in church, 'washing-up — cleaning — saucepans — and — dishes — preparing — the — vegetables — for — the — family — meals — and — the — staff — meals — and — scrubbing — down — the kitchen. If you progress,' she said in a normal voice, 'you will become an under kitchen-maid under Cook's guidance. You will do the kitchen fires and grates and if that goes well we might move you to be considered as third housemaid — we keep only three. You will at all times be under the upper servants and do their bidding.'

I thought it was time to bob a curtsy and did so.

I thought also of asking if George Starling was an 'upper' servant, but she swept on:

'It usually takes six months to a year to progress from scullery to kitchen and a year from kitchen to house depending on other staff. Some girls prefer to stay in the kitchens.'

She took another breath, but thought better of describing the duties of a third housemaid.

I was to find them out soon enough for I was to 'progress' quite rapidly. By the time I was fifteen I was able to be trusted with opening shutters, taking up hearth-rugs, sweeping the breakfast-room, removing the ash from the fire, black-leading the grates, and fetching and carrying coal — all this before the family was up.

But today I was to dust and polish. I liked cleaning and polishing.

I was to work until six o'clock with half an hour for my dinner in the middle of the day, which she said I was to take with the other girls. Usually they gave their servants a fortnight's holiday in the summer but since my home was so near they might let me have Sundays off instead.

She dismissed me to the corridor and told

me to walk along it and enter the third door on the left. This I did and saw a young woman working in the room making some sort of polish, I think, for it smelled of methylated sperrits. She looked up and said:

'Amelia will take you to the back sitting-rooms.'

I saw another smaller younger girl in the corner. She turned and came up to me and I saw she had a birthmark on her cheek.

Well, that morning Amelia set me off dusting table-legs and chair-legs mainly, which were not very dusty. I was not yet to be trusted with tabletops. I suppose they thought I might break whatever was on them. It was strange being at the hall without anyone I knew, and no Mam in the kitchen like I remembered there had been before when I was there. Everything was different. So far I had seen none of the servants I had once known, or any of the women from Stow Bedon I knew worked there.

Amelia gave me a brown duster and told me to shake it every few minutes at the open window. Obviously this was not a very important room. Amelia began to work on the table-tops and the chimbley piece and was quite silent.

I learned later that 'Melia Fenn never said much whilst she was working. I hoped they would give me some polishing soon, for at least you could see the result of your labours if you started on something dull or tarnished. But I didn't mind dusting. It was better than sweeping out the kitchens or wet-cleaning the floors. I supposed they would give me this once they thought I was strong enough, for I had glimpsed a big raw-boned woman on her knees in the passage beyond the far end of the room of my interview, slarting water from a bucket all over the stone floor and then mopping it with an enormous mop. Had I had better pretend I was delicate? No, I couldn't do that!

The rest of the day passed in work, apart from the half-hour in the servants' kitchen where I was given a bowl of broth and some bread and water. I sat next to Amelia and I did try to be friendly but I think she was very shy and maybe — I believe now — embarrassed about her birthmark which I was determined not to stare at. I got to know her better later, as I did most of the maids and some of the young men who were eating at the long tables, women and girls at one, men and boys at the other. The men drank small beer.

After this, I dusted and dusted all afternoon and when I finished the furniture in one sitting-room I was put into another with furniture all curly bits that were the d — l to dust! At about five o'clock the maid who had shown me the room came in again and said, 'The mistress wants to see you. Mind your hair's tidy and your hands clean.'

Well, I didn't think I could be looking clean and tidy — they hadn't let me wash my hands at the pump after dinner, or I'd been too shy to ask — so I plucked up my courage now and asked,

'Please can I wash my hands? — I have a comb in my pinny if you will let me use it.'

'What's it to me?' said this maid who, I later discovered was called Hepzibah Knights but we called her Heppie.

'Well, you said I must be clean,' I replied.

I suppose I had a tendency to argue but I wasn't letting another servant not much older than me get away with it. Mam had always told me to stick up for myself. Reluctantly she dragged me down the corridor and pushed me into a little room where there was one of those newfangled water closets *and* a tap *and* a glass!

'Don't let anyone see,' she said. 'It's not allowed for us to come here!'

Well, I washed my hands and combed my hair. I looked a sight with my hair needing a wash and no ribbon.

I followed Heppie down to the other end of the corridor and then past a big green door and then up some stairs. She put her finger to her lips, telling me, I suppose, not to open my mouth. At the top of the stairs we turned left again and soon I was being thrust into a large room.

Mrs Upcraft, whom I knew Mam had liked, was seated in a little chair near the window drinking from a small cup. There was a teapot on a tray.

Heppie said, 'Here she is, ma'am,' and curtsied before turning and fleeing.

'Well, Eliza — er, Emma — I hope you will be a good worker and then I'm sure you will be happy here at the hall,' said the lady.

'Oh yes, ma'am,' I breathed. I thought she was prettier than the housekeeper though she was older.

'I was so sorry to hear about your mother,' she added, not looking at me. She sounded as though she meant it.

I swallowed, not knowing what to say, so I just said, 'Yes ma'am.'

'You can go home early today, Saunders,' she said. 'That will be your new name here,' she added.

'Please ma'am, Mrs Foster said she wanted

to see my work before I left,' I ventured.

'I will tell her I sent you home,' said Mrs Upcraft.

So I was dismissed — and I ran all the way home.

4

There began then for me what would in the end add up to about seven years working for Mrs Upcraft. Sometimes when I look back on it those years all seem to have happened in a flash but when I have time to sit and really think about my time at the hall I marvel at how much I changed between the ages of thirteen and twenty. I was learning my 'trades': cleaning and polishing and 'turning out' rooms, washing and ironing and goffering, and observing Cook make pies and fancy puddings, though I was never allowed to do more than help to mix and stir. I already knew how to bake bread. Of course it took me several years to become proficient in all these household duties — as well as learning how to deal with nasty folk as well as nice ones. I hadn't a lot of time to dream of what Heppie called 'romance', not to speak of meeting a future husband.

One day I was in the kitchen cleaning some pans. I had been at the hall for about three months and each day they had given me something different to be getting on with. I had not seen George Starling since that first morning. I believe he took the mistress out in a small carriage if she had anything she wanted to buy in Watton or further away in Thetford. I learned afterwards that if she was feeling well she would just go out for the ride, for a bit of fresh air. She was a widow and they said her husband had left her a lot of money. As she had no sons, only three daughters, there was a lot of talk about who would inherit the hall after she died. Some said a nephew, as it must be a man, others said it would be the eldest daughter and her husband. But Mrs Upcraft was only in her fifties, I suppose, when I first worked for her.

In the coachhouse there were all sorts of carriages for him to drive: a landau and pair for visiting grand houses, a barouche for less important occasions, a gig, even an old-fashioned post-chaise, as well as several governess carts and traps like the one our Uncle George had brought us back home in.

Well, as I say, I finished my pan-cleaning, and showed them to a servant higher up than I was in the system. Naturally everyone at that time was higher up than me! The under-cook said they would 'do' and I could go and have my dinner.

I went into the servants' dining-room; two other young maids were already there tucking into their stew as well as Amelia and Heppie, and there was the footman, the odd-job boy, and one of the gardeners who came in for a pasty since Cook was his auntie and let him. I must say we ate quite well at the hall.

I was finishing my plate and wiping it with bread — I was always hungry — when in came George. Everyone greeted him.

'There you are, Mr Jarge. I say, you'd better ask Cook for a big helping,' said the footman.

George smiled, and greeted everyone and Cook came over from her kitchen with a plate for him. He smiled over at me and said:

'Hello, young Emma. How's a-doing?'

I had hardly uttered a word so far to anyone, so paralysed I was with shyness but I did not find it too hard to talk to George. After all, Mam knew his family.

'I'm a-going on fine, thank'ee,' I said.

He laughed and replied, 'Well, I'm glad. Your Uncle Banham asked me to keep an eye on you, but I've been away on errands. What shall I tell him, then?'

'Please send him my love and tell him Myra's with Gran, and Dad's managing,' I said in a low voice after reflection.

'Do you know him?' whispered one of the maids, a big fat girl called Emmeline who looked clumsy but was not.

'His family knew my mam's,' I replied.

Amelia asked, 'What was your mam called?'

'Eliza,' I said. 'Eliza Banham. She used to work here years ago.'

'Did she come from Caston?' asked Heppie.

'Yes,' I said shortly.

'My grandma came from there,' said Amelia.

I thought, if she comes from Mam's village perhaps she'll know about the man who built the windmill. I could ask if he'd ever worked here. I'd hoped that there would be talk of it in servants' hall, or of the young man who built it, if he'd worked here, but I had heard nothing.

George was munching away. He ate tidily and didn't say anything further until he had finished.

I said to Amelia, 'Did you know the young man who built the Caston windmill? They say he worked here too after he'd finished it.'

'No, I haven't been over home for a long while.'

George took a long draught of water before saying:

'You saw our windmill, then?'

'Oh yes — and my cousin told me that one man had built it all by himself.'

I wanted to ask George Starling about the

man. I wasn't quite sure why. I was far too shy to mention the name Jabez to him.

George looked at me without saying anything and then he came out with:

'He was a darned good worker, even if folk thought he was a gypsy! He did come on here afterwards. There were some repairs to do to the roof, but they couldn't find enough of the bricks they needed so he went off to another job. He was the sort to wander all over the place for work.'

He looked at me speculatively. Oh, I did want to ask him what the man was called. Had it really been Jabez? But I'd wait a bit longer when I could talk to him without all the others there.

George added: 'I believe he's been a bell-ringer over in Thompson. My brother James rings the bells in Caston.'

My heart gave a little jump. Bell-ringing might mean he was musical, mightn't it? I wanted to ask him if the young man had played the penny-whistle but just then George got up and wiped his mouth and I couldn't ask him then. But I kept thinking Jabez? Baz? They might not be the same name at all.

When George had gone, Amelia said, 'His wife used to work here for years, you know — but after she had the baby — little

Ann — she was poorly, so she went back to her own family for a bit.' Amelia apparently knew everything.

Soon Mrs Foster came in from what she called her 'little sanktum' — that was her own room — and made us girls all go straight back to work. We could tell the time only from the big clock on the stable building in the back courtyard but Mrs F had an instinct for knowing when our half-hour was up.

⋆ ⋆ ⋆

I almost forgot about the windmill and I hardly had time to think about Jabez Smith. I had decided, however, not to pester George about bell-ringers or whistle-players. I didn't often see him in any case as he was always so busy. So was I.

It was about nine months after I'd started there that Mrs Upcraft asked me if one day I'd like to live in at the hall. I'd still be very pleased to get away and live at the hall so long as I knew the lads were behaving themselves, but I worried about Dad, and I didn't think he would want me to leave home yet. I did a lot for him and the lads when I got back at night. I made Dad a cup of tea in the mornings before he went off to work and if we had some oats I made the boys' porridge. Gran looked after them all when I was at the hall but she was getting on and wouldn't want even more responsibility. Myra was headstrong and a handful.

I told Mrs Upcraft I would ask my father. I didn't get another chance to talk to George about anything for ages. He was always out doing our employer's business, and I was told by Amelia, who knew the other groom, that George's wife was still away.

I asked Dad about living in the hall and, as I had thought, he replied that he didn't want me to leave home yet. I could go when I was nearly fifteen if I still wanted to and if his mother was willing to go on looking after Myra, but there was no hurry.

'Soon Myra could go to school along with Bob and Percy.' I said. Then, 'Dad, do make sure the boys go to school. Mam wanted them to learn things.'

Dad said, 'Well, so long as they're not wanted in the fields,' and I knew it was hopeless. Percy — he wanted to be called by his proper name now — liked working outdoors and getting a little money for his labours, and Dad liked it too. I had the feeling though that Percy had rather liked school and was only doing what he felt was his duty. Bob was less keen on school work but tagged along with whatever his brother did. He was still only a little boy, only seven years old, and a strong child. I thought I might ask George Starling what to do about it. If Dad insisted Myra went to school soon it might be a way of forcing Bob there and helping Percy to go back too.

Every so often George would go on reading aloud to the other servants when they were having their fourses, from one of Mr Dickens's magazines. I don't know where he got it from — perhaps the mistress lent it to him or gave it him, for she knew he could read right well. Nobody else among the servants could read like that and we would all gather round to listen if we could steal a little time to ourselves.

I did one day have the opportunity to ask George his opinion. I was sweeping, then washing down, the passage that led from the tack room on the ground floor of the house through another door into a covered walk that led to the stable building. It was raining and George was walking into the house this way, coming for his dinner, I suppose. We maids did not always eat at exactly the same time as the outdoor staff and I had another half an hour before I could stop my work.

'Hello there, little Emmie!' he said. 'How are you getting on?'

I straightened up from my task.

'The mistress has asked me to live in,' I replied. 'But I'm not sure. My dad wants me to wait till next year.'

'And what do you think?'

'Oh,' I said, 'I wouldn't mind living in soon.'

I didn't need to say that I was kept just as busy at home with the boys, but I did say, 'I wonder, could you give me some advice?'

I sounded rather self-important to myself as I said this but he waited with a smile.

'It's my brothers — they often won't go to school — and Mam did want them to.'

'How old are they?'

'Well, our Bot — Percy is ten and Bob is seven . . . '

'It's hard to keep a ten-year-old in school,' he said, 'They like to be out working for money. But the younger one can't do very much yet, can he?'

'It's just that Dad isn't too bothered. I think Percy should be at school — he did like going there. I thought if they sent our Myra, then Percy and Bob'd have to go with her. But what can I do about it?'

'Aye. Nobody's yet made a child attend when there's something better to do and his dad doesn't mind! But why don't you tell your Bedon schoolmistress?'

'Dad mightn't like it,' I said.

'My sister knows her,' said George. 'What if I just tell her to let slip there's a child waiting to go to school in Caston with her brother? How old is your little sister?'

'She's four and a half. They'd take her, wouldn't they? She's a real handful. My Gran has her with her now I'm at work.'

He looked at me and said, 'Don't you worry, Emmy. Our fambly and your mother's were close years ago, and I'll do you a good turn when I can. Learning to cipher and read's very important, you know.'

'I know. I wish I could read like you do,' I said boldly.

He did give the impression of not quite belonging to the servants, though I wouldn't have thought he was exactly on the side of the masters or on their level.

But then he added, 'You should come to chapel — doesn't your dad go any more?'

He meant the Methodist chapel.

Caston folk sometimes came now to our chapel in Bedon because the singing was good. I loved it still but I didn't have much time to go. I knew that Mrs Upcraft would want me to go one day to the church with her other servants who lived in, and I knew folk didn't like the vicar of Breckles much, nor did the folk in Caston or Bedon. The servants agreed with my father and said the vicar here was always 'putting you in your place.'

'I'll try to go,' I said. 'But in the morning I have to cook our dinner. I wish chapel had a service in the evening like they do in the church. And bells!'

'We can all hear *them*,' he said, 'but the church has more money for a curate, so they can have more services. Never mind. See if you can go to chapel with your dad and your brothers. I won't forget to mention your Myra to my sister,' he added, as he went off for his dinner.

I'd wager they didn't have to make *him* go to school, I thought as he went into the house.

* * *

I did try to get Dad to go to chapel with us. I asked Grandma Saunders to come too — I knew she would be pleased that I cared about going — and to ask Dad to come along. I also told her that Myra ought to be going to school and that the boys would take her along with them.

In the next few months Dad did take us twice to chapel, along with Grandma, but then she found her rheumatism getting much worse and it was too painful for her to walk very far. By now it was winter, and a cold wet one too. I had enjoyed singing hymns and our Percy loved singing too though Bob was less keen. I went by myself once or twice but obviously George Starling had gone back to Caston chapel.

I heard Grandma and Dad talking one December evening when she had come over, bringing Myra back with her. She was saying that Myra ought to be going to school with the boys after Christmas. It would be easier for her as Myra was 'quite a handful' — but they could all go to her after school for their tea.

Dad said, 'The lads have been busy helping James Osborn all summer — he says they're good workers. I know they should get on with their book-learning now winter's come. I'll see they do, Mother.'

'And Emmie could live in at the hall in the spring. She'd get all her victuals there.'

My heart missed a beat. Truth to tell I wanted even more now to 'live in'. I felt much older now. But I loved my brothers and Dad and Myra. I'd have stayed at home and looked after them all if I could. Why did I have to work 'out'? I enjoyed it pretty well — since work had made me feel grown up, but I wished that I could stay at home until I was sixteen or so. But I gave all my money to Dad, not that it was much, but it helped with all his expenses.

Now Grandma said, 'She can still help out, though she must begin to save soon for her bottom drawer. I know Perce and even little Bob have brought you in a few pence but you should manage now if I take on your meals. It's no trouble cooking a bit, it's walking that does me in, and I can rest during the day if the little one is at school.'

I knew what she meant by my 'bottom drawer' but I was incredulous. I wasn't yet fifteen and she was already thinking of me getting wed one day! I knew Granny had married Ben Saunders at eighteen. Those days must have been more prosperous, because she did have a little chest with a drawer at the bottom full of hand-stitched nappery! *I* wasn't ready for no 'bottom drawer', yet. Talk of such things made me think again of Jabez Smith who I hadn't had time to think about since that conversation with George.

5

I went as a live-in maid to the hall a few months later. I was in my fifteenth year. Mrs Upcraft was very kind, 'cos she let me walk home once a month on Sunday afternoons, provided I accompanied her and all her live-in servants to church in the morning. This was very unusual. Most girls only got home once or twice a year. In course, Dad and the others wasn't very far away, not like some girls who came over from foreign parts. One, Emmeline, came from Suffolk and another, Mary Frances, from north Norfolk where there wasn't much work to be had.

I did look forward to those Sundays, though I had to promise to be back by seven o'clock. I so missed seeing my little Myra, who was now at school. Even Bob said the new schoolmaster was 'not so bad' and they were learning more interesting things now at school. Grandma Saunders was still giving the family something to eat at six o'clock and the children went to her first when they got back from school, though the boys were sometimes delayed, she told me, by games and fights and ramblings off. Myra always went with her brothers in the morning but came home with Hannah Tooke who was still at school. They said she was going to be a pupil-teacher.

Mrs Upcraft was a religious woman and a friend of the rector of Caston, the Reverend Mr Partridge, who had a rivalry with the vicar of Bedon. The Breckles living had just become empty so my mistress now preferred to go to Caston. The servants were conveyed there in a trap as it was a bit further away. Mr Partridge had this idea that servants should sit in the same pews as their masters or mistresses, that is, in the sittings the family owned. Most of us would rather have sat away by ourselves where we needn't be on our best behaviour. The rector was always talking about Judgement Day and telling the parents to set a good example to their children. I had the idea he had a low opinion of some of the village folk because he kept saying how disobedient their children were. I expect he really did want them all to go to Heaven. He often said if we didn't do our Christian duties we'd have to answer for it. I did listen to him carefully, though I still didn't enjoy the service as much as I had the chapel ones where the hymns were so much better, and sung so much more lustily. Some of the servant girls did get permission to go to chapel instead, and I ought to have done so, but I would always seize any opportunity to go to Caston for I had the fancy that Mam's spirit might be there. Sometimes, I'd see some of the Banhams in Caston church. If it was on one of my free Sunday afternoons, Mrs Upcraft let me stay in Caston for the afternoon and then I'd go for a walk with my cousin Elizabeth and one of the other cousins would take me as far as the road to the hall in his cart. That's how I got to know the village better. Everyone seemed to know me because they'd known Mam when she was my age, I suppose.

As soon as I was free and grown up I'd go back to chapel, I thought, and then I could spend more free Sundays in Bedon. I wanted to keep in with Mrs U, so I went along to the church with her for the time being.

* * *

One thing I did like about the church was the bells. They had been rung this particular Sunday morning and I'd wondered if my Uncle George or Cousin Isaac or George Starling's brother James had been one of the bell-ringers. Dad said they didn't stay for the service but went off to the inn afterwards, they were so exhausted and thirsty with their labours! I hadn't known whether to believe him but it was true I'd never seen my uncle in church.

This Sunday morning as we came out after matins, Mrs Upcraft heading the line of her servants, the rector was as usual waiting to shake her hand. He always had a few words with her and this morning I heard him asking her once again the names of those who accompanied her. He never seemed to remember from one Sunday to the next. Afterwards, he would shake hands with us and say our names as he did so, as though he knew us intimately.

I had very good hearing, and that morning I was sure I heard him say, 'Oh, is that the little Saunders girl? I remember now that I married her mother.'

I thought at first he meant he had been my mother's husband, before I realized he meant he had been the clergyman who had officiated at Mam and Dad's wedding. Fancy him remembering though! Mr Partridge must surely know that Dad's family were chapelers?

As I came up and curtsied to him I thought he looked at me rather sharply, but he said nothing about Mam. It had not been him who had been there for Mam's funeral; his curate had taken the service in Bedon that day.

The rest of that Sunday I had to accompany Mrs Upcraft back to the hall where I was kept busy trying to please Mrs Foster. I was told that she had conveyed to the mistress that I was a good worker. When I got back to the hall I was free for an hour or two and explored a bit. I glimpsed, in a corner of the tack room, ready to be put somewhere else, a treadle sewing-machine like the one my old teacher had owned! I remembered that Aunt Mary Ann, on a visit to us, had once showed Mam a picture of one, and I had just known I wanted to use one, and that I would be good at it. I don't know how I knew but it might have been because Mam was so good at mending lamps. Perhaps it might be a similar sort of talent. That morning the rector had preached on the parable of the talents and I'd thought about how I could one day approach the housekeeper to ask her about it.

I've often wondered what would have happened to me much later in life if I hadn't succeeded in getting Jemima the under-housekeeper to teach me how to use the Singer sewing-machine. I was hoping to become a sewing-maid and linen-maid rather than having to be promoted to ordinary housemaid.

But I might soon have no job at all. Times were hard and getting harder. When I was fifteen, Mrs Upcraft had to cut down on servants, and by then I'd been scullery-maid and kitchen-maid and laundry-maid. The next step would be to become housemaid or chambermaid, and then if I were very lucky, and didn't get wed, lady's maid! I wouldn't have minded that — but Jemima was soon to be given that post. The under-housekeeper was not replaced, though Mrs Foster and Cook were kept on. Our mistress got rid of the footman. There was to be no chambermaid, but if I did the sewing and mended the linen I supposed I would have reached that level myself and would be paid a little more.

Well, to cut a long story short, I made rapid strides with the Singer machine and was soon busy, starting with making uniforms for the servants — quite cheap to make if you knew how.

* * *

By the time I was sixteen I had learned a lot. Chiefly about cleaning and sewing and washing and ironing, and even looking after children, for now and again when Mrs

Upcraft's grandchildren visited the hall without their nursemaid, she would ask me to play with them in the garden. I knew this was regarded as a great treat for me. It was true she didn't ask any of the other young servants.

I had never found any of the other male servants at the hall in any way handsome or interesting though they acted the goat with us girls. George Starling was the only one I had ever had what you might call a conversation with, and he was still often away on errands. I noticed that he kept himself to himself among the men. He was always polite to them, laughed along with them when necessary, and was certainly never stuck up, which they would have regarded as the worst sin, but I could tell he was not really one of them. In course, he was married and lived away from the hall. I heard his wife had given birth to another daughter they were calling Mary Ann — Polly for short. The first had been an Ann too! I liked my own name better, though I liked Eliza, Mam's name, best.

We had a knap-kneed groom, Houghton, who they said had once been a jockey, and 'Mr' Hawkes the old boss-eyed butler was still there. 'Melia said he had been squinting at the silver so long while he cleaned it that his eyes had stuck. None of the other menservants were young. Even when I had passed my sixteenth birthday, though, I did not feel myself in need of a young man. On the whole, I liked the girls I worked with; 'Melia and Heppy and Emmeline and Jemima were the ones I was closest to, though sometimes I realized I was wishing there was a bit more excitement in our lives. I don't quite know what — a fair, a song, a story, I suppose.

One Sunday afternoon I was walking to Bedon along the long lane on my monthly Sunday visit home. Mrs Upcraft had fallen out with the rector of Caston, they said, and was now going over to yet another church, though there was talk of the hall church being revived. That day my feet were tired as I'd been standing around all the previous afternoon being handed jars of conserves by Cook who was standing on a chair to reach the high shelves of one of the pantries where they were kept, and my boots had been pinching me. I knew I was still a-growing.

Before I passed the mere I sat down to rest for a moment on the old oak-tree stump by the crossroads. It was a warm afternoon and I remember thinking I'd pick some daisies from the field or celandines from down by the stream so that when I got home Myra could make some daisy chains or play

‘Do you like butter?’

I’d have liked to take off my boots and paddle in the stream but then I’d be late for dinner with the family. It was not often I had any time for sitting down and just thinking and I must have been half asleep when I was roused by the dull sound of slow hoofs coming down the lane from the direction of Caston where a sideroad cuts across the fields.

I looked up and saw a donkey with a long chimbley-sweep’s brush and a bag on his back. A young man was walking slowly by the animal’s side. Not anyone I knew, and neither had I ever heard of anyone using a donkey to carry the tools of his trade. And it was Sunday too! He couldn’t be going to work. The man half-raised his cap and said, ‘Arternoon’. A little surprised, I replied.

I was still young enough to be rather pleased that any man should raise his hat when he passed me in the lane, especially as I was only a servant-girl, and everybody said I looked younger than my age.

I got up then, deciding to get on with my journey, but I could not resist turning round at the fork in the road to see him plodding on.

* * *

Norfolk land is so flat you can see quite far in some directions, so after this I used to see the 'sweep as I called him, occasionally plodding along some distant lane with the donkey at his side. But I never saw him closer than that.

I think almost a year had passed, and I was still living at the hall, before I saw him again to speak to. I used to be sent now to Caston on foot, and sometimes, more rarely, in the pony and trap to Watton, a great treat, to do some purchasing for Mrs Upcraft. I don't know why she sent me rather than the other girls but I was pleased. If I went in the governess-cart it was usually George Starling, now head groom and coachman, who took me and dropped me off at the market before going on his own errands.

One summer afternoon I was in Caston feeling rather tired and dusty. I had gone there with a message about new harness, as George was away in Norwich on business for our employer. Mr Gooch the saddler was however also away, and now I had to walk back. My boots were hurting; I had had a new pair only in the spring, but they too had always pinched, so I intended to go down by the stream on my way back and bathe my feet before returning to the hall.

I was seventeen now but they did not need me so much at home. Myra was content to go to school along with Percy who had developed into quite a keen scholar and a good singer, though he'd have to leave school very soon. Bob still didn't like school so much and often helped Dad in the fields as well as earning a bit of extra money working for Dad's cousin. Grandma was now in her seventies. Her rheumatics having got a lot worse, she had consented to come to live with Dad and the boys if they would let her 'housekeep'. She wouldn't take hospitality for nothing, that was not our grandma! She decided to invite her much younger son, our Uncle Jonathan, usually called Joe, to take his bride to live in her old house. Jonathan was in his late forties but had just got wed to Fanny Young, like her name a much younger woman, and they needed a place. Grandma didn't want to live with them.

'I don't know the woman!' she wailed.

I think she knew she would no longer come first with Joe, but she wanted to be fair. As Joe had always been her favourite child she decided to lease him the cottage that had once been owned by her husband for a half-crown a year. Then he need not 'work away' as he had been forced to do for many years.

If she could see them all now, I used to think, Mam would be relieved, for the boys were good lads, I was still in decent employment, and Myra — well, Myra was just Myra, a little madam, if ever there was one, singing and dancing and speechifying all over the place.

I was still thinking such thoughts as I took my boots off down by the stream that meandered from the mere to the river which I had never seen, far away.

I was day-dreaming, I suppose, for I started when suddenly I heard a voice say:

'I thought you lived in Bedon — or perhaps Breckles?'

I looked up and it was the donkey man! or rather, the 'sweep, but today he didn't have his brushes with him. He tethered the donkey to a tree.

'How would *you* know where I live?' I asked rather sharply.

I had been brought up not to talk in too forward a fashion to young men unless you knew them quite well. He was busy tying the rope and did not look round.

'I'm sorry, I don't know you, do I?' I said and looked down in the water at my feet.

He laughed, and sat down a few feet away from me. I saw that there were several people on the other bank of the stream and I thought, really I need not be afraid of this person.

The sun was shining and his voice was friendly. He still had the flat cap on his head.

'I see you sometimes on the lane to Breckles Hall,' he said.

'Well, it still doesn't mean I know you, does it?' I answered. He looked a mite upset but replied:

'I suppose not. But I know *you*. You are Emmy Saunders. Am I right?'

'Quite right, but you must tell me *your* name,' I said.

'Jabez Smith,' he answered, and doffed his cap.

I had almost but not quite forgotten that name and that he had built the windmill, and why, in any case, long ago I had wanted to know about him. But I found my heart suddenly missed a beat and my throat constricted as I said:

'You built the windmill? I thought you were a chimbley-sweep?'

'I am a jack-of-all-trades,' he replied with a grin, and scratched his head unselfconsciously.

'Well you'd best be careful if you sweep the chimneys up at the hall,' I said. 'There might be a dead priest hidden behind a panel by the fireplace brickwork!'

'I know,' he said, 'There's no priest, but there used to be a secret passage. A man I know went down it once.'

We were silent for a minute and then I said: 'I did hear that a young man called Jabez built the windmill.'

'Who told you?'

'Well, my cousin Sarah Banham told me ages ago the name of the young man who built the windmill. It's not a very common Christian name, is it?'

And now suddenly it all came back to me and I remembered exactly why I had once been so interested in the name, I had not forgotten about Baz but life had carried me on and I was always so busy. Baz had returned only in the dreams when I dreamt of my childhood. You know how quickly dreams fade. I wondered sometimes whether I had dreamed my childhood. But I knew I had not dreamed Mam. This young man, whoever he was, appeared friendly and kind.

'How do you know my name?' I asked him curiously.

'Oh, I expect someone told me,' he said.

Then he must have asked who I was.

We went on chatting for a bit and I told him I sometimes ran errands for the lady at the hall here in Caston and that today there was some harness that needed mending and that less often I went with George Starling to Watton.

'George Starling will see to the harness, I expect,' he said.

'He's away at present — that's why I'm here instead. You know George, then?'

'I know one or two of his brothers better,' he replied.

There seemed to be a cloud over his face now, and so I did not pursue the subject. I rose to make my way back from Caston to Breckles.

'You can sit on the donkey if you want,' said this Jabez Smith.

I was sorely tempted, for my feet were still feeling pinched when I pulled my boots back on but I did not know him well enough so declined the offer.

'Maybe I'll see you one day in Watton when I go to market there,' he said, when we made our goodbyes.

I walked back thoughtfully.

* * *

I was given the opportunity a week or two later. George was back and was to go in the trap to Watton so I asked my lady a little timorously if there was anything I could purchase for her in the town. Unless there was urgent work to do that afternoon at the hall, I might perhaps accompany Mr Starling?

She looked at me and, with the ghost of a smile, she said:

'I suppose you want a change? Well, you might buy me some embroidery silks at Browne's opposite the church. George will be pleased to take you, I'm sure!'

I didn't tell George that I hoped that as it was market day Jabez Smith might be in the town. I hardly dared tell myself!

We arrived about half past two at the clock tower near the market-place. I knew where to go for the silks as I had been before, and I told George I had other things to purchase for Mistress Upcraft as well. I knew he liked to look around himself and sometimes he'd meet a friend for a chat. We arranged to meet each other by the old market cross at five o'clock and I went straight to the haberdashers in Middle Street to buy the silks so that after that I'd have an hour or so free. The colours were lovely — six different violets and purples with the new mauve, as well as a new dark pink and a sky blue and sunshine yellow and primrose yellow — I could never have enough of looking at them.

I bought Mistress Upcraft the ones she wanted, and I nearly bought a blue cotton ribbon with the money I'd saved from what was over when I'd given Dad my wages, but I'd sworn to myself I'd save it for a velvet or a silk one and I managed to hold on to my sixpence. Then I looked at some kitchen bowls and basins in the market and heard the medicine man selling his black drops and his red cough-syrup — or trying to. I never saw anyone buy any of his wares that afternoon.

It was just as I was turning away, thinking I'd walk a bit by the other side of the market-place that I heard an 'Emmy!' then felt hands over my eyes and heard a 'Guess who!'

I knew who it was of course and turned to look at Jabez who was laughing. He had a goose under his arm!

'Oh, Mr Smith, you gave me such a fright!' I said, but he hadn't really, even though he had been cheeky enough to cover my eyes. I was just pleased to see him.

'Let's take a walk to the bridge and then sit down — if you have time,' he suggested.

It was whilst we were sitting quite comfortably together on the grass by the bridge in the sun, the goose, poor thing, a-lying at our feet that he said something strange.

I suppose I was looking at him quite closely, not even thinking about the fact that I was probably staring a bit, when he said:

'I'd like to be your friend, Emmie.'

I wasn't quite sure what he meant by those

words. It was true that — unusually enough for me — I already felt he was a friend. Even if we didn't really know each other, he felt familiar. Yet that word 'friend.'

What had I called Baz when I was little? *My Friend*. Had Jabez Smith really once been My Friend?

I was never really coy, so I replied:

'I'd like to be your friend, Jabez Smith, if you'll be *my* good friend.'

'That I will,' he said, 'But I expect you've got a sweetheart who wouldn't want you having a friend?'

'No, I have not!'

'It's better to be *friends*, I think,' he said.

We sat on companionably enough for a good half-hour, throwing pebbles into the stream and chatting, but I pondered those words long after. Maybe it was he who had a sweetheart.

He told me about the many odd jobs he had done. As he had no fear of heights he had sometimes been a steeplejack and put weathercocks on churches but his great ambition was to be a bell-ringer and a sexton. I thought being a sexton was a queer ambition for a young man, and said so.

'Nay, the churchyard is a peaceful place to work, and there are always jobs to be done there or for the parson,' he said. He intended to give up the chimbley-sweeping if a better job could be found.

I almost asked him then if he had ever lodged with my family in Bedon, but something held me back. Surely he would tell me if that had been the case.

He had taken his cap off and I observed that his hair was not red. It was dark, but perhaps there was a glint of auburn in it.

We went on talking for what seemed hours. It was truly as if I had known him all my life and I'm sure he felt the same. I had never spoken to a young man like this before.

After we had made our goodbyes, finally parting with a handshake that I for my part wished could have lasted longer, I walked across the market-place and came up to George by the market cross. He must have seen me shaking hands with Jabez Smith for he said:

'Who was that, Emmie, that you were talking to?

I thought it none of his business but I said:

'Oh, it is a friend from Bedon — you may know him — the chimbley — I mean — *chimney*-sweep?' I thought that perhaps George Starling, who had so much contact with the gentry, might be more impressed if I spoke proper English.

George said nothing, so I went on, 'He

does other jobs too, you know. I see him with his donkey in the lanes, and it turns out he is the man who built the Caston windmill.'

I intended to find out more about the windmill next time I saw him. George did not however look impressed. Instead he appeared rather displeased.

'Yes, I thought it was,' he said. 'If I were you I'd give him a wide berth.'

I gaped at him, and then I felt angry. I replied, 'I do not know him well, yet I find him very pleasant to talk to.'

I did not say that he wanted me to be his friend. I did not say that I felt I *did* know him. 'We like to talk together,' I added, as if we had the habit of talking to each other. But what could George have against that?

He said nothing more but was very quiet all the way back to the hall.

I knew that though I thought of Jabez as a friend I also found him a mystery, and that attracted me.

* * *

All us female servants at the hall slept in the attics and I shared a room in the eaves at that time with 'Melia. I had hoped to share with Heppie but she, being older than us and having also worked longer at the hall, had the luxury of a tiny room to herself. I couldn't stop thinking about Jabez Smith when I went to bed that night. I suppose I needed to fix my thoughts on someone, until then having only had my family to think about and worry about. Jabez had seemed so pleased to see me and had treated me in a friendly fashion, yet not too familiarly, as some of the male servants did if they got the chance with us maids.

I *would* like to see Jabez again as his 'friend'. He was a hard worker, you could tell that. He was the sort of young man you knew would make a good impression upon good people, but might make lazy or unpleasant people jealous. I don't know how I knew that but it was in my thoughts. George was neither lazy nor unpleasant so I couldn't understand why he should have warned me off Jabez. George had always been nice to me, and easy-going, and he had only seen me shake hands with the young man! I resolved to confront him with it.

I fell asleep late and had a mixture of happy and disturbing dreams. Mam was there in the first dream, Mam just as she had been when I was a little girl. She was sweeping the room with a large broom and I was playing outside the cottage making marks in the dust with a small stick. Jabez Smith was inside talking to Mam. Though I could not see him I knew it was him. Neither could I hear in my dream what they were saying.

Then the dream changed as dreams do and I was standing in a field with someone and looking at a windmill. It was a much bigger windmill than the real one in Caston, and I said to someone, I can't remember who, 'They are telling fibs — one boy could not build that by himself!' There was an atmosphere of sadness that contrasted with the happiness of the first dream so that when I woke I felt sad too.

When I got up at half past five and splashed cold water from the ewer on to my face to make me more awake I realized that the first dream must have been saying that Jabez really was my long-lost babyhood friend Baz. But if he *had* known me as a child, why had he not said anything about it when we met? Perhaps not at first, but when we talked in Caston? Or yesterday in Watton? Of course, I had not said anything too personal myself. Truth to tell, the old memory of 'Baz' was one thing, and this young man was something else, even if he had been Baz once. It had not at first occurred to me that the chimney-sweep was a person I had once known. Anyway, he didn't have red hair. But I was puzzled. He had raised his cap to me that time, hadn't he? *He* had recognized *me*, I was sure!

I had to prepare the morning-room grate and bring in the coal from the passage where it had been left by a manservant, but I was still trying to hold on to my dreams of the night. What were they telling me?

'Melia said, 'What were you dreaming about? You were shouting out in your sleep!'

Now 'Melia snored, and I had had to beg her to stop more than once so I felt she was justified in taxing me with this, yet I felt uncomfortable during the following days and still determined upon asking George Starling what he knew 'bout Mr Jabez Smith.

6

I didn't find time to talk to George Starling again for several days. The weather was overcast and thundery. Mrs Upcraft did not like the horses to be taken out unless absolutely necessary for they were afraid of thunder and lightning, so George was busy in the harness room, and I was turning out a room at the top of the big house which had not been swept or tidied for — it seemed to me — a hundred years or so. There was no point in going over to Caston either in the rain, though I intended to make sure I ran some more errands there eventually. For the time being I would have to be content with waiting for the weather to turn, and hoping Mrs Upcraft would soon find me a job to do away from the house. I had said to Jabez Smith that I might occasionally be in Caston but could not tell him when. If he wanted to talk to me he would have to find himself on the lane from Breckles to Bedon on a Sunday afternoon! Or he might perhaps ask for work at the hall.

* * *

The weather improved the following week but George was still elusive. His wife had been ill and he had had to take her and their year-old daughter, Polly, along with the elder daughter, Ann, to stay with her parents in Saham. I learned all this from Emmeline whose cousin lived in Saham where at present George's wife's family owned a house. Now that he was chief groom and coachman he had a bed above the stables at the hall, but being often on the road he was allowed to see his family when now and again he was not needed by Mrs Upcraft. In this she was an unusually kind employer. George stabled an old horse in Caston for this purpose; he could be at the hall in ten minutes, and in Saham Toney in less than an hour. I was sure that he would now bring his wife and children to live nearer the hall but I had never enquired about his arrangements. His own parents still lived in Caston.

The girls gossiped a good deal and it was from Heppie that I learned he was back.

'Emmeline's cousin told her on Sunday when she went over that Mrs Starling had lost a babby and was right poorly. It's a pity — but now perhaps he'll try to find work a bit nearer her family.'

I did see George for a moment the next day at dinner-time. I asked him how his wife was.

'A bit better,' he said quietly. I didn't want to say anything else whilst he was still worried about his Elizabeth Ann.

Next Sunday was my free afternoon and I walked along the lane wondering if Jabez Smith would be around. If he were, I'd like to have a nice long chat with him at home in Bedon. But that would be impossible. They would all think he was courting me and I was sure he was not. He liked me, I was sure about that, and even surer that I liked him. I'd better not show it though. I knew from talking with my fellow maidservants that the one thing the lads didn't like was a girl who made a beeline for him. Still, I wished . . . I wasn't sure what I wished, but I'd ask him more about the windmill next time I saw him. Then I might gather the courage to ask him if Jabez had been Baz, if he might ever have been the boy I'd called My Friend when I was only a babby.

But he didn't appear on the lane nor anywhere in the distance as I walked along home.

They were always pleased to see me at the cottage. I gave Dad the month's wages I'd saved for him.

'You're a good girl Emmy,' he said.

I knew it didn't amount to much but I was

proud I could help them all a bit. Myra was very talkative that day but I noticed how tired Grandma was. Bob and Percy were their usual selves. Percy sang a hymn for us all that he'd learned at chapel. He'd just left school. They'd kept him on as long as Dad could manage but Percy wanted to earn a few shillings for himself as well as for the family now. There was talk of his working away and learning a trade.

I left them at six as I had to be back at half past seven.

It was as I was trudging along the back lane by the fields that I heard music coming from something or someone. A pipe, it sounded like. I turned but could see nobody and there was nobody ahead.

Then I started and stopped, for a face appeared from behind a hedge on the right and the face was of Jabez Smith, grinning.

'Oh, you did give me a fright!' I cried.

'I'm sorry. I was up the oak tree playing my pipe when you walked along this afternoon but you looked to be in a hurry and I didn't want to hold you up and cut your visit home. And now you've got to get back?' He sounded regretful.

He came round through a gap in the hedge holding a little tin whistle in one hand.

'I'm sorry if I gave you a fright.'

'No,' I said, 'It was the music.'

Now I felt sure I'd known him before, but was still cautious about saying so. Instead, I said as we walked along:

'Did you really build the Caston windmill all by yourself?'

'Yes', he said, 'It wasn't too hard — you need a good head — I enjoyed doing it all by myself. That was four years ago . . . ' He paused. 'I wanted to tell you that I'm going away for a time. I've found a job, see. That's why I was playing that tune — did you recognize it? — because I have to go away again.'

I didn't know the tune, but I felt a lump in my throat.

'Oh,' I said, 'I'm sorry to hear that.'

'Well,' he said 'I've been offered a good job in Norwich — for a year or so . . . '

'Is it another windmill?'

'No, Emmy, it's helping with some bricklaying at the cathedral.'

I suddenly had the fear that this wasn't true, that he had a sweetheart in Norwich and this was just a way of being kind to me. But why should I feel that? He *was* my 'Old Friend', wasn't he? And a New Friend. Nothing more. I hardly knew him! And yet . . .

'What tune were you playing?' I asked him.

'It was a Scots tune. I can't remember what it's called exactly.'

We were walking along together now and I felt suddenly that if I were not to see him again for a year or longer there'd be no harm in asking him the two things that bothered me.

'Why did George Starling warn me off you?' I asked him boldly. 'You know him, don't you?'

'Oh I know George. I like him. I reckon he was a-thinking of you being so young and thinking I might want to . . . to . . . take advantage of you.'

I felt myself blushing.

We'd both stopped walking for a moment at the bend in the lane.

The other thing I wanted to ask stuck in my throat. After a few moments, I said, 'Well, you are my friend and I shall tell him so!'

He repeated, 'I *am* your friend, Emmy — and always will be!'

We walked on.

Soon we were standing before the gates of the hall, the long drive winding down to the hollow where it stood.

'Shall I see you before you go?' I asked him. I knew it was forward but I was right miserable knowing he'd soon be off and away.

'I'll find you when I come back,' he said.

I didn't know why I should feel so forlorn. After all, I had only known Jabez for a few weeks but it seemed I had always known him.

'Jabez,' I asked in a small voice, 'did you know me when I was little? Were you a lodger at our house? I seem to remember calling a boy like you My Friend long ago. But that boy had red hair.'

He started, but said quickly, 'I might have bin. I lodged in Bedon once but it was only for a year or so. I've lived all over the shop.'

'Then you don't remember *me*? I was only a babby. That boy played tunes on his pipe. I know I didn't imagine it though the others always said I'd dreamed it.'

I looked at him as I said that and he had a strange look, a mixture of guilt and embarrassment.

Then he took off his cap and smiled. The hair was dark but the eyes that looked at me were a brilliant blue. For sure he remembered it, but for some reason didn't want to say so. He stood there and neither confirmed nor denied it.

I knew I had to tear myself away.

'I'm late — I've got to go in. Good luck with your job.'

'Emmy, now you'll look after yourself, won't you?' he said.

I wished he would not go away and that he

would look after me. There was nobody else now who did. I had been so busy ever since Mam died, and even before, looking after folk. But I tried to smile, and wished him luck. We shook hands awkwardly.

Then he walked away but turned and waved, and then he stopped in the lane and played that tune again.

* * *

Without thinking, I was humming the tune Jabez had played as I set a late supper for Mrs Upcraft on a tray. I have always been able to reproduce a tune if I hear it once or twice.

'That's a sad air,' said 'Melia.

'It's one my dad sings,' said Heppie. 'It's 'Will Ye No Come Back Again'.'

A few days later when Heppie and I were working together I asked to her to sing the words for me.

'Let me get my breath,' she said. We had been beating the cushions from the morning-room.

I waited, and Heppie sang for me. She had a good memory but not a very powerful voice. I listened carefully and then sang it with her.

'Oh Emmy,' she exclaimed. 'You ought to be in a choir!'

I knew that the words 'Better loved ye canna be' would always remind me of Jabez Smith. Had he specially chosen to play that? Or had I gone and fallen in love with him as folk say? If I had, was it because he really *was* my friend, of long ago?

I thought about him a lot after this, but I didn't dare call him Baz, even to myself. My feelings were going up and down as the weeks passed, but I began to wonder if he *was* a gypsy. I knew there had been gypsies with the name of Smith in Caston at one time because I had once heard Granny Saunders talking about them with my Aunt Mary Ann. They had shut up when they knew I was listening but that was what they always did: 'Little pitchers have big ears', was what they used to say to me. I heard that remark quite a lot when I was a child for I loved listening to the grown-ups talking.

Had Baz been a gypsy? Was he still? Had I *imagined* that he lived with us? Had he perhaps only been doing a job in the garden or more than once trying to sell pegs to Mam? If he were a gypsy, that would account for his disappearing and reappearing and having so many different jobs. Yet they always said gypsies were lazy and Jabez Smith was certainly not that.

I thought I might ask George, even if he

did not think it a good idea for me to know Mr Smith. Maybe that was the reason. Even if they were poor, respectable village folk did not usually mix with the Romanies. George was the only person who seemed to know anything about Jabez. He was often away though, and if I ever did ask him I'd have to be a good actress to give him the impression that I was not particularly interested in Mr Smith.

In the end my curiosity triumphed over my caution and one day as he was in the yard cleaning harness and I was returning from the kitchen-garden where I'd been gathering herbs for Cook, I stopped for a moment by him and said:

'I do hope your wife is feeling better, George.'

'She's still weak,' he replied, straightening up and looking at me. 'She's back with my parents but I believe Mrs Upcraft is going to lease a cottage near here for her so that I can look after her better. You knew she once worked here?'

I had a sudden notion. Perhaps I could offer to look after their childer on my free day — take them round the village perhaps, so she could have a rest.

'I wish I could help her,' I said. 'I like little childer. I could come over to Caston on my next free day and take them to visit my Uncle and Aunt Banham?'

'Nay, Emma,' he said, 'It's kind of you to have the notion but there's enough folk in Caston will mind them now and then and you have only your one free Sunday.'

But I could tell he was touched at my offering. We went on for a bit chatting and then I said brightly:

'Mr Smith has gone to work in Norwich.' Then I added the fib: 'I heard it from one of the girls whose father used to ring bells with him. He's off again.'

I tried to look unconcerned; George should be pleased that I was out of the way of Jabez Smith.

'He's as bad as a gypsy,' I went on. 'Always here and there.'

He looked at me sharply. 'Maybe he is from one of those families,' he said, neither agreeing nor denying, but the grave way he looked at me gave me the idea that perhaps good men were afeared their wives might be led astray by Romanies in caravans. Good girls might run away with such men. Or gypsies might put a curse on them. George however was not a silly man. I'd even heard him telling the maids not to believe a fortune-teller, after one of them had had her hand read by a gypsy in Thompson village.

But maybe Baz really was a gypsy. I decided that George was 'having regard for my welfare' as the minister used to say in chapel: 'Have regard for the welfare of your children . . . '

I was not George Starling's *daughter*, however; he was just caring about me!

I wondered if Jabez had arrived in Norwich and how long he would stay there. The world seemed empty when I knew I was not likely to see him on the lanes any more. Yet it was only a few months since I had first seen the Donkey Man as I had first called him to myself. I could not believe it was so short a time, yet as the weeks passed, my conviction was strengthened that I had certainly known him as a child. To think of him made me now both happy and miserable.

Every time I tried to recall those very early memories I feared that they would be made vaguer and cloudier if I thought of them too often. The reality of My Friend was never so present as when I had heard the music played on Jabez Smith's pipe, and sometimes other music. Music meant a lot to me. I would sometimes hear the gentry playing on the pianoforte in their drawing-room at the hall and would try to linger there outside the door.

Remembering My Friend also made me

remember Mam, which made me sad. I realized that I had never mourned my mother properly. I'd had to survive without her, and when I was thirteen it had been too painful to think my thoughts through. Her death had been too much to take in aright. Now that I was older I could mourn her more deeply. But that did not make it easier. Harder, in fact, for it was all too late. I began to realize how much she had suffered and how much she had not wanted to leave us all.

I tried to remember only happy times, to remember my very early years even before Percy was born and sometimes I succeeded. I wondered whether Percy or Bob felt like that, but they never spoke to me of their deepest feelings. They preferred to live in the present, liked to keep themselves busy, not sit remembering. Dad was a man of few words too. Maybe if I talked to Mam's sister Mary Ann or to her brother, Uncle George they might tell me more of my mother.

You don't understand. your parents till you grow up. I wasn't yet properly grown up but I felt older and older! I was being given more responsibility now at the hall too. They might soon start training me up to be a lady's maid!

* * *

I did not hear anything of Jabez Smith for many months. Indeed I did not expect to hear from him again at all. It was from 'Melia that I heard. The father of a friend of hers in Caston was a miller and was searching, she said, for the man who built the village mill for advice over something that had gone wrong with one of the sails after a storm.

'Why, that was Jabez Smith!' I said.

'Aye, he said that, but they can't find him.'

'He's in Norwich,' I said, after a pause during which I wondered if I should tell her. But what harm could it do for 'Melia to know that I was acquainted with Jabez? It might bring Jabez back to Caston.

'Who might have his address, then? I could tell Mr King. Put me in good with him 'twould!'

Emmeline, who was listening to this conversation, said: 'Go on 'Melia. We all know you're sweet on Tom King! Courting you yet, is he?'

'I don't know Mr Smith's address,' I said slowly, 'but I do know he's working at the cathedral. Something to do with the brick-work.'

'How do you know? Is he a friend of yourn?'

'Oh, he's just a family acquaintance,' I said, and felt my heart give a jump. It was possibly true, I thought. 'Tell Mr King to ask in Norwich, he must take his flour around a bit?'

'I will that,' said. 'Melia. 'Ta, Emmy. Dark horse, aren't you.'

I pretended not to know what she meant by this, but I added, 'Oh, you can tell Mr King that you had the information from Emma Saunders.' Perhaps if she did, Jabez would arrange to see me again, I thought.

Before I heard anything more about Jabez Smith I had surprising news when I went home to Stow Bedon the following Sunday afternoon. There was an offer of work for Dad now in Caston. Old Granfer Banham had been approached to see if he knew of a man who would be willing to take on the job of village rat-catcher, at the mill and in village barns. Grandpa was getting on but there was still plenty of shepherding to do along with his youngest son, whom he had trained up to follow him. He loved his sheep, did not want to leave them. He had had the idea of asking Dad if he would like to move into Caston and take the job of vermin destroyer.

Before I could stop myself I cried:

'Oh Dad, you wouldn't want to be a rat-catcher!'

Dad looked grim and it was then I realized there was at present little work for him or

Percy to do in Stow Bedon. The price of corn had gone down and labourers were being given lower wages. Things were looking bad.

'Your Uncle George Banham has offered us a cottage at Northacre, one your mam's family used to live in and which they own. The family who lives there is leaving — going North for work, they say. We could all go and live there!' Dad said.

'Couldn't you go on here and just walk to Caston each day?' I asked him.

'If I take on the job I lose this cottage. I'd pay less rent to your Uncle George Banham over in Caston.'

But there was still Grandma Saunders to look after, I thought. Would there be room for her with us over there? We could surely never leave Grandma?

'I don't want to leave Bedon,' said my grandma now. 'I can manage fine by myself, or I could go back to live with Jonathan if they wouldn't let me stay on here,' she kept on saying, but not very convincingly.

I thought, but she does not want to stay with her younger son. She is just trying to make things easy for Dad. The idea did occur to me that perhaps Mam's family had always been a bit better off than Dad. Not better off than Grandma, but Dad had never earned much. Mam must have loved him a lot to marry him.

'We needn't decide till next week,' said Dad.

I went outside with Percy and Bob after a cup of tea.

'What do you think, Sis?' Perce asked me.

'We don't know if Uncle would want Grandma back. She ought to come with us if we do go,' I said.

I had always liked Caston better — it was Mam's place after all. And there was the windmill . . .

'Dad'll make his mind up,' said Bob.

But I knew that Dad found it hard to make up his mind, and he wouldn't want to leave Grandma if she wouldn't go with us. Yet he must find a job that paid better. Nobody liked being a rat-catcher but Dad would be better paid for that than he was for labouring, even if a farmer needed a man to work the land in Stow in future.

'Uncle said that there'd be work for a ploughboy too!' said Bob. 'I could do that, couldn't I?' Bob was now eleven and a good worker, but it was our Percy who needed a job.

'It all depends on Uncle Joe Saunders's wife,' I said. 'If she can do with Gran.'

Well, to cut a long story short, Dad decided to take on the Caston work and to accept the offer of a cottage in Caston at Northacre, a row of cottages at the end of the lane from the church. Gran did go to live with her son Jonathan. I suspect she'd promised his wife to leave them her best bits of furniture and chiney. Of course, it didn't affect me so much at first since I hadn't lived at home for some time and I wouldn't miss the old cottage. I'd never really felt at home there since Mam died. I said to Myra that Caston was Mam's place, but she didn't remember her so well. She was seven now and growing right bonny.

'I can go to school in Caston now,' she said. 'I don't like the mistress at our school!'

I reported the move to George Starling when next I saw him at work. Nothing more had been heard of Jabez — at least, nothing had been said to me. I still continued to hope he would soon turn up again.

'Aye,' said George, and he no longer looked cross, 'I know all about it. Whole village is glad your mam's family have moved back over. Eliza was always for Caston.'

'I know. She got married in your church,' I said, 'And I was christened there.'

'Banhams have always been in Caston, along with Starlings,' he said.

7

Dad and the lads and Myra were soon settled in the new place. It was better than our old home, less damp for one thing. Myra was thrilled — till the other children made up nasty rhymes about Dad's job.

Rat-catcher will snatch yer.

She told me this when I found her in tears on Caston Green the first Sunday I visited them all, after walking the mile and a half from the hall.

'But, Myra, he doesn't catch little field mice or the voles,' I said. I knew she liked them. 'It's only the rats — and he doesn't 'snatch' them, he puts poison down to kill them.'

'I know. He tells us all every day not to go near the top shelf of the outhouse. It would kill us all!' she answered dramatically. Myra was always one for making things sound horrible — or exciting. I thought then — and I think even more now — that she was very like Mam in that.

I knew it was a nasty death for the rats but

rats were the bane of all farmers' lives. It was the unpleasant ideas that have always been associated with rats, I suppose, that put the children off. They thought the rat-catcher the lowest of the low. Dad was the gentlest of men and I dare say he didn't really like killing anything but it was his job and he took it seriously.

It was certainly better than being on parish relief. They said many people were going on it now with the lack of work. Of course we had always had many old people who were paupers, even if some managed to live with a son or a daughter. Anyway, Dad wasn't old and he could have asked for help from his younger brother, but he would never have done that.

We passed George Starling's parents' house in The Street on our walk back to the new family home, the cottage on Northacre. I loved Caston but I never thought of Northacre as my home, even though many of Mam's relatives still lived around there. But then, ever since Mam died, the cottage in Bedon hadn't been my home either.

The sun had come out and we saw George's two little girls playing outside. There was no sign of their mother or of George. When we got back, Dad was out. 'On a job,' they said.

He worked every day if necessary. Percy had now found work — the ploughboy offer had needed a lad of at least fifteen, so Bob was being forced to go on a bit longer at school. But I had the impression that our Perce didn't much like the farmer he was working for, over in Thompson village.

'How does Gran get on with our Aunt Fan?' asked Percy. He was always more observant than his brother and thought about other people more.

'I don't suppose she really likes living back in what is really her own cottage,' I said.

'She could have come with us,' said Bob.

'Folk don't like change when they're old,' I replied. 'She belongs to Stow, like we really belong here.'

Perce looked surprised when I said that.

'Mam belonged in Caston, and I like the place myself,' I went on, 'but the house needs a bit of mammucking up!' There was one room downstairs, and the kitchen, and upstairs two rooms reached by a ladder. Things were all haywire in the room. Myra wasn't really old enough to see to the housework. I found a dwile (a kitchen cloth), wiped things down, then washed the pots in the tiny kitchen and sided them on to a shelf, and finally sorted the beds upstairs. Perce was sleeping 'out' now and Bob and Myra shared a bedroom. Dad had a little room of his own. Soon they'd have to swap round.

I shone up what I could and cooked them a stew from some carrots and onions I found on the table along with a bit of bacon they said Mrs Holcombe had left them. With plenty potatoes it made a good meal.

Bob said, 'If Grandma were here she'd have made things nice!'

'Dad wants you to come back home and look after us when he's saved a bit,' said Percy. 'I told him we could manage.'

I knew I could earn enough to help them out. What they needed was a mother. I found that I did not really want to come to live with them again. But where *was* my home?

'Perhaps Dad will marry again,' said Bob hopefully.

'Tell him I'm leaving some money here for you — and remember, you must help him.'

'Mrs Holcombe comes in on weekdays and Dad pays her for the cooking if she brings it over,' said Percy. 'Myra likes her.'

'Mrs Holcombe is nice,' said Myra. 'She tidies us up. But I wish I didn't have to go to school!'

'Look, Myra,' I said, 'next time they sing that silly song, you sing them another. They'll all know then how you well you can sing.'

'I can read too,' said Myra complacently.

'Teacher said I was the best reader. That's why they don't like me!'

* * *

I saw Jabez Smith once more that year I was seventeen, and it was almost the last time I saw him for a long time. I hadn't been able to go very often to Bedon to see Grandma as I felt I ought to go to Caston to help out with cleaning the house. I always cooked their Sunday dinner now as well. Mrs Upcraft was aware of our family's move for Mrs Foster had heard me telling 'Melia about it all, and how the neighbour was cooking for them when she could. She must have asked Mrs Upcraft, for I was given permission to take the whole of Sunday off rather than just the afternoon so that we could eat a midday dinner together. Mrs Foster knew I worked hard the rest of the week. She had turned out to be quite a kind woman once you got over her forbidding appearance and strange sing-song voice, and so long as she knew you worked hard.

Sometimes, Dad was able to eat with us, sometimes not. He did not much like his new work but 'twas a steady wage. He was all over the place and now he had an old horse to take him to outlying farms.

One Sunday in early autumn, still having heard nothing from or about Jabez Smith, not even aware whether he was still in Norwich, I promised myself to go to Stow Bedon to see Grandma and my Uncle Jonathan.

It was strange arriving there now, with our cottage still empty. I thought it unfair the landlord would not allow Grandma to stay in it. He was looking for another tenant, I suppose, for when work picked up.

I was greeted by my Aunt Fanny at the gate of Grandma's old house. Fanny looked still a very young woman, almost a girl, but she and Uncle Jonathan had as yet no children. Fanny was a mite untidy and I thought, Oh dear, Gran will not like that, for if there was one thing she couldn't do with, it was a 'slammocky' woman. At the door I asked Fanny how my grandmother was keeping.

Grandma appeared to have made her peace with her, or at least made the best of a bad job, for Fanny said:

'Oh we're rubbing along all right. But she's not well. Joe believes she's failing.'

'Is it the rheumatics?' I asked before we went in. Grandma was old, and most old people in our village died of that, along with bronchitis, as I well knew, that having been partly the matter with Mam. But Mam had only been forty-six.

'It's her chest,' replied Fanny. 'I does my best and rubs her back but she coughs something awful.'

I thought, Gran has always been so strong, except for the rheumatics, when she lived along with us in that damp cottage. Before that, she'd kept a good fire going here.

'We keep warm,' said Fanny, guessing my thoughts.

We went in and I found Grandma dozing by the fire in her old chair. I remembered how I had loved coming here to see her when I was little. I pulled a chair up and sat down beside her. I did not want to wake her but she opened her eyes and said in a croaky voice:

'Is it Emmy?'

'Hello, Gran,' I said, trying to sound cheerful. 'I brought you a bag of humbugs — and love from all the family.'

'How are they all? Your dad come over once but he's that busy now.'

'They miss you,' I said. I wasn't going to go into details about the difficulties of housekeeping over in Caston. But she knew they would have liked her with them for she said:

'I couldn't have gone, Emmy, I'm too old — and you see Fanny's looking after me in my little old place.'

Just then my Uncle Jonathan came in through the door at the back. He was a taller man than Dad and had a beard and sidelines (whiskers) and curly hair. I liked him but I hardly knew him. I could tell that he was the apple of his mother's eye though, for when he went up to her and took her hand she smiled up at him with *such* a look.

Fanny was busy making a cup of tea, a great luxury for me. I imagined Jonathan's work paid regularly. As well as working for a farmer in Lower Stow Bedon he had started up a little market garden where he grew vegetables and had some apple trees. Why had our dad not thought of that, I wondered?

Grandma began to cough over her tea and I could hear her chest wheezing.

'Tell your dad I'm well looked after,' she said as I left.

Fanny accompanied me once more to the gate. 'There was a young man come looking for you in the village,' she said. 'I forgot to tell you. I didn't know 'im but 'e went to your old cottage and folk must have told 'im to look for you here. I said you'd all gone over to Caston. 'Is she still at the hall?' he arst me, and I sez, Yes, you were. He was a right nice-looking man — he had a red spotted 'ankerchief on a stick over his shoulder . . . '

'Did he have a donkey?' I asked.

'Nay, no donkey, but 'e said 'e'd 'ope to see you soon.

It could not have been anyone but Jabez. I didn't know any other young men. I wondered why he hadn't gone to the hall, then I remembered he probably did not want George Starling to see him.

I walked away slowly from Grandma's cottage, wondering if I would ever see her alive again. It was only when I was already on the lane to the hall that someone pushed through the hedge.

He stopped before me. I stood stock-still.

'Emmy! I did hope to see you! Was it you who sent the message to that man King who needed help with his mill?'

'Oh, Jabez,' I said, and could hardly speak for the feelings that welled up within me.

'I wanted to say, thank you,' Jabez went on, 'I got a good stint of work from that fellow — but now I've to go off again. I wanted to say goodbye properly to 'ee.'

'Why didn't you call in at the hall? They would have let you speak to me — or you could have done some work for them.'

'Because I didn't want to get across George. I can't see you again, Emmy. I wish I could but it's better not.'

'What has George got to do with it?' I said angrily. 'He's not my keeper!'

He ignored this and just said, 'Never mind,' and took my hand as we began to walk along.

'I know we'll always be friends, Emmy. I wanted to know you were all right.'

After a pause he said, 'Not courting yet?'

He tried a smile but I could tell his heart was not in it.

I wanted to say, No, I'm not and I don't want to because I love you. Instead, I found myself saying, 'Baz, I don't care if you are a gypsy — I know you are *Baz*! I *know* that I met you when I was a babby! Why didn't you tell me? Had you forgotten?'

He looked bit afeared then and he said, 'What if I did? It's a long time ago, and nobody remembers now.'

'I remember,' I said.

'I'd better confess then and tell you I *am* half gypsy — and I have a sweetheart now.'

His last words came out in a rush and the odd thing was that I didn't believe a word of it, even the gypsy part, and why should I care about that?

I tried to sound dignified. I said, 'I won't bother you Baz, if that's what you want, but if I ever do need to get in touch with you, how can I do it?'

I don't know why I said that. I just felt I might need him one day.

'You can rely on me if you are ever in a spot of danger,' he said slowly. 'You can write me a letter care of Mr Thompson at the

Cathedral — but I hope you won't ever need to do that. Marry a good man, Elly.'

I saw with amazement that tears stood in his eyes as he said this. I did not understand them because I knew he knew I was fond of him, and I believed he was fond of me. He would not have bothered to seek me out again otherwise. He was like no one I had ever met except for the old Baz. We had hardly seen very much of each other since I'd seen him months before with his donkey and his chimbley brushes, and yet I felt I knew him. I wondered if he felt that too.

I said, 'I hope you will be happy, Baz, with your sweetheart.'

I don't know how I managed to get this out, but I trusted him in a funny sort of way. I didn't want his idea of me to be that I was a poor weak thing that couldn't look after herself. And men don't usually have tears in their eyes unless there is a good reason for them.

I too was choking with tears that I fought back. I knew there was something he was not telling me, and I also realized that I had to make the best of a bad job. But somehow at the bottom of my heart I was sure that I *would* see him again one day. We are taught to mistrust our instincts, and I expect many are the times when our feelings betray us and lead us to expect something better than what really happens, but I can't explain it except to say I felt sure that the old Baz would one day recognize me and all would be well between us. I wished I could say something that would show him my real feelings but not ask anything of him he was not prepared to give. I said:

'*You* might need *me*, Baz — you won't stop me calling you that will you, as we are to part?'

All he said was, 'Goodbye, Elly.'

He turned and almost ran from me, and never looked back once.

I walked slowly back to the hall.

Two things kept repeating themselves in my head. One was, Oh how I shall miss you, how I shall miss you! Which was stupid, for I had hardly seen much of him. But when you part with someone you love you feel wretched. It was a little like losing Mam again.

The other thing was that he had called me 'Elly'.

Nobody but Mam had ever called me Elly, and that was a long, long time ago.

⋆ ⋆ ⋆

I did not have much time to feel unhappy during the following weeks and months, and when, the following year, I had my eighteenth birthday. Only when I finally put my head on the pillow at night did I find myself depressed, with the realization come upon me that Baz was gone and would not be coming back. During the day I was kept busy with one task after another and perhaps that was best. It was not that I forgot him in the daytime, for I would often listen to the conversation of the other servants in case I might overhear his name. The very word 'chimney-sweep' or 'windmill' uttered aloud would make my heart jump.

I dreaded lest Mrs Upcraft or George Starling should introduce the subject of repairs or chimneys in case I trembled or blushed. But George never mentioned the name of Jabez Smith. He had other matters to worry him. His wife was ailing again and he looked overburdened with troubles. 'Melia told me that they thought Mrs Starling had the consumption. I was horrified.

Trouble was not far from our own family either, for Grandma Saunders had taken to her bed and we did not expect her to get up again. I went round about once a month as she lingered on, saying little to any of us now. On my other free Sunday afternoons I visited

Dad in Caston. I dreaded seeing Grandma but forced myself to go.

It was just before Christmas that she died. A hard winter had set in and Grandma had shrunk to nothing but a cough and a wheeze. Dad had gone over to see her during the week before, and on the following Sunday when I arrived in Caston they were all waiting for me with the news that Grandma had passed away the previous night. Uncle Jonathan had ridden over to tell them all.

'It will be brother Jonathan's task to arrange the funeral,' said Dad. 'You must ask your mistress for permission to attend.'

Myra's usual high sperrits had been dampened down and her chatter reduced by the news. I saw her looking frightened. Perhaps she did remember the time Mam died. I told them I would ask for leave; the funeral would probably be on the Wednesday and I would see that my brothers and Myra were cleanly and neatly turned out when I came to collect them.

Dad said, 'Ask George Starling if he will bring you over to us in his cart, then your Uncle Isaac will take us all over to Bedon.'

That was what I did. Mrs Upcraft allowed me to take a few hours off work and Dad said the vermin could wait while he bade his mother farewell.

'I should ha' insisted she came with us,' he kept saying. I knew it was not guilt that made him say it, since his mother had flatly refused to go with him to Caston. It was just the sorrow that always accompanies death. We wonder if we ought to have done more, always believe things might have turned out differently. But Grandma had used up more than her threescore years and ten, even if she had not enjoyed her last few years.

It was snowing the day she was buried and we were all frozen. George Starling looked ill himself when he took me over to Uncle Isaac's where the others were waiting. I felt like an icicle as we were conveyed to Stow Bedon by my Uncle Isaac, and the icicle did not really melt even in church. I tried to feel sad, and I knew I'd feel sad later but for the present I was frozen.

After Grandma's funeral other revelations were awaiting me. It was when we arrived back in Caston that my father said he had something to tell me. He looked a bit shamefaced.

'Well, Emmy,' he began, 'I met a widder woman when I was working over in Griston and the long and the short of it is that I've asked her to be my wife. She's accepted me. I was going to tell 'ee last week, but then we had all this worriting — over my mam's funeral,' he added, not very tactfully.

'Do the children know?' I asked. I was not really surprised.

'It's no disrespect to your mam,' he said, not answering my question at first. 'A man needs a wife — specially when there's a home to keep.'

'I know, Dad. Mam would have wanted you to marry again,' I said. I was not sure as I said it, but thinking it over later I decided that she would have been glad to know he was well looked after. Mam had always done her duty by Dad. But I did wonder whether she had really loved him. Not the way I loved Baz, I thought!

We knew nothing about our future stepmother yet, of course.

'She's called Hannah, and the children do know but I arsked 'em to say nothing to you,' said Dad, heavily. I was surprised that Myra had kept the secret.

'What do they say?' I asked him.

'Oh, they are pleased,' he replied vaguely.

I met Hannah a week or two later. She was quite a bit younger than Dad, about thirty-five, and she had a boy from her first marriage, a lad called William who was fourteen.

Dad and I were in The Room sipping a cup of tea, waiting for her arrival. The others had gone next door. When she came in, alone, I was quite surprised for she was a good-looking woman. I was sure that it was only circumstances that had made her accept Dad. He had a home and a job and it was not much fun being a servant, and not having your own little place, especially with a boy of your own. Dad was nervous but I made some more tea and she was quite pleasant towards me. I decided I would never see her as a mother.

It was not quite true that all the children were pleased. Percy was of course already working in Thompson village so felt fairly indifferent about it.

Bob said, 'Why couldn't he marry Mrs Holcombe?'

'Mrs Holcombe has a cottage of her own,' I answered. Myra was annoyed. Not in front of her father I am glad to say.

'I don't need another Mam,' she said.

She told me this on a cold Sunday the following month. It had stopped snowing the day before and the short-lived sun was bright in the sky as we walked round Caston. We went down The Street, her hand in mine. I wanted to ask her what she thought of Hannah but she forestalled me, saying:

'She's all right I suppose, but you know what will happen. She'll have more babies and I shall have to look after 'em! Well, I won't!' Myra was old for her age.

I calmed her down a bit and we made our way back. We passed George's house as usual and I saw he was with his two little girls just going into his parents' house. We crossed the road to him. The little girls were both tall for their age, but very unalike. The elder, Ann, had a long nose and rather small eyes and ears, whereas Polly, the little girl, had big eyes, large ears and a full curly mouth. She looked more like George. Ann looked cross but Polly smiled at me.

'I wanted to thank you for bringing me over the other week,' I said.

'Think nothing of it. But I shan't be able to help you much longer for I've found a job as groom in Snetterton. Mrs Upcraft has offered one of the church cottages on the Hall Farm estate. My wife can take the girls there to live and do a bit of schoolmistressing.'

I gaped at him. Was everyone going away or getting married? I seemed to be the only one who was to have just the same old life. Was his wife a schoolmistress then? I had never heard that before.

George went on, 'Caston don't suit her, and Breckles is only four mile from Snetterton. I can lodge over there for the time being.'

'But what will Mrs Upcraft do without you?' I exclaimed.

'They have their problems, the Upcrafts,' replied George. They're cutting down on the carriages and she can't pay me what I could earn as groom to a richer man over in Snetterton. She understands. I can help her out now and then when I come over. My brother Henry will go on living here to help my parents.

'You must think it over for yourself too, Emmy. If you worked at Hall Farm rather than the hall you'd be nicely near my wife and the girls. Farmer Oldfield would find you work if Mrs Upcraft spoke for you. They say he needs another maid; his sister and niece have come over to live with him. He's a widower and he's over four hundred acres to farm — a right big amount of land!'

I thought it strange that this farmer who rented his land from my mistress seemed better off than the family at the hall.

'But she wants to train me up to be lady's maid!' I exclaimed.

'There'll be no lady's maid, Emmy. That's a luxury, gal! You can earn more if you move, now you've had the experience.'

Were his suggestions a plot to get me to be handy to help his wife and children if he was to live away? I had no desire to leave Mrs

Upcraft, but I was worried that George found it needful to warn me she was losing money. I'd always thought if you had money it stayed with you and that was that.

I had all this to ponder when I got back. Nobody said anything about it for a few days and then Mrs Upcraft asked me to see her.

'I'm afraid I have bad news, Saunders,' she said. 'We are having to rein in our expenses.' She looked out of the window as she spoke, not directly at me. 'As you came last, you will have to be the first to go. I am extremely sorry to have to tell you this. You have been a very satisfactory worker here and I shall give you a good reference. I gather that my groom, Starling, has spoken to you about work at Hall Farm? Oldfield needs another maid-servant. He knows about you and will see you tomorrow.'

What could I say? I felt terribly worried. But I'd need this new post as soon as possible.

'I shall pay your wages to the end of next week,' said my mistress.

Even less time than I'd imagined! I resolved to walk over to Hall Farm the next day. Would they have me as live-in servant at the farm?

I curtsied and she looked quite sad when I went out. 'Melia and the others said they would be next and I'd be sure of a good job with Oldfield. But I knew how women farm-servants were regarded. Lowest of the low. Once a farmhouse servant always a farmhouse servant, they said.

I realized that it would be rougher work than at the Hall, but I had not then taken in that I would actually be paid the same — seven pounds a year — as if I had stayed on at the hall, where a housemaid could eventually earn twelve pounds. We had even heard of a housemaid who was earning thirty pounds by the time she was forty. Of course she would have been in a place over twenty-five years. All that talk of lady's maid and all they had promised Mam! But I knew that Mrs Upcraft had had no choice. Apart from my family, the hall was a link with Mam. They'd known her there.

Things were all changing too quickly. I admit that my worst fear was that Baz would not know where to look for me if he did come round these parts again. Yet Mrs Foster would tell him where I was, wouldn't she? It was only half a mile away after all!

8

I went to be looked over the very next day. Hall Farm was a nice roomy old place, with fields all around. What surprised me was that Church Cottages, where George's wife had already moved with her girls, was so near the farm, at the edge of the nearest field, on a lane near the hall church.

I decided I'd better go over and see Mrs Starling and her children on my way back from my 'looking over'. I ought to get to know them better.

I'll pass over what the housekeeper at the Hall had called my 'interview' with Mrs Boulding, the farmer's sister. All Mrs Boulding had said was:

'We don't have the hall fancy ways here.'

And I replied 'No, ma'am,' but my heart had sunk.

There had been a little girl of about eight called Jane in the room with us whom I presumed to be her daughter. I smiled at the child though she looked rather sulky.

'You'll do,' was all Mrs Boulding said, and I was dismissed, to return in a week.

Later I discovered there was an older

servant called Lydia Kettle and one even younger than myself called Eliza. I'd miss 'Melia and Heppie and the others.

* * *

I walked over to Church Cottages feeling rather nervous. I'd never met George's wife, seen her only in the distance, but she received me very kindly. She was a tall woman, very thin and pale except for two spots of red on her cheekbones. Her hair was dark. I was dying to ask her if she was really a schoolmistress but did not know how to turn the conversation round until she did it herself.

'I am to teach little Jane over at the farm,' she said huskily, 'Along with Polly and Ann.' Polly and Ann, hearing their names, peeped round the door.

'Come in children,' she said. 'This is Miss Saunders, a friend of the family.'

They advanced, the smaller child cheerfully, the elder, darker-haired Ann, hanging back. I saw now that she had a hint of what her mother might have looked like when she was younger and stronger.

'I heard a lot about your mother,' Mrs Starling went on. 'George told me about you as well. Are you to take the post at the farm?'

She had a nice voice. I wondered how she had met George. She seemed older than him. She enlightened me about this too until she began to cough. Polly ran into the pantry for a glass of water which her mother sipped gratefully.

George had worked in Watton when he was in his early twenties and she had been a sort of parlour-maid to the family where he was coachman. They had got together because she had seen him one day waiting for the lady of the house, sitting on the driver's seat reading! It turned out to be a copy of *Household Words*.

'Mr Dickens, you see,' she explained.

I was at a loss to know what to say. I knew George was a great reader but he was only a working man and she seemed somehow different.

'You look surprised,' she said. 'My father was a cottager like yours. It was just that my aunt, who had married her wealthy employer, paid for me to go to a school for a year or two so that I could find myself work. When George came to the hall here they found me a post — not as a governess but as lady's maid to Mrs Upcraft's daughters.'

Otherwise, I thought, she'd have started off at the hall the way I did.

Mrs Starling was so easy to talk to that I

soon found out about their courtship and marriage and her move to Breckles and about Ann and Polly who were both 'clever girls'.

I have since found that women who have the consumption are often very talkative. It may not be their real nature, just their heightened nerves, like their heightened colour. Anyway, after this I visited the family whenever I could and nobody said a word about illness.

Her husband came over every other week but I did not see much of him. Mrs Starling always told me he sent his regards.

By then I was too busy baking and cleaning and feeding the nine young men who worked for Farmer Oldfield, all with hearty appetites. Two things that were good about this post in spite of my wages and lowly position, were that the place was warm — fires were always kept going — and the food was plentiful.

The farmer's niece, Jane Boulding, went over for lessons with Mrs Starling as there was too much going on at the farm and I believe her mother was glad to get her out of the way. I cannot say I made any other real friends. Lydia was too old and Eliza too young for me and the work was never ending. It stopped me thinking too much but I already had the notion that it would be nice if our Percy could come and work here. It would be someone for me to talk to.

I did see George one spring morning. I'd been sent over to the village for some yeast — we baked scores of loaves every Thursday. He looked worried but he stopped and gave me a lift in the little carriage. He was off back to Snetterton.

'Can you look in on my wife, on Elizabeth?' he asked me.

George had only ever said 'my wife' before this and his saying her given name made me sorrier for him in a strange way. He was working very hard in Snetterton and could not always get home. I wanted to ask him if he really needed to work away but I supposed he knew best, though I had noticed how ambitious he was.

I liked little Polly, but Mrs Starling probably lacked company too, though she'd never complained to me of feeling lonely.

'She's not well — gets easily tired,' he added.

I knew that. I said, 'Have you had the apothecary round?'

Not many folk could afford an apothecary but I thought George would if he could.

'There's naught to be done,' he said sadly, and it was the first time I'd heard him speak like that about his wife.

'I thought the quiet would suit her and she

likes the cottage but I worry about her cough. She's always been delicate.'

I had my nineteenth birthday that spring and I was hard-worked too. As I had expected, it was rougher work than my cleaning and 'mammucking' at Breckles Hall but it would stand me in good stead, I thought, if I ever had a home of my own. I think I could have made pies if I were blindfold. The men who worked the farm were all so hungry, and I too ate better than I ever had before. One thing I did miss that surprised me was the beautiful crockery and plate at the hall. I thought I'd never see such lovely things again, for the farm crocks and mugs were of rough earthenware. I had loved cleaning Mrs Upcraft's precious objects.

By this time our Percy had joined me at the farm and was a great comfort. He was now one of Oldfield's ploughboys but, like George, he wanted a better job.

Myra was the one I worried about most, especially when, as she had forecast, my father's new wife had a baby. Not just one baby, though, but twins, a boy and a girl! It was a bit of a disaster for Dad, though he did not complain, but Myra was really jealous. No longer the youngest of our father's children she had taken to disappearing when she was on an errand and not telling anyone where she was. She was needed to help with the babies and Dad asked me if I would speak to her. What with being needed to speak to Myra and being asked to look in on Elizabeth Starling I felt I was in great demand. I liked to help but I myself did not have much time for others. Dad would never raise his hand to Myra but I knew how provoking she could be.

I got Percy to bring Myra over to us one Saturday afternoon — the farm work continued on Sundays as far as the animals were concerned so it was not always a Sunday I had off now. This May afternoon was lovely and warm and sunny, but I was determined to have it out with my little sister. I might even ask if she could work in the kitchens with me though I did not hold out much hope and Myra herself was not very handy.

When she came that afternoon Percy very tactfully disappeared on one of his walks. I should have thought he had enough walking whilst working but he liked to go off by himself. Nobody worried about him. After all he was sixteen, but Myra was only nine.

I had a little room, a sort of cupboard really, next to Eliza's, but as it was such a pleasant day I suggested we went outside.

'Oh, can't we stay in here?' said my sister.

'I'd like to dress up in your clothes. Let me wear your apron!'

Myra had always liked the idea of dressing up: she had once 'borrowed' Bob's trousers. I did not understand my sister. I had never wanted to wear any clothes but my own! I remembered though that once when she was only about six she had found an old petticoat of Mam's that I was going to cut down for myself and had worn it tucked round her waist. She had put on my boots and pretended she was someone else, and she had looked a picture. She was still a very pretty child with long auburn ringlets and blue eyes. She still had a temper too.

'Our stepmother's brother has promised to take me and William and Bob to Thetford to see the travelling players!' she announced. I was surprised. Perhaps Hannah's family were a bit more enterprising than I had thought. I had learned that word from George's wife.

'William doesn't want to go, but I do! He's a silly boy — he's found work at the forge now with our uncle. A girl at school told me about the players. Have you ever been to Thetford, Emmy?'

'No,' I replied. 'Never the once. But I have been over to Watton many a time.'

'You should get your Mr Starling to take you in the trap,' she suggested. I had told her

I'd walk over with her to Mrs Starling's so she could meet the little girls.

'I'd be glad to go to Thetford — I wish I could get out more,' I replied, 'but I'm too busy and Mr Starling is now in Snetterton.'

I could not drop in on Elizabeth Starling whenever I felt like it but I'd got used to taking Jane Boulding, the farmer's niece, there for her lessons.

On the way there I ventured to say to Myra that she must help more at home.

'I don't like babies,' she said. 'How old do you have to be to leave home?'

Oh dear. 'You might find work when you are twelve,' I said.

'I don't mean a *post*!' said Myra crossly. 'I just want to leave home. I shall run away, you know!'

I changed the subject, and when we got to Church Cottages I was relieved to find that Myra could be perfectly delightful. It was all part of her pretending to be someone else, I thought. She was so attractive, rounder faced than the girls who now joined us, and I saw that Mrs Starling was impressed by her. They all went out at the back of the cottage where there was a little garden and I was relieved to hear laughter as they ran around. I knew I must soon speak to my sister again about helping more at home. I knew she would then suggest she might leave school and would not have put it past her suggesting she could be paid for helping out with her half brother and sister!

Elizabeth Ann Starling and I chatted cheerfully enough though I could see that she was tired. I asked her how Jane Boulding was getting on with her school work.

'I'm afraid she is not very clever,' sighed Mrs Starling. 'I do my best, but it makes for bad blood with the child's mother when our two girls are so clever.'

'They both look very capable,' I said, for lack of anything to counter that with, for I knew I was not clever myself, except in the matter of sewing and making things, and there was nothing in that line for me to do at the farm as there had been at the hall.

Mrs Starling brightened up.

'Oh they are both so good. George has told them to look after me and they do help me a good deal. If only George could have found work over in Saham Toney where all my family still is . . . '

I realized she knew she was really ill.

The girls came in soon after this.

'How are your little brother and sister?' Mrs Starling asked Myra. I had told her of the recent twin births to my father and his wife.

Myra's face clouded over. 'They are horrible. They cry all the time!'

Mrs Starling laughed. 'I know — babies can be hard to get on with at first.'

I was surprised. Perhaps she had not found them easy herself.

'Twins must be very hard work,' she added.

I thought she might be just the person to talk sense into my sister.

Myra however was soon back on her favourite subject: herself. 'I am going to be an actress!' she stated.

'That is very hard work too,' said Mrs Stone, not at all shocked.

'I can sing and recite to you now if you like,' said Myra.

Polly said, 'Oh, do! do!' but Ann looked sour.

'No, Myra, Mrs Starling is tired . . .' I began.

'You must come to see us again soon,' Mrs Starling said to Myra as we left. 'My husband could call for you in Caston on his free day if you would like to stay here overnight.'

'Oh, yes please!' said Myra.

After our visit, my sister said, 'She is very elegant, that lady, isn't she?'

'Polly and Ann are nice too,' I said.

'Yes, they are all right. They are not babies,' said Myra.

There was however little chance of Myra visiting Breckles again for some time. I was hard pressed with work and George Starling did not always know when he could be spared by his employer. I thought he should take his wife and the girls to Snetterton in lodgings so she would be less lonely. She told me she missed him but would rather be in this little place at least for another year.

I got to know both her girls well. They were very different. Ann was a serious child, not very talkative but very sharp underneath. Polly was always cheerful and smiling, a kind child, very helpful to her mother though she was only four. George appeared to prefer Ann, who possibly looked more like her mother than Polly did but he was always firm and just with both of them. Fortunately, the girls did not get on too badly with each other. I used to drop in on my way back from the village on a 'narrand' or taking fourses to the fields for the men, and Mrs Starling was always glad to see me.

I imagined she would rather have had George stay in the cottage with them and earn less with Farmer Oldfield than go seeking a fortune for his family in Snetterton. But then George had always had a lot of ambition. What he did, he did for his family. Once or twice, later, Elizabeth Starling mentioned to me what I knew she dreaded above all . . .

But I must not get too far ahead with my story. Elizabeth's decline was at first very slow, and there were days when she appeared much better. But in the end she seemed to struggle not to lose heart.

George came over more frequently in the autumn of that year. He begged me to keep on visiting her until he could find another coachman's job over in Breckles that paid as well as his present one. I knew he sent almost every penny of his earnings over to her and the girls.

In November he asked me if I could go and live with Elizabeth and the children at Church Cottages whilst continuing with my work at the farm. I asked Oldfield but he refused. He said he needed me to live at the farmhouse; it would be too inconvenient if I lived half a mile away. Jane Boulding had given up her lessons but I still took every opportunity to go over to visit Elizabeth and succeeded occasionally in taking the girls for a walk, or over to the farm, to give her a rest.

By the time I had my twenty-first birthday in the April of 1872 Elizabeth Starling was visibly failing. After that, her decline was rapid. I remember thinking, surely those clever people in London you heard about from the newspapers George used sometimes to read could find a cure for the decline. I wondered whether Mam had died from it too but they had said with Mam it was bronchitis. Church Cottages here were not as damp as ours in Bedon had been; there seemed no reason for her death.

When she died it was in June in her husband's arms, Polly and Ann in the next room. George sent for me the day after she died, and I tried to comfort the weeping girls; a wisewoman from Breckles had laid their mother out. George took the children over for the time being to Watton to their grandfather's, where their mother's older, unmarried sister lived; George himself went on working and saving in Snetterton.

The week after she died, my own dear Granfer Banham died. William the Shepherd, as everyone called him, was eighty-seven, a great age, having outlived many of his own children. All his live children and most of his grandchildren were there at the funeral; a big family. I did not know them all well, for some of Mam's sisters had moved to other villages when they got married. I knew Uncle George, of course, and Aunt Elizabeth, and my cousins, Sarah and Alfred and Isaac and young William, and Aunt Mary Ann of course, who cried. I cried a little too, sitting with Myra and Bob and Percy, but I do not know if it was for Mam, or for Elizabeth Starling, or for my grandfather.

Dad's new family was not there. I felt very low, but it seemed to me that the rector of Caston made a special effort to look as if he meant his word: the sermon was about the sheep who strayed.

My low spirits were compounded by the sadness I still felt over Baz. As we came out of the church to walk round to the graveyard, my eyes still full of tears, I had a kind of strange fancy that my childhood, along with Mam and Baz, was waiting for me, hiding behind a gravestone. But I had to pull myself together for Myra and the boys, who were all looking very upset. A younger brother of George, Henry, came on afterwards when Mary Ann Banham gave the village mourners cups of tea and bread and butter, but his father and mother did not.

They all spoke solemnly to me, first about my grandfather and then about their sister-in-law who had just died. George was not there; he was not easily spared from his work.

9

It was August and I was still working at the farm. I was feeling increasingly restless, and worried about the two little orphans, Polly and Ann. George had buried his wife in Saham Toney, her home village, and had come over to clear the cottage two Sundays later.

I found the girls slumped in the cottage garden that hot afternoon. I was surprised to see them for I had thought they were still with their aunt. But George came out into the porch and whispered that the girls were now to stay with him. There was no further explanation, but I imagined that the aunt had found them too much for her.

'I am to take them to my lodgings in Snetterton,' he said. 'My landlady will keep an eye on them if I pay her enough.' But he sounded really despairing.

Their mother had known she would die and she had made herself feel worse over what would happen to her children when she was no longer there to look after them. She had told me as much, and I had not been able to help showing my distress.

'Could they not live here?' I said. 'It would not cost more than your lodgings.'

'No, the cottage will have to go back to the hall — I have already ascertained that.'

I had liked George's wife and was fond of his children, especially Polly. I knew that I could offer to look after them in Snetterton, but anything further had been miles away from my mind. It was true that I might be ready to leave the farm, find new work somewhere else, now that I had a bit of experience of work, now that I was older, and could see my father and his family were more or less settled. I might have admitted also to a little bit of what a new song going round — from the music halls, I suppose — called 'Wanderlust'. If I were never to see Baz again I wanted a life of my own. But of course I had no money and would have to find work. George couldn't afford to pay me, in addition to the rent he paid the Snetterton landlady.

I remember thinking that what he really needed was a wife who would look after the girls. Yet I never connected this idea with myself! Not even when the idea came to me of being paid for looking after children.

Nobody could have been more surprised than I was when a week or two later George asked me if I would think about being a mother to his motherless girls. That was all that he said.

He'd seen me walking back to the farm from the hall where I had called on 'Melia for a chat, and he offered me a lift in the trap. He was on his way back to his lodgings in Snetterton, having been to Saham to see the children's grandfather. He had left the girls for a few days with his sister in Caston, he said. Perhaps things were not working out too well in his lodgings.

It was after I had got down from the cart, just as I was turning to go through the farm gates that he spoke. Even then I wasn't sure if he meant a job or a marriage! I think he was at his wits' end and appeared mighty embarrassed. 'Just think about it, Emmy, will you?' That was all.

The following week I happened to be in Caston on a Sunday visit to see Myra, when there was a knock at Dad's door.

I opened it and there was little Polly Starling standing in her Sunday best with a white pinny over her draggly skirt.

'Dad says, can we play with Myra?' she said.

'Where is your father then?'

'He's in at my grandma's but he has to go back to work at seven o'clock. Please can we stay with you for an hour?'

I saw Ann lurking behind the bend in the street. 'Come along in, Ann!' I shouted, holding the door open for Polly.

Myra came up and took her over with a great show of fussy friendliness that was over Polly's head, before Ann sidled in and stared at me.

Although Myra was twelve and Ann only six I could see that Myra might have met her match here. I prayed she was not going to say 'Your mother is dead', for I knew that was what the 'show' was about, and the girls might burst out crying and remain uncomforted. But Myra said nothing and I think that Polly and her sister were relieved they could just be ordinary again.

The girls' father came over about an hour later to fetch them. As it happened, my father was back, and I saw him drawing himself up to comment upon his neighbour's wife's death.

'I was sorry to hear of your trouble,' was all he said and George replied, 'Thank 'ee'.

The twins were bawling as usual but were then shown off to the visitor who looked a little nonplussed. Then my father put his foot in it by saying:

'We was wondering how you was going to manage with your lasses now.'

I saw George look over at my stepmother

as if to say, well, you found one way out, but then he said:

'I am thinking of emigratin'. Elizabeth was willing, but we left it too late for it to be done together.'

'Where was you a-thinking of going then?' my father asked. 'Australly? Canada?'

'Nay, not now. I am considerin' going where a neighbour once went a few years back. Up North. There's work there he says . . . '

'And you would cut off and go — and never return?' my father asked, sounding quite shocked. Of course he was a much older man than George who was himself about thirty-six, probably, I thought; not yet too old himself to be feared of change and upheaval.

'There's others of the same mind,' replied George. I wondered who they were and what his ideas were. I had not heard such 'emigration' mentioned by him before.

'When she was seventeen, Mam wanted to go to America,' I put in. 'She once told me.'

'Aye, well, your mam didn't go. It's different for the men,' my father began, but George interrupted him.

'Oh, there's many a girl too who's all for settlin' far away — so long as there's work and bread.' And he looked at me so searchingly that I began to wonder what he was up to.

They left soon afterwards and Dad said, 'There used to be talk of it twenty, twenty-five years ago — and some folk did go — it was around the time there was trouble over corn just before your Mam and me got wed.'

'What became of them then, Dad?' I asked him.

'Oh, we never heard but once — at least I didn't, but 'twas said they were living in coal heaps, all black, and working day and night. There weren't no fortunes to be made, girl!'

'But there might have been a bit more to eat,' I said. I was beginning to find the idea quite attractive, though I hadn't really thought it out. I knew I was now old enough to know my own mind and to go to work wherever I wanted.

No longer a child, they said.

I saw Dad looking at me speculatively just then and it was the next week that George, in the kitchen of number three Church Cottages, where I had gone to help him finish packing up some flour and pans and bowls he had left there, got round to offering me his hand in marriage.

He didn't pretend it was a love match. He just began in a very honourable way by saying that he had noticed how good I was with his girls and that Elizabeth Ann had said I was a hard-working woman, and that his family was all urging him to find a wife. He wanted to marry again one day, to someone who had never been married before, and he would try to look after her. He could offer a wage to be shared, a settled life, children, and married 'comfort' — and he would take care of me.

Well!

He went on, 'Your mother's family and mine are village families who have known each other for many years. We belong to the place, and' — here he looked at me directly, 'you might agree, as you are so young, Emma, to make a new start in the North?'

My heart missed a beat. I did not think any the less of him for not talking in a fancy way. He was direct, and the truth was that for me he was a good proposition. I was poor, had no mother, and a father who had other responsibilities, but I possessed two good hands and bodily strength.

'If you will think about it, Emma — I'm sorry I sprang it on you the other day — I wasn't thinking straight — but if you agree that we might make a life together one day we could begin to get to know each other? I can't court you, you know that, but we could become friends first.'

I thought he sounded a bit like the folks he used to read to us about in Mr Dickens, but I saw he was trying hard to clear things up his own way. I respected him, that was true, and I knew him to be honourable. I also knew that he was very unhappy, and being unhappy is not a good frame of mind for decisions, so in spite of my shock I replied:

'I'm taken aback, George.' I almost called him Mr Starling. 'I will think about being friends and I will help you with the girls.'

I thought, I could go into lodgings in Snetterton with them so he could get on with earning money.

George looked a bit bewildered but we shook hands and then we went into the garden where I fetched the girls from the gate where they were swinging and prepared their return to Snetterton.

Could I marry George?

I had never seen him as a possible husband, or even as a friend of my own age, only as a man older than myself who was spoken well of at the hall and in Caston. He was respectable, appeared to have married a woman a little above his own family in gentility, and even if he was just a village man, was above me in the pecking order. He was, in short, a good prospect, the kind of man Mam would have wanted me to wed.

But how could I *marry* him?

What did I really want?

I wanted Baz. That was the truth.

There was nobody I could consult, or at least there were plenty who would have liked to give their opinion but whose business it was not. Dad was ruled out. He would have been pleased for me to marry *anybody*, now that he had other worries and duties. The boys were too young; Grandma was dead; Uncle and Aunt Saunders did not know me well; Uncle George Banham would most likely have said, 'Why, of course you must wed George! I've known him since he was a nipper.' Aunt Mary Ann would probably have advised against my marrying at all. I could ask my older cousins, but I hesitated. The other maids at the farm would have giggled and asked if I was 'in love'. The maids who were still at the hall, however, Amelia and Heppie and Emmeline, were probably available for the most sensible opinions.

I went round my next free Sunday to see them and found them all in their kitchen. Mrs Foster was away on a week's holiday. Not that I would have wanted to ask for *her* advice, for I had always found her unapproachable unless it was a question about work. It was always strange being back at the hall and it struck me that Mrs Upcraft would have been the ideal person to ask for advice if she had not had to cast me off, unwilling as that had been. Yet if she had kept her word to Mam I would not have had to go. The girls had been very angry at my dismissal and it still rankled a little with me, but they knew that belts had to be tightened and one of them might be next.

I had chatted with Amelia recently, along with Heppie, here and at the market and they knew all about George's wife and about my work at the farm. After we had embraced and gossiped a bit, I introduced the subject of the motherless children and they asked for news of Mr Starling.

'Oh, he has asked me to marry him,' I said nonchalantly.

I thought if I surprised them I'd get an honest answer. But they were not going to commit themselves until they knew which way the wind was blowing.

'And you have accepted?' asked Emmeline, the boldest.

'No. I have given myself six months to think it over,' I said, adding, 'I might offer to help with the girls.'

'I bet you are fed up with work on the farm,' said Heppie. 'He will get you that way!'

'How do you mean? I get on well with Ann and little Polly.'

'I wouldn't marry such an old man!' said Emmeline. 'He must be thirty-five at least!'

'Nobody has asked you,' said 'Melia unexpectedly. 'You must think it over, Emmy. He's a good proposition.'

'She doesn't *love* him,' said Emmeline, 'do you, Emmy? She's thinking of her gypsy lover!'

I said, 'Nobody else has asked me to marry them.'

'Talking of gypsies,' said Heppie, 'I heard that Jabez Smith went away to build another windmill.'

'No, he's most likely working in Norwich,' I said.

'So she knows where he is! Well, Emmy, you will never marry till that chimbley-sweeper jack-of-all-trades comes back!' said Emmeline.

'Hush,' said 'Melia.

I felt slightly annoyed because they had brought up the very reason I felt I could never marry George Starling, yet I had never said anything to them about being 'in love' with Jabez.

I decided I would give myself six months and in the meantime write to Baz. He would advise me! I know I was being rather silly wanting the man who fascinated me to tell me what to do — which would certainly not be to marry *him* — but it would be one way of seeing him again. Baz had my interests at heart I felt sure, and he would tell me whether George was the right man — or if perhaps nobody was.

In spite of having made myself do as he asked, and give him up, I had never stopped longing to see Baz again. This latest development with George Starling only intensified my desire. I could no more marry George, or anyone, without telling Baz first, than fly.

I thought over what was the best way of doing it. George must never find out, that was the main thing. No good asking my family in Caston about Baz, for they would be curious. No good going by rumours that he was a-building another windmill. I had helped that miller Mr King find him once, and Baz had said that in case of urgency I could send a message to the cathedral. Was this urgent enough? It might be to me, if not to My Friend, but it would mean writing a letter, and I was not a great writer.

There was nobody I could ask to help me. The schoolmistress might, but she would not approve of me writing to a young man. Elizabeth Starling would have helped me, I thought. What a strange twist that only because she had died did I need to write to

Jabez Smith! Well, I would take my courage in both hands. What could I lose? It might take months for him to receive it, or he might have gone away for good. I would have to leave it to chance. All I could do was to wait, and meanwhile tell George I was still thinking it over.

I wrote as long a letter as I could manage with, I'm sure, many misspellings. I'd like to have said more, but it took me long enough writing this one. I found some paper at Mrs Starling's cottage, the door of which had not yet been locked. I felt like a thief, but I remembered where she had kept it. Then I begged an envelope from the farmer's sister saying I needed to write to my father. I don't think she believed me but I had never got across her so was in her good books.

'Dear Baz (I wrote)

Mr George Starling's wife has died and George has asked me to marry him. I do not know what to do. I know the dead lady's children. I am working at Hall Farm but may go to Snetterton to look after the girls, whether I marry or not. George says he will leave Norfolk and go to Yorkshire. If we were married I would have to go with him. Will you please advise me.

I added after some thought,

I hope you and your sweetheart are well. I am well. I do not love George but I would do my duty by him.

I did not tell Baz that I loved him. I suppose that last time we spoke together he must have guessed. I was frightened the letter might be found by someone. If you write things down you take risks.

I ended: Elly.

* * *

I addressed the envelope: Mr Jabez Smith, bricklayer, care of Mr Thompson, The Cathedral, Norwich, and I put Please keep for Mr Smith.

Then I waited, and I had to wait a long time. On my free Sundays, whilst I was thinking things over, I went across to Snetterton. I saw that Ann and Polly were not very happy in lodgings. Though George had moved the girls to be near him he had almost no time to be with them, never mind look after them, and they had learned to look after themselves almost too well. I was frightened that they would become too quiet and too sad. As soon as I arrived George had to go out to his work. He apologized, but I knew he had to keep his job.

One day I was working in the farm dairy. It was a cold November day and I had to carry two heavy buckets back to the kitchen.

Mrs Boulding shouted from the kitchen door, 'There's a letter for you!' and pointed the table.

I have kept that letter all my life.

Baz sounded very anxious but I could tell he was all choked up.

Dear little Elly,

Thank you for writing to me.

George is a good man and I think you must marry him. It will be for the best.

I will try to see your sister whenever I am in these parts. I expect she will tell me about you if you do go away. I am busy here and well paid.

I am very fond of you, little Elly, if not the sort of fondness for a wedding. Better not mention this, or even my name, to George. Nothing must get in the way of your happy future.

I am your sincere Friend,
Jabez Smith.

I knew that Baz knew I wished it were he who wanted to marry me, rather than

George, though I had taken care not to write that down.

After this I was cast between despair and sorrow over never seeing Baz again, and over the plight of the little girls. But these feelings were blended with excitement and alarm and anxiety over George. I knew I should make up my mind quickly to accept or reject him, and I wanted to do that before I spoke to Dad or anyone of our family. It would be no good giving Dad or my uncles the chance to dictate to me. Once I had made my mind up, that would be that.

I decided also that it would not be a good idea to go and help in Snetterton for too long before I married him — if that was what I was going to do. I ought really to find work there first so that I was not under any obligation to be supported, but there was no way of finding out if there were any posts available. George would know, and would find me work, I was sure.

I realized that I might soon be dependent on a husband. For so long I'd worked hard for others, but been in a curious way my own mistress. It would be lovely to be looked after, though it had been Mam who had looked after Dad, not the other way round. I had enough common sense, I suppose, to want to get my marriage lines sorted out as quickly as possible. I knew George would not intend to take advantage of me but I had observed that men were strange creatures.

I suppose all my thinking and planning led me to accept in my heart that I was going to say yes to George. It was easier to make the big decision by planning lots of little things first, like finding a new post. But that was easier said than done and I knew nobody in Snetterton. Things were going from bad to worse in the countryside around; there was very little work, which was in any case seasonal. Another servant would soon have to leave the hall.

I would not have decided as quickly as I did if George had had no children. They would be part of the bargain, and what had I to lose? I was genuinely fond of little Polly, and she made me want a child or two of my own. I was led by a sort of instinct. I was not what Emmeline would call 'in love', but I felt that if I could never have Baz I would have to resign myself to accepting a good man. And George surely needed the help of a woman in bringing up his daughters, as well as a female companion. I knew that Elizabeth Ann had not been his true companion for some years, ever since the consumption had taken hold of her.

I had no savings or nest-egg, and no

expectations, and I was not fond of being a farm-servant. I would rather work for a family of my own. Yet I still longed for Mam to come back and advise me. I even carried on conversations with her in my head. Once I had told George, I would write and tell Baz what I had decided, for after I was wed I would not be able to communicate with him without a husband becoming suspicious.

George came over again a few weeks later. He had been too busy to come before and I was getting anxious. But he came straight over to the farm and took me out. He looked a bit worried himself. He apologized for not coming before and then waited for me to say something.

I could not at first get anything out. It all seemed so sudden now. But then he said, 'Polly sends you her love,' and then it was all right.

I took my courage in both hands. It was a cold day and we were walking in the direction of Bedon on the lane where Baz and I had walked.

'Well, Emmy,' he said, and stopped and took my hand. 'What is it to be?'

'I will marry you,' I said in a rush. 'But I must find work in Snetterton.'

'Oh, Emmy, that makes me very happy,' he said. 'I will try and make *you* happy. I am sorry I cannot say all the right things but . . .' He stopped. I knew he was still grieving for Elizabeth Ann.

'I will do my best,' I said.

'We must tell your father,' he said, and took my other hand.

I was pleased in a way that he was not going to make a long speech about love.

'I want to leave the farm and find work in Snetterton,' I said.

'Nay, it will not be necessary. We only have to call the banns for three weeks and you can lodge with the girls, unless you want us to wed in Caston?'

For some reason I thought, No, I don't want to get married in Caston — I want to cut away properly from the old life. Would my father have to give me away? I would ask the farm servants and those at the hall to come to my wedding, and Myra of course, and my brothers, but I wanted to get it over!

I told George that I preferred to wed in Snetterton and if I lived there for at least three weeks I could.

He kept saying, 'I shall tell the girls, they will be so pleased.'

I thought, we will never be without them now. I would have to tell Oldfield straight away. Strictly speaking he needed a month's notice.

George said, 'I will speak to Oldfield,' and I felt relieved. This is what happened.

When I told Mrs Boulding, Bob Oldfield's sister, that I was to be wed she looked at me carefully and I guessed she was asking herself if I was expecting. I was pleased to be able to show I was not. She knew I had not had any 'followers'.

I seemed to be walking slightly above ground as I went around telling Uncle Jonathan, who would tell Dad when he could get over to Caston with his cart, and of course all my friends. Dad and Myra would tell Mam's family in Caston. I would leave it to George to call the banns and fix a date.

When I went over to Bedon I looked out my 'bottom drawer' the contents of which I had emptied into one of Aunt Fanny's drawers when Grandma moved. There were the sheets Mam and her sister had sewn long ago, and a cotton nightdress, and two mats Mam had crocheted. Well, I was not completely without a wedding trousseau!

George had said I must have a best dress for the ceremony. I only had my blue one that had been sewn in Caston by Mary Ann the previous year, so that would have to do. I had Mam's little ring she had left to me, and the little girls sewed me a blue handkerchief. When I went over to Caston Dad took me aside and gave me a hair brooch that had been Mam's and had belonged to her own mother.

Dad was really pleased I was marrying George, but I wasn't sure if George's parents were. They must have had a conscience over Polly and Emma, had perhaps not made the children's mother as welcome as they should have done, her being a 'foreigner' from another village and a 'reader' to boot. My father said if needed he would come over to the wedding to give me away but he did not look very enthusiastic. I guessed his wife would want to come and they did not have the clothes in which to show themselves off. In the end Dad said his wife was expecting again and was not too well. They must have had an argument about it for he suggested my Uncle Jonathan gave me away. Myra would come 'for the family', he said.

I had very few possessions: a little box of Mam's, a few ribbons and a cotton bag, a few knick-knacks. My boots were, as usual, old and ugly. George had me measured for a new pair. I saw that though he did not have a great deal of money, what little he had he had saved whilst he was in Snetterton hoping that Elizabeth Ann would soon be well and they could be together with nice things. *She* had owned a few superior objects: a Bible, a sewing-basket, and one or two dresses that were unfortunately too long for me but which I would cut down and alter for the girls. We could not afford to waste anything. With all these preparations, as I worked out my time at Hall Farm I hardly saw George, but when I did he was always attentive. I did worry a bit about the intimate side of marriage for I had no experience. In a way it would be a relief to marry a man who had already been a husband.

George kissed me on the forehead, and held my hand, and once or twice took me in his arms and muttered a little. But that was all.

* * *

Well, there I was for a month in Snetterton in the lodgings with the girls. George had moved there too, as I have said, to look after them, but we did not share a room. Instead, the little ones were with me. I tried hard to make them understand I was going to marry their dad and would be their stepmother, and that I loved them even if I was not their real mother. I think they were by now too tired and dreary to take it all in, and at first they were quiet and did not even quarrel with each other.

Gradually, after I had taken them to church with me to hear the first banns, they thawed out a bit. I did wish that Myra could join us if we actually left to go north but I knew Dad wouldn't hear of it. He wanted Myra to work in the rectory kitchen in the village and bring in a shilling. I think too that she was his last real connection with Mam. She did look a bit like her — more than I did, anyway.

One evening, during my second week in Snetterton, I had eaten together with the children at the table in our room, when Ann asked me:

'Will you come with us wherever we go?'

George had said no more for a month or two about his plans to go to Yorkshire for work and my heart did jump a bit.

'Of course, if you are married you stay together,' I replied.

When George came in and the girls were in bed in my room I tackled him over it.

'Is it sure that we shall leave Norfolk?'

'Yes,' he said, 'I was going to speak to you about it but I never seemed to find the time. My plan is to move with you and the girls along with my younger brother Henry and some Caston neighbours I've known all my life. I've sounded out the Sayers and the Hoys, and Solomon Gapp and Mary Bambridge who are to wed soon. Possibly the

Murrells too — they're a bit older than the others. I was waiting to hear what they all said. They'll all have to save the fare — or borrow it. It's not all yet completely fixed but it won't take long. I've already warned my boss. Soon we can make proper arrangements.'

'Ann was asking me if I would go wherever you went.'

'I wouldn't go if you were dead against it.'

For answer I said, 'I think we ought to ask my two brothers as well.'

'Why not? My brother Henry is keen to go,' said George. He was smiling. Relieved, I suppose.

'I'm sure Dad wouldn't mind if Bob and Percy left with us,' I said.

Dad had enough mouths to feed, and though Bob brought in a little, Percy in any case lived away.

'Why not?' he replied. 'The more the merrier!'

'Are you sure there will be work for them all?'

'Oh yes, no doubt about it. My friend Bill Jackson — he went up north last year — has written to me again. He says there's work in the mills for all who want it.'

I was not at all sure what sort of mill he meant but I knew my future husband had set his heart for a long time on a new life and I'd guessed he'd been sounding out the Caston neighbours more thoroughly. George was a man who did nothing by halves, and there was nothing on the land here for any of the Caston labourers. But I wondered whether Elizabeth Ann would have really wanted to go.

I waited for George to tell the girls when we might be leaving — preparing them, like. Polly and her sister didn't like Snetterton much, and neither did I. I wasn't sure how long it would be before we left, but by then I'd be married!

10

After the last banns there was no going back.

What I remember most about my wedding-day, a Friday morning in February, is that it was cold and wet and that Ann had felt sick that morning. George hadn't slept very well, having come in late from a carriage-drive from Attleborough. He had told his employer Mr Soames of his intention to go north and his employer had been displeased. This meant he now took every opportunity to overwork him. But George had insisted on a day off for his wedding, so long as he worked at the weekend, and I suppose Mr Soames knew he had a good groom. If George left earlier than expected he would have even more difficulty in finding a replacement who was as efficient. He had several racehorses and George looked after them, as well as going all over the place on errands for him.

I don't remember much about the service except that it was quite short. I had the sneaking feeling that it was somehow not real and that Elizabeth Ann was watching us. George looked solemn and worried. He did hold my hand though and I felt a sort of gratitude to him. I thought the guests would know he was a serious man. I wore my best dress though I can't remember much about how I must have looked in it. I had a prayer-book from my young Aunt Fanny and a little nosegay of Christmas roses from Uncle Jonathan who gave me away. Aunt Mary Ann said that Isaac was to write my name and George's in the Banham family Bible and that George must start to do the same in his own Bible.

The little girls behaved well, though Polly had a cough. Their father had bought them each a new short grey cloak. My father sent a message with my brothers to say that he could not be spared from his work. Percy brought along Bob and Myra. George's father and mother were said to be indisposed. I had met them only once a week or two before and they had seemed to me rather cool. They had looked me up and down, especially his father, and his mother asked me if there was consumption in my family. Their eldest son James was working away but two of George's sisters came, and his brother Henry who was only two years older than me. My Aunt Mary Ann was there of course and my Uncle Isaac. Mary Ann had already asked me if I was sure I wanted to marry a Starling; she seemed to have some grudge against them though she was always polite to George.

There were fourteen of us together afterwards at our lodgings and Mary Ann saw to the children so that I could have a bit of a rest and celebration with them all. The landlady allowed us her front parlour and we paid for her to produce some ham and beer and tea.

Myra was very excited. She really looked lovely, her auburn hair down her back. She was wearing a blue dress that Mary Ann had made for her out of stuff her sister Matilda had once kept. Matilda had died young and I think that Mary Ann had forgotten the stuff in the chest. Myra had found it and wheedled it out of her. She was often round at our aunt's. Myra had brought some white heather — I don't know where she'd got it from — and she insisted on 'toasting' me. She wasn't yet thirteen so wasn't allowed even small beer, but she had made up a poem for me which she recited. It began:

> Dear Sister Em.
> I am so happy
> To kiss the hem
> Of your dress today . . .

but I don't recall what came next. Some of the men sniggered but George said, 'Thank you — that was very fine,' and smiled and shook her hand.

Myra really always wanted to do things 'proper'. I think I remember that the best of all my wedding because it was as if Mam were there.

The men were generally on their best behaviour though I believe they all stopped on their way back home at a little inn in Snetterton for another drink. They toasted us, but not noisily. I suppose everyone but Myra felt this wedding was the result of a death and a funeral and so it was not like I was marrying a young bachelor. I didn't mind that, indeed preferred it, because there was still only one young bachelor I wanted to marry and that was impossible. Now I was married it was even more impossible.

I shed a secret tear on my wedding-night thinking of this, but I bore up. George had soon fallen asleep and I heard Polly cough. She'd be wishing I were there in her room with her and Ann but now I was to share their father's room. I must confess that Myra had brought the thought of Baz back as well as the memory of Mam and I found that whenever in the future I thought of Baz I always found myself thinking also of my mother. Naturally I didn't tell George any of this.

* * *

When I thought of leaving all the familiar places and almost all of the people I knew, I was a little frightened. It bewildered me to think about all the plans and preparations. How could I have ever considered doing such a thing? How would we do it? Yet I remembered that Mam had once wanted to emigrate, and that was to America or Australia, not just to the north of our own country. But I didn't have any idea of where Yorkshire was and how far away it was. We had had an atlas in school, but it had never seemed anything to do with me.

I thought I was very stupid. George was so clever to know what to do, and to know about such things as railways, and where to find work. I had no experience of anything like that. All I was trained for was housework and looking after babies, so I just let George get on with it, trusted he would manage, and hoped and prayed for the best.

I had to cheer up the little girls so that took my mind off cheering myself up. I don't think George ever understood how uneasy I was for a few months. Also, just the day before he announced that we were to leave in two weeks, after I had thought we were to wait a bit, I found I might be expecting! Two weeks!

I said nothing to George until I was quite sure. He had enough to think about. As I was not sick in the morning, like I remembered Mam had been before Myra was born, I thought I might be wrong.

We had been married at the end of February, and we left Norfolk in late June. I remember the day we left and the long, long journey much more clearly than I remember my wedding-day. I did wish later that I had looked longer at our lovely fields and skies and lanes to remember them better, and that I had said goodbye to everything properly. I suppose I always thought we would come back soon, though that would mean we had failed and had no work. You can't believe till the last moment that your life is going to change completely. I often ask myself, would I have gone if I had known all there was in store. But it's no good thinking that. I couldn't have gone alone, but with George I felt secure, even if I had scarcely got used to being married. And now I'd have to get used to living far away — and maybe becoming a mother.

It had taken weeks to make sure of who was going with us, or before us or just after us, and to save up for and buy the tickets, check the trains, pack our possessions and say goodbye to so many people, but all this business took my mind off the future. I was taken up with Ann, who had got herself a nasty chest that worried George. I felt now the better weather had arrived, her cough would go.

One thing that did please me and reassure me was that Hannah Sayer, a woman of about forty-five, was going north too. She had acted as midwife at home so I knew I'd be in good hands. Her husband was a gamekeeper fallen on hard times but he had already visited Calderbrigg in search of work and applied to a grand baronet living near the town who needed a man to look after his grounds and go grouse-shooting with him. Hannah sounded optimistic about it all.

I had always realized that our Percy was coming along with us. The big surprise was that Bob had persuaded Dad that he could find work along of Percy, and that Dad had believed him and let him go. He was fifteen now, was Bob, and strong — he'd take anything going. All there was for him in Caston was ploughboy, and the wages had actually gone down. Bob enjoyed working the land, though we told him there'd be little enough of that where we were going. Bob was adventurous.

'I shall learn a trade,' he said.

George said the trade would most likely be in a mill.

'What sort of mills are there up there?' I asked him.

I'd never really understood what people meant by mill-work. Did they mean a mill like the flour-mill in Caston, or even a wind-mill?

'There are corn mills,' he replied. 'But mostly they are factories for manufacturing. There are great big flour-mills though that send their bags of flour to other towns in barges on canals.' I had to be content for the time being.

Percy wanted something better than a mill, he said. He wrote a good hand and wished there was a job where he could show his mettle.

The worse thing for me was to say goodbye to Myra. I was a bit surprised that she did not make more fuss, so I knew something must be brewing in her head. She had meekly agreed to start work at the rectory in the kitchens. I guessed she had plans.

'I'd rather go work in the rectory than stay at home with *her*,' she said to me, meaning her stepmother, Dad's wife. 'And I'll be so glad not to hear those babies bawling away. I guess there'll be more of them soon!'

I tut-tutted as she said this, though as it

turned out she was right, for Father's wife was to have three more children after the twins. Neither was Myra to stay in the rectory kitchen for long.

I guessed there had been big rows between Dad and Myra about her coming with us until finally even Myra had had to give in.

'Dad has promised on the twins' heads that I can go North when I'm sixteen if you will find me work,' she said.

I was surprised that she had consented to this but I had a vague idea that she would try to find a post in a rich family where she could work on her employers. Myra was different from the rest of my family, full of confidence. The funny thing was that she did often get her own way and met people who were fascinated by her. But I knew the traps for a girl like her and I had to warn her against the menfolk, had to say what a mother would have said. I knew our stepmother would be only too glad to see Myra leave, whether ruined or not. It was to Dad's credit that he had said she must stay for the time being.

'Yes, I know about *men*,' she said scornfully. 'Don't worry — I shan't be a bad girl — but you have to look out for yourself, you know, and I ain't having a rich man's bastards!'

I was shocked, did not know where she

could have heard such talk.

'There's jobs in London, Emmy!' she went on. 'I shall probably get the rector's wife to speak for me one day. It's a pity your Mrs Upcraft doesn't want me, but there you are.'

I was glad that I had spoken of her to Jabez Smith and now I had to tell her about him.

'I want you to promise that if a young man called Jabez Smith, a bricklayer, the man who built the windmill, ever comes back to Caston you will listen to him. He's a friend, and if you are ever in any sort of trouble, he will help you.'

'Oh, Emmy,' she said, 'was he sweet on you?'

'No, nothing like that,' I said hurriedly. 'He's a good man though. He knows 'bout you, but I want your promise to say nothing about him — don't bring his name up in conversation. Just remember he might help you one day. You can write to me if you ever do see him.'

She looked at me old-fashioned like, but said:

'I promise, Emmy — and I will write to you anyway. Nobody else will. I'll keep in touch with you, I promise.' I had to be content with that.

We were to leave on the train that went from Stow Bedon to Thetford, where we had to change to go on to Ely and March, and then catch the train to Peterborough. George had enjoyed long discussions with the station master in Snetterton about all this. I had never heard of the next places we'd go through after Peterborough. On and on to Grantham and Newark and Retford and Doncaster and then to Wakefield. Here we had to get out of the train, find a cab and go to another Wakefield station which would take us directly to a station that served Calderbrigg. That was the name of the town where we were to live. All I could think about was, what if we could not find a cab, with so many people and so much luggage?

I felt very nervous. I'd never even been on a train before, though I had seen plenty of them at Stow Bedon station which was about a mile from the village. I had never even gone on one to Swaffham, never mind Thetford.

With all the changes, the journey would take all day and some of the evening before we arrived. I was worried about how Polly and Ann would manage. Would the train make them feel sick? Polly was always sick, her father told me, on a drive with the pony and trap.

I had helped George pack up most of our things to send on ahead — clothes, pots and pans and dishes, sheets and blankets. We decided to give some of Elizabeth Ann's things to her sister and her cousin Rose. We kept her Bible and sewing-basket for the girls, and sold some small things to make money for the journey, things which could not be handed on to Polly and Ann. The rest of George's furniture, a table and chairs, was given to his sister and we sent on his wooden chest. We'd have to get another table and chairs in Calderbrigg. George's friend Bill Jackson was to buy us a bed ready for our arrival, and George had already given him the money for that. Mr Jackson said there were lots of second-hand shops in Yorkshire towns where pawnbrokers sold off what folk hadn't been able to redeem. I was amazed that people had to pawn their furniture! Not that my family had much but we'd never have thought of selling it. It made me worry that we were not going to be any better off up North, but George said some of the people there who had work drank their wages, so were always in and out of the pawnshop.

I didn't own much of anything myself, as I have said, but I did have Mam's box where she used to put her ribbons and her hair brooch, made of her mother's hair, which I now owned, and my cotton bag with my hairbrush and comb. Dad had taken my birth certificate, so I got it back from him and put it with my marriage lines in Mam's box. Dad promised he'd be at the station with Myra to see us off and I dreaded that, in case I never saw them again. But my duty and loyalty were now to my husband. I was discovering I had married a careful man, not a hard one but a determined one. Dad had told me I had made a good match and everybody else seemed to think so too.

I resolved to put the past behind me.

* * *

Some of those neighbours of George who had decided to go up to Calderbrigg to work had also decided to travel the week before we did, though there were some we didn't know so well who were going to work in Woolsford and were travelling the same day. Other Caston folk — John Sayer and his wife, and Solomon Gapp with his bride that was Mary Bambridge who had lived next door but one to Dad, and Richard Hoy and his wife, and the Murrells had already gone. George's 'baby brother', Henry, was to follow us in six months or so. Our family with all our possessions would make a whole carriage leaving from Bedon and I hoped we'd all find seats.

'Don't you worry, Emmy — we'll all get

there in the end,' said George. He'd been on trains before, to Norwich, and had gone once to Cambridge, so I trusted him. Marriage was taking some worries away from me, besides adding others.

I was not sorry to leave Snetterton the afternoon before we took the train from Stow Bedon to Thetford. We were to stop overnight in Bedon at Uncle Jonathan's so we could go along to the station in his cart.

I didn't sleep much that night. George was on the couch and I was with the girls in the spare bed, and Ann kept saying she was too hot, and moving around.

It was a lovely summer day that dawned for our departure. I looked round the cottage, the same cottage Grandma had lived in and where I'd been so happy as a child. I'd said goodbye to so many people that I was tired of saying the word, but I wished I'd said goodbye to Mam and Dad's old place. There was a new family living there now.

I didn't feel hungry for the porridge that Aunt Fan had kindly made for us but I had to give a good example and encourage the girls to eat. I wasn't sure where we'd eat next, apart from the bread and cheese and apples I'd packed. Uncle Jonathan had already harnessed the horse and all the things we hadn't sent on were piled up in the cart. Bob and Percy were round with us by seven o'clock; they'd walked over from Caston together. Percy looked very solemn, Bob excited. Polly and Ann liked the lads, so they chattered with them whilst I got on with checking everything. I whispered to Aunt Fanny my secret as we washed the pots in the kitchen. I hadn't told anyone else yet. She looked quite sad — so far they hadn't any children.

Well, we all managed to fit in the trap with the boxes and bags, except for Bob who walked on behind us. I must say I was too preoccupied worrying about not missing the train and not forgetting anything that I hadn't time to cry or feel sad except when Myra arrived with Dad. She looked a bit forlorn, I thought, so I took her aside and made her promise to write and tell me all the news.

'I'll write to you as long as I live, Emmy!' she said, which sounded a bit excessive but that was her way.

'We'll find room for you one day, I'm sure,' I said. 'In the meantime, be a good girl.'

Then I told her my secret too. 'You can tell Dad later,' I said. 'He'll be a grandfather one day!'

She put her hand to her mouth and said, 'Oh Emmy, I hope you have a baby that doesn't cry!'

The platform was full of the folk who were going to Woolsford, and their relatives there to bid them godspeed. There was *such* a hubbub on the station but quite soon we heard the train puffing along from Hockham.

We had a bit of a scramble finding and getting into an empty compartment but I remember that George was very calm. Dad suddenly arrived and wanted to shake hands with him. My husband then busied himself getting bags into the compartment, whilst I hugged Dad and kissed Myra, hugging *her* even tighter. It was strange hugging Dad and saying goodbye. I couldn't remember when I'd last hugged him, not for a long time I don't think. Not even at Mam's funeral. If I had known that I was never to see him again . . . but we are spared such knowledge. Neither did I know then that my stepmother Hannah would soon have another son, John, then two more little girls — another half-brother for Myra and me and the boys and two more half-sisters.

Percy was looking after Ann and Polly. He got them sitting down in the train and then helped stow the rest of the baggage. I kissed my sister again and then got in quickly in case I cried. Myra had borne up well and was dry-eyed.

The station master waited for us all to

embark. There were just the six of us in our compartment with all our things around our feet. As I got in I saw a Caston couple making final farewells. I knew that one or two of those who had already gone didn't intend to stay in Yorkshire for ever, but I had the feeling that we would. Ann was staring out of the window. At least there was glass now, though we were third class. George had told me they used to be open to the air.

Finally our family was settled, our bags and boxes around us. The guard blew his whistle, and waved his flag and we were off, at first crawling along. I waved out of the window to Myra, George holding on to me, and Bob squeezing in at my side, taller than me now. Then the train gathered speed and we were away. The crowd of people vanished, and that was it.

Both my stepdaughters had been on a train before, but Polly huddled up to Percy. Bob began to whistle.

George said to Percy, 'We shall have to move again when we arrive in Thetford. You help me with the baggage and then Em can look after all the rest!'

Bob looked cross. As if *he* needed looking after! I could see we were going to have our hands full with him. But now I had George, who wouldn't stand for any nonsense, and whom I imagined Bob respected. He'd never got on with Dad.

The rest of the journey took so long and we passed so many places all bathed in sunshine, that it made me think how big the world was and it was about time I saw a bit of it, even if it frightened me a bit. But now I didn't want us to go travelling on for ever, only to find a place to rest our heads, for George to find a good job and the children to settle down. Somewhere I might bring up my children decent-like.

By the time we got to Doncaster the girls were asleep. We'd eaten our apples and bread and cheese at noon having made our next to last change of train and my hands were red and sore from carrying my overloaded baskets whose handles dug into me.

'Not be long now,' said George. 'Wakefield next.'

I looked out of the window. It was all gloomy and smoky and the sun appeared to have gone away though it was still only early evening.

We had to wake the girls when we arrived in Wakefield. Fortunately Bob and Percy turned up trumps and helped carry everything and there was even a cab waiting at the bottom of the station approach. It was not the first time I'd been glad to have two strong brothers. George had enquired in advance how much it would cost. The cabman was not cross when he saw us and all our luggage but laughed and called me 'Love'! It was the first time I'd ever been called that by a stranger but I soon learned it was their usual way of addressing you in Yorkshire.

The next part of our long journey was the worst part. The girls were tired and even Bob was silent, and when we had gathered all our possessions up we found we had to walk over a bridge to wait for the train to Calderbrigg which went by a roundabout route.

At last it came, a small train puffing a lot of smoke. We were all tired. George tried to cheer us all up. I was apprehensive about what I'd find when we finally got to our new home. I knew the previous tenants had been obliged to leave on account of being behind with their rent to the landlord. Would they have left the place dirty? Might our bed not have been delivered? Would there be any clean water, any coal? What would we have to eat that first night?

'Nearly here!' said my husband to cheer us up as we passed gaunt-looking buildings he said were cotton- and silk-mills. Soon after, when I heard the guard shout: 'Calderbrigg! Calderbrigg!' I knew we had at last reached our destination. I was sorry in a way to leave that last train, since for me Calderbrigg was shrouded in mystery.

We all piled off and made a big heap of all we owned. George found a little cart we could borrow, and negotiated with the station master to return it the next day. He was always able to convince a man he was honest, so we trundled out of the station and down a cobbled alleyway. I had never seen cobblestones before.

We had a long stumbling walk along another cobbled pavement, the children almost asleep on their feet. I felt more weary than usual myself, I suppose because of the baby I was now sure I was expecting. It was colder too than it would have been at home, and everything smelled of smoke. It seemed such a big place and there were shops selling many things I'd never seen before. I was to get used to them of course but I remember the first time I saw a clogger's shop. All the mill-workers, men, women, and children wore wooden clogs. I saw a barrel outside a shop and a man working inside making tuns. The shops and houses were of stone that had become black. I found that out later; at first I thought it must be a new kind of stone. We crossed two bridges, over a river and then a canal and finally turned left on to a street called Commercial Street which led eventually to the road where we were to live, from which a hill began to climb. There seemed to be lots of hills in this town. We arrived at a line of stone houses in terraces built closely together, behind which the land fell down through woods to the bottom where, George said, were both the river and the canal. But it was beginning to be dark now so I'd have to wait till morning to look at the view, if there was one.

Summer nightfall in Calderbrigg, our new home town, and all of us in the end were out of breath 'cause the house too was on a slope.

It was number 28, stone like the others, and George's friend Mr Jackson was waiting at the open door! I was never more relieved to see anyone in my life.

A lady was standing behind him, who turned out to be Tabitha Jackson. I hadn't ever seen her before but she seemed a kind soul, and I thought, she'll know there'll be lot of cleaning to do, us taking over from other folk, and it seeming a very dirty smoky town.

They both greeted us cheerfully, and she said:

'We got a fire going — you'll find it colder than home — and we've brought you your water from the pump — there'll be enough for you till tomorrow.'

We went in — and that was the beginning of our Calderbrigg life. And yet for a month or two I couldn't really believe we were there for good. What Tabby Jackson had said about the cold was true and what I had felt about the amount of cleaning I'd have to do in future was even truer. The smoke from the mill chimneys made everything dirty — walls and curtains and furniture and clothes. As soon as you'd got them clean again they were back filthy. It was a good thing I'd learned how to clean and wash properly at the hall, I thought!

11

It was a great comfort during those first strange weeks in Calderbrigg to be able to talk to Norfolk women who had come just before us. After a week or two I got to know Isabella King who was living a bit further down our street on the same side of the road and who was just my age, and also Mrs Gapp, who had just got wed and had reluctantly come North with her husband. The Murrells were much more cheerful and had found a place not far away. I discovered they were actually related to George. I was delighted when George told me that Hannah Sayer and her husband and one of her sons were also living a few streets away, and I longed to have a word with her. A few months after us Martha Flegg arrived with her sister and brother in law. Martha was so homesick, poor girl, that she cried and cried and lost her appetite for weeks. But in the end she perked up. Years later she was to die of a sore on her breast but you couldn't blame that on Calderbrigg.

I was too busy to be homesick. First of all there were days of unpacking and cleaning and scrubbing and laying in coal and wood and going down the road for water from the pump. Then I had to find out where the markets were, the closed one and the smaller open-air one where I discovered you could buy cheese and tripe and sweetbreads and udder a lot more cheaply than at the butcher's.

I walked to the stores every day for such things as we could afford and cooked them on the fire with its big grate, a sort I hadn't seen afore. I seemed to have dozens of things to learn, as well as settling the others, and scores of tasks to attend to. I always had soup on the hob and tossed in my Norfolk dumplings that I made with flour and water and a pinch of salt and a little onion if I had it or a carrot or a swede — which the Calderbriggers called a turnip. I did my baking on a Thursday. George could bring home half a stone of flour for that at a cheaper price for workers at the big mill.

One of my jobs was to find out about school for Polly and Ann after August. I was determined they should not lose their knowledge, for their mother had taught them well. Poor scraps, they took ages getting used to the place. Ann lost her appetite and Polly kept saying, 'When are we going back?' I knew that when they were not much older they'd have to go out to work, for George's wage would not be enough to keep us all comfortably once his savings were gone, even with the addition of what Bob and Percy could bring in. And there'd be another mouth to feed eventually.

George had lost no time going for that job at the big corn- and flour-mill where he was to help look after the horses, some of whom pulled barges on the canal, often stopping to go on further to Wakefield and other smaller towns. Other horses pulled the carts that took flour to the station. I found out what people meant by a mill for 'manufacturing', and soon learned the town was full of many kinds of 'factories' — great tall buildings with long windows. They were mostly for cotton but there were quite a lot of silk-mills too. I soon discovered that all the workers, spinners and weavers, including children, went in early in the morning to work. The women all wore long shawls that they passed round twice, so cold it was. We were just on the edge of the centre of town, and you'd see them all streaming in the same direction, and hear their clogs on the road setts. They worked till six o'clock at night. Young girls in Calderbrigg usually went into 'the mill' rather than into service. I thought a silk-mill would be the best for I was told by Mrs Jackson that for silk-spinning and weaving girls had to be handy and neat but they started children off on easier jobs.

After the first few days I plucked up my courage to go and explore the town a little more. On the other side of each house in the terrace there was a flight of stone steps going down to a lane. From the back I could see in the near distance that water which I'd glimpsed on our first night; it must be the river or the canal. Later, I found that you could walk very pleasantly by the canal — it was harder to get to the river.

The first day that I walked out from the front door down the road into the town with Polly and Ann, to go to the market, I was quite frightened. We walked to the main street, then along it and found that the river and the canal ran side by side. There were two bridges one after the other, one for the river, one for the canal and there were mills everywhere. The river was a dirty-looking thing, not a bit like a river at home. We crossed by the canal bridge. I knew George worked for the enormous corn-mill by the riverside. He'd told me that the river gave the mill water for power though they were soon going to change over to steam power. I saw his mill for the first time that morning, with a yard leading down to the canal on the far side, a bit further up from where we were standing.

On the canal there were barges carrying big loads of corn and sand and coal and flour all pulled by horses. Of course when I had finished my shopping the children wanted to watch the horses. We walked down to the canal bank and I let them have ten minutes or so staring at a barge with a big old horse pulling it along on the other bank before we had to walk back home. I could see as we neared our house that there was a piece of land, almost an island, in between the canal and the river. There were just a few trees and patches of green.

When we got home, I had to get on with cooking the dinner and then carry on cleaning after we'd eaten. This became the pattern of my days before the girls went off to school. Things got so dirty inside the house, though we still hadn't much furniture. It was the smoke everywhere. I swept the stone floor and then washed over it with hot water and soda, and brushed the wooden stairs like mad, and polished the windows. I'd watched the Yorkshire women kneeling on their doorsteps whitening the edges with a donkey-stone. I'd have to do that. Our house had been neglected.

Mr Jackson showed us where to go to buy

some sticks of furniture. There were lots of second-hand shops, some with their goods out on the pavement, which they called 'causeway shops', and after work on the first Saturday, when George came home in the late afternoon, we all went out to buy a table and four chairs, and stools for the little ones. George had tried to save, and though he'd been charged a lot for the fare we had just enough left to buy a few goods. I thought of Elizabeth Ann and their little home and all the nice things in it and I felt so homesick. George had saved all this really for her and their children, even taken that job of groom in Snetterton, which paid better. I wanted to say, you must keep some money for the girls, but I daren't say nothing. Before I spoke of anything else, I had to tell him I was expecting. I thought he might be angry because of that 'other mouth to feed'. Also, I often wondered whether it was really an improvement to live up here in all the dirt even with the work. I so missed the fields and the lanes.

I noticed from listening to conversations first at the butcher's and then at the grocer's that we were what Yorkshire folk call *offcomers*. I imagined they might try to cheat us, thinking we were so foreign we didn't understand about money, which they called 'brass'. But George said that once he made friends at work we'd be accepted. The town was full of 'offcomers' — lots of them Fenians, which was their name for the Irish.

It would be a tight squeeze financially, not to mention sleeping arrangements in the house! But soon Percy and Bob began to bring in brass. Bob found work at a wool-mill at first and Percy began helping to unload from the barges, sometimes even to George's mill. He hoped he might get a job inside in a mill office one day. Later, Bob got fed up with factory work and went to a stone-quarry a mile or so away to delve.

There was so much going on in this town. I didn't find it all out at first but discovered it bit by bit. There was wool-weaving and cotton-weaving and silk-spinning and weaving, and carpet-making and mills where material they called 'stuff' was dyed, and 'engineering' where they made some of the machines for the mills, and even mills for something called 'wire-drawing'.

There were three Methodist chapels too. I was surprised when our Percy decided to attend one of them, and then said he wanted to sing in the choir.

'How do you know they'll want you, lad?' I asked him.

He just smiled and replied, 'They'll find

out I can sing!' And they did, and it was a home from home for Percy ever after that.

I must go back to those few weeks after our arrival in Calderbrigg. I hadn't found time to write to Myra but one morning I got a letter from her. Getting a letter addressed to me cheered me up even if it reminded me of everything I'd left at home and made me feel homesick. I suppose I'd just been too busy to feel too much of that before. I could tell that Myra was a bit low but trying to sound cheerful for my sake. She told me Dad's wife was going to have another baby soon, and wondered if mine and our stepmother's would be born about the same time.

I decided I must reply. George might help me with the spelling. I'd often said to him I wished I could read better and he'd promised when we got ourselves sorted out a bit better to help me with it. But if he was going to help me he'd have to know what I wanted to say and I wanted to mention *my* baby to my sister. I'd have to tell him, I really would. A better way might be to give him Myra's letter to read as she had written about it already.

It took me a few more days to pluck up my courage. One night, the girls were tucked up in their makeshift 'bed' — we'd bought an old couch, a real bargain. Ann slept at one end and Polly at the other. The boys were out waiting for the mushy-pea shop to open. That was one thing we didn't have at home and it was very useful. We were in the kitchen. George had washed after work and was getting the wood fire to burn. He'd just been telling me how there was an open-cast coal-mine not far away and how you could get coal from the land nearby just by picking it up off the ground. Lots of people took prams or wheelbarrows and regularly walked two miles there and back. It wasn't the best coal but it was better than nothing.

I began by saying: 'I got a letter from my sister the other day. Would you like to read it? Then I've got something to tell you.'

He looked up at me, a bit surprised.

'Perhaps Myra don't want me reading her letters?' he said.

'Oh, she means her news for both of us. Here you are.'

I handed him the letter and he got up and took it near the candle on the table. It was almost dark already at nine o'clock, now that it was August. Not that the house was ever very light. We hadn't yet got the gas to work in the kitchen but the mantle man was coming soon to fix it. We had lamps upstairs, and candles.

He read the letter carefully, his arms propped on the table. He looked up.

'So your stepmother's having another baby?'

Hadn't he read what Myra had written about me? I waited and then he said, 'And what's this about you?' But he was smiling, so I knew he wasn't angry. He came over to me and I said, 'It's what you read — we're to have one of our own — I think at the beginning of the New Year.'

'Well, Emmy,' he said, 'is that such a surprise?'

I knew he was joking but it made me blush.

George was never a man to show his feelings over much and it sometimes worried me that I didn't always understand him. His first wife was so different from me and I think he'd learned many things from her. I was just a young ignorant woman, grateful that my husband was kind to me, and quite willing to look after his children as part of the bargain. *He* already had two children so it could not be such an excitement for him as it was for me.

'It'll be a boy!' he said, and he put his arms round me.

The following evening he helped me reply to Myra. He gave me a sheet of notepaper and a sharpened pencil — he possessed such things for writing to his family, not that he'd had much time to do that yet, apart from sending a message by Mr Jackson whose brother lived in Caston.

I said what I wanted to say, and wrote it down, and then he corrected it for me. I couldn't help thinking of the other time I'd written a letter. I wondered now if Baz had thought my writing ill-spelled.

George had not yet had time to find out where you sent your letters off. I was shy of speaking to the townsfolk at first. They didn't seem to understand what I said and I found their answers hard to understand too. But they were kind and would point out things to me, especially if I was accompanied by two little girls. By asking a woman in the street I discovered that the postal service was at a saddler's shop not far away.

Isabella came round quite often and we used to go to the market together. I made a new friend who was not from Norfolk, Harriet Bracegirdle, who was living next door to Isabella King. Harriet was a bit older than me and though she was much taller and didn't have a birthmark, she reminded me a little of Amelia in character. She was really a very good-looking girl, seeming quiet but obviously very competent. She told us that she was not really from Calderbrigg but from the country, not far from York. She said it was lovely country over there and showed me and

Isabella how to cook tripe — we'd never eaten that before. I cooked a rabbit pie when Percy came home one day with a rabbit he'd been given by a mate at the mill and the next day Harriet said, 'Your house always smells right nice.'

I had been asking around about a school for Ann and Polly. I knew I hadn't learned much at the village school I'd attended, it seemed to me now hundreds of years ago, but I knew that George wanted his children to do well. When we first arrived in Calderbrigg you had to pay a several pence a week for each child at school. Of course you weren't obliged to send your children to school, though by the time our own first child was five you had to. I was told that lots of folk couldn't, or wouldn't, pay. At home, as far as I can remember, Dad did not pay for us at the parish school. If he had had to pay I should have had even less time at school than I did! When our very last child was ready for school, he got it free!

In the end we decided to send Polly and Ann to the Catholic school, St Joseph's, on Martin Street. I was told by my new friend Harriet that the children there were better mannered. They were mostly Irish and I loved the way their parents talked — softer than this Yorkshire speech, more like the way we spoke at home. George's girls — I hadn't quite got round yet to calling them 'our' girls — would stay on at school till they were ten or twelve when they could be half-timers at a new silk-mill. It would cost us fourpence a week for each of them rather than the threepence the Church of England required, but George said he could afford eightpence. Their mother would have wanted them to go on learning. Mrs Jackson said that the school was stricter than the other schools they could have gone to. I'd seen some little gangs of lads roaming round the town and didn't like the look of them.

The girls would be taught in a separate classroom at 'St Joe's'. It was a pity there was no Methodist school, though, I thought, but you didn't have to be a Roman to go to St Joseph's. Later on, we were to wonder about our choice when the Fenian riots took place in the town, but we thought it would be nice for the girls to be together in a religious school They'd been gently brought up by their mother. I expect I could have coped with the rough boys, but I doubted Polly could. As for Ann, she'd tell them where they got off and make life hard for herself.

* * *

I was determined our house and ourselves would always be clean and warm and spent most of my time cleaning and washing and trying to keep a fire going. We found that the folk in Calderbrigg used what they called 'shale' to bank a fire up when they couldn't always have — or afford — coal. You could buy that cheaper. Before winter Bob went down a few times to the wood near us at Brookfoot to gather kindling we could dry out for the fire. He had a good business head, my little brother, in spite of his heedless ways and he had the idea of selling kindling to other Norfolk families. But he had nowhere to keep it dry, so that idea was 'put in cold storage' as you might say until better weather came again.

'But we wouldn't need a fire then, would we?' asked Ann.

'Folks have told me,' said Bob, 'that the summer can be very cold up here.'

I shuddered. I had been looking forward to the sun reappearing — if it ever did — from behind all the smoke, and one day taking my baby out for a walk. If Percy could knock up a little box on wheels I could pad it with what they called 'shoddy'. I'd seen it sold in the market — bits of woollen clothes all cut up to be re-used. I intended also to get some old carpet remnants for rug-making.

George said, 'There are always a few good warm days. We shall all be able to go for a country walk — at Whitsuntide perhaps or on bank holiday. There are six of those holidays now!'

He was always a mine of information, my husband. I don't know how he found out all he did but I knew they passed round a newspaper at work and read it in their meal-break. Or rather it was George who read it aloud, for even up here a lot of men couldn't read. He hadn't changed much. I wondered if he was liking this new life better than the one at the hall. I was glad I was married, in spite of everything, and half glad we'd come here and now rented a house of our own. It had been a hard life being a servant, specially on the farm — though this life was just as hard and even busier when you were responsible for other people.

I began to knit for the baby and to sew a layette, mostly from sheet material they sold off cheap. I was helped by the little girls whose mother had taught them plain hemming as well as knitting. How I wished I had one of those sewing-machines they'd had at the hall. Heppie had once told me you could get one on the 'hire system'. I vowed that even if it took me fifty years to save up for the deposit I'd save up for one.

George wanted to grow onions and cabbage and potatoes but he was very weary after his long day with the horses. It was Percy who began to dig the heavy clay soil that was behind the house. Nobody else seemed to want this small piece of land. It was true it was on a slope, but we got permission from the landlord, a Mr Crowther, to make a vegetable garden out of it. Mr Crowther came once a week for the rent. He thought we were a bit mad to try to grow stuff there and said, 'You Southerners miss your fields?' I'd never thought of us as 'Southerners' before but we certainly weren't Northerners!

* * *

Those first months after leaving Norfolk will always remain in my memory. Although everything was new and strange, I was young and full of energy, in spite of getting tired in the last month before our little boy, little Herbert that we called Harbie was born at the New Year of 1874. I knew George wanted a boy as he already had two girls but I didn't mind whether I had a boy or a girl so long as it was healthy and I was all right. I didn't look forward much to the birth. All the women I knew took delight in telling me how painful it was and how they'd sworn never to have another. Of course they always did, as it wasn't really up to them.

I went one morning just before Christmas to see Mrs Sayer. She already knew about me from her husband. George had told him about the coming baby, and that I would need a midwife. He'd asked him how much she charged. He had replied, 'Better ask the wife.'

'Bless you,' she said, when I went to see her a few streets away that cold December morning, 'I don't ask Norfolkers for nothing. It isn't as if you were at home and you'd saved up — we must all help each other up here.'

I knew George would insist on giving her something but perhaps we could arrange a shawl or a rug.

When I stepped into her house I'd seen that Hannah Sayer, although she was small, was a strong-looking woman with nice blue eyes. I noticed her clean nails and hands too and there was the smell of dumplings cooking in a big saucepan on the fire. There was a little girl playing with a tin and a pebble on the floor under the window, and she looked up and smiled. Later I discovered she was Mrs Sayer's granddaughter.

On the wall there was a picture of a big

Shire horse like the ones we used to have working in the fields at home.

'Do ye like my Dandy then?' asked Mrs Sayer, when she saw me looking at it. 'My brother painted him to remind us of home.'

I learned she'd already helped another young woman who'd arrived after us already eight months gone and all had ended well.

'You must lay in some raspberry tea,' she said, 'and plenty clean rags. Keep going till you feel the first pains and even then keep going as long as you can. Have you got a fire? A kettle?'

I told her we had laid in some coal Bob had collected from up Norwood and some old logs he'd found too. We had a kettle, and a bed — and I'd made the baby-clothes.

'Let's have a look at you,' she said and felt me all over my belly.

'You'll do,' she said finally. 'I think about another month.'

I told her that was my opinion too.

'What does George think about it? Is he glad?' she asked.

I thought that was a bit forward but that she was very shrewd. Girls whose husbands were not pleased might tell her about it and she'd be on their side. But she'd met George at home in Caston, and when she said, 'He's a steady fellow,' I was glad to agree with her.

'That poor Elizabeth Ann of his — mind that warn't any way his fault — she were frail. Did he tell you she lost two little babbies?'

I didn't know she had lost two. I knew about one miscarriage.

'You're stronger nor her,' she went on. 'She'd never have lasted up here!'

It was true the winter weather had turned very cold. I wished it were summer and I could have my first little one with the sun shining and warm air all around. Mrs Sayer told me not to send for her till I'd been having pains for six hours and then she'd come and see how I was getting along. Isabella King had promised to stay with me during labour and to keep an eye on Ann and Polly. George was more nervous than I was, I think because he'd been through it all before. Perhaps I was being too easy-going about it all.

* * *

Our first Christmas in Calderbrigg was a happy time. George was given the day off and we all went to chapel in the morning after Ann and Polly had opened their stockings. I had put an orange in each stocking along with some monkey-nuts, and George had put each girl a shining sixpence wrapped in paper from the wages he'd been given that evening.

It was the first time I'd been to this chapel though our Percy was already a keen worshipper there. They called it Bethel. Oh, I did enjoy the rousing singing that Christmas morning! We sang 'While shepherds watched' and 'O come all ye faithful' and the choir sang the Hallelujah Chorus. The folk were all very friendly, most of them Yorkshire of course, but Mrs Murrell was there and Isabella King with her husband.

George said as we walked home, 'You enjoyed that, Em?'

'Oh, I did!' I answered and he said,

'You've had a hard time of it all. How are you feeling?'

Well of course I said I was fine. After all, he'd had a harder time than I had. Percy came up alongside of us and said:

'They've asked me to sing a solo soon! I sang for them last week after the service — a sort of test.'

'Oh, I'm so pleased, Botty,' I said.

I knew that he at least was going to be all right.

I think Herbert's birth — we called him Harbie because that was the way we Norfolkers said his name — was the end of one part of my life. More than Mam dying when I was thirteen, more even than getting wed. After Harbie I was never carefree again till my youngest child got wed and then there was no more looking after others for me. That was over forty years later, believe it or not.

I wouldn't like to give the impression that I thought of my life like this when I was young; it's only looking back that I see it in this way. When you are older you can give names to your feelings, but whilst you are experiencing them you are too busy to think about yourself. Neither was I a careworn sort of woman, or at least I don't think so. Folk used to say that I always looked busy and that's because I *was* busy! but I don't think I looked burdened, the way I now realize Mam had been when I think about her. For one thing I was a lot stronger woman than Mam.

We wives and mothers took it for granted we'd be overworked for years and years and years, that there'd never be enough money — or 'brass' as I learned to call it, and that the main thing you could look forward to if you were lucky was your children growing up and making a good job of their lives.

Well, Herbert — our Harbie — was born at the beginning of the New Year, in 1874.

And then my real new life really began.

PART TWO

Yorkshire

1873 – 1935

12

The birth wasn't as bad as she'd feared. She'd heard so much from other women about these things and had thought they liked to stress the painful side of it, maybe wanted you to suffer the way some of them had suffered. She'd thought, well, I'll be prepared, that's all I can do. But would she be like the other mothers after she had had a baby, scaring young wives off it all?

Although she was not a big woman she was quite a strong one and she was only twenty-two. All the hard work she had done for so long had prepared her body well.

She felt she was lucky. She had a good husband, even if he was fifteen years older than her and a trifle set in his ways. She had soon realized he'd never change and that was in some way a comfort. She'd had enough change in her life with the move to Calderbrigg.

* * *

Several mildly niggling pains came on early one January morning. Bob and Percy and

George had already gone off to work when Isabella King called round. She often came round in the morning to see if she could get her friend anything from the market if Emma was not going into the centre of the town. Usually Emma would buy potted meat for George's tea and some muffins for the girls' tea, unless she had baked some tea-cakes the previous day. This morning she needed a little buttermilk, a few eggs, some scrag-end of mutton and some yeast so she could bake the following week. George always brought the flour back from his work at the flour-mill where it was packed in bags each weighing a stone.

'Oh, would you tell Mrs Sayer I think it has begun,' she added to Isabella on the doorstep.

She felt a little stupid. Why couldn't women have babies the way cats did, with no interference? But she'd better take care and accept help, she supposed.

'It'll be hours yet!' said Mrs King. 'But I'll tell her.'

How long would it take, Emma Eliza was asking herself after Isabella had left. She felt almost certain the birth had begun and her belief became a certainty when she suddenly felt a great gush of water rush down from between her legs. That was annoying for she'd have to mop it all up.

After she'd done this, interrupted a few times by the nagging ache that had become more insistent, she brewed some raspberry-tea that was said to hurry things on a bit. Then Polly and Ann could be heard stirring. She gave them a cup of buttermilk each and some bread.

Isabella returned about an hour later. 'Hannah Sayer will be round soon to look you over. Shall I take Polly and Ann over to number seventy for the day?' Little Ann looked mutinous, Polly worried.

'I could do with a bit of a rest,' Emma said to them. 'When you come back this evening there might be a little brother or sister arrived for you.'

Ann said, 'I hope it's a boy,' and looked rather crossly at Polly. Polly said, '*I'd* like a sister — but littler than me!'

Off they went with Isabella, though not before Polly had given her stepmother a hug. She was a very loving child. How much did she now remember of her own mother?

The pains were still bearable. She concentrated on them when they came, but got on with her housework. George had raked up the fire and relit it that morning, so she swept the room, washed the dishes, and cleaned the kitchen floor, before stoking up the fire, filling the big kettle and putting it on the hob. Then she went upstairs to tidy the girls' cots.

By the time Hannah Sayer arrived, also intoning: 'Oh you'll be ages yet!' Emma was finding the sensations a bit stronger and closer together.

Mrs Sayer made her sit in the only armchair and felt her 'bump' all over, carefully. She said in a surprised sort of way,

'You'd best get to bed, my dear — it's not going to take as long as I thought!'

Emma did not want to go to bed but thought she had better do as she was told. Once again, she toiled up the stairs to the floor above where they had the two 'proper' bedrooms and one sort of cubby-hole over the back kitchen, with a mattress where the boys slept.

Hannah left her pacing up and down, wondering if she'd got everything ready. She'd already put the basin she'd been told to provide, into the downstairs hearth, and the big iron kettle was waiting.

Then she just waited herself. It was strange not knowing what was going to happen to you. A bit like dreaming. You didn't know what you were going to dream. Certainly you did not choose your dreams. There were one or two longer pains now that made her catch her breath but she looked out at the sky through the window and breathed deep. It seemed that made her feel better. When Hannah Sayer came up for the second time the young woman consented to lie on the bed. Then Hannah fixed long rags made out of old sheets to the bedposts.

'They're for you to pull on,' she explained. 'When you need to.'

Hannah went downstairs again to fetch water and everything seemed to pause for a moment. Then suddenly there was a really long pain that made Emma wonder, oh dear, how long is this going on? A minute later, another. It seemed she'd lost count of time for she could hear children's voices outside going back to school after dinner, or coming home for it.

The thought of Baz was suddenly with her. Not for long, but definitely there and he seemed to be encouraging her. Maybe too there was Mam's voice that kept saying, 'It's all right, it's all right . . .'

After she had been lying on the bed for some time breathing along with the long, deep, twisting pains and making the most of the intervals between, the pains began to feel different. When Hannah came up with the ewer and the clean cotton pieces she'd got ready, Emma said:

'I think I must push!'

Hannah felt her again, this time even more

intimately. She looked up. 'Next time you can!' she said.

It felt quite comfortable between the times when the knot tightened and she wanted to push, and the rests in between. The intervals were long and it was even a little boring, all quite slow now and not painful, which surprised her. Mrs Sayer looked resigned when nothing seemed to be happening, or just chatted, half to herself, half to Emma. Emma was then overcome several times with a much stronger urge.

'Push it out!' shouted Hannah.

Now she saw the point of the rags. She pulled down on them, beginning to expel the unknown at the same time as something began to push itself out. It was like the marble that stoppered up a bottle of lemonade being very slowly ejected by some impersonal force from inside the bottle. She felt for an instant that she might split in two. But Hannah was ready with the wet cloths, waiting for the baby to be ready to leave what had been its home for nine months.

Emma closed her eyes and held her breath each time for a long minute as three times she pushed the baby completely out into the world. Hannah lifted first one shoulder and then turned the next.

'Now!' she shouted, but Emma kept her

eyes shut. The big moment had arrived.

Apart from her puffing and blowing, everything had been quiet, but suddenly she heard a wail that got louder and louder and, when she dared open her eyes, there squirming on the sheet in front of her was a red-looking baby with white stuff all over him, and a long wriggly shiny affair looking like a sausage joined to his belly.

'There you are,' said Hannah Sayer. 'And it's a boy!'

After that there was an interval, then some more pushing, but by that time she had held him close. She put her finger on to his palm and his own fingers closed round it.

'You know your own mam then?' she said. But his eyes were for the present tight shut.

Then Hannah took him and swaddled him and put him in the drawer that had been lined with wool, and placed it on two chairs next to the bed.

It brought back to Emma the time when her mother had given birth to Myra. She leaned over and stared and stared at the little face. He had almost no hair at all but his eyes were now open. Hannah went downstairs to make them both a cup of tea.

'Percy's just home from his shift. I'll tell him to run and tell Mr Starling,' she shouted up. She always called George Mr Starling.

Goodness, it was later than she'd thought if Percy was back. She'd spent all afternoon in labour! Still, it hadn't been too bad. She must have woken about half past five that morning and the whole thing from start to finish had taken less than twelve hours, and for much of that time she'd been on her feet.

Hannah came back upstairs with the tea and a big enamel basin of hot water to wash her with.

'I've known two women who were over two days and two nights in labour and then only bringing out dead babies — or the babe killed the mother,' said Hannah over her cup of tea. 'You're a natural!'

'Isabella will be bringing the girls home after tea,' said Emma. 'Little Ann will be pleased it's a boy. George will too, of course, since he's only had girls so far.'

She couldn't stop looking at his crumpled little face peeping over the swaddling.

'You might as well give him suck,' said the older woman. Emma found the baby appeared to know what to do, and was amused.

The two women sipped the hot tea and Emma said, 'Thank 'ee, Mrs Sayer.'

'You can call me Hannah if you like,' she said. She was a good twenty years older than the young mother and although Emma Eliza thought of her as Hannah she felt shy of saying it to her face. But still, she supposed she'd been closer to her than any other woman since her own mother.

'Let's get you straight,' said Hannah. She rolled her over and pulled the bloodied sheet from under and put a clean darned one in its place. It was one she'd brought from that 'bottom drawer' she'd once saved up for and kept at Grandma Saunders'.

The baby was asleep now and Hannah said again, 'You did right well. Aren't you proud of yourself?'

'Yes I am!' she replied. She didn't even feel tired. 'I think he'll have ginger hair,' said Mrs Sayer. 'They often look like that when they're going to be red-haired or fair.'

Red hair! Was he going to look like Myra? George had quite dark brown hair. It would please him if his son looked like him. Polly did — but she was a girl.

Suddenly, she could not help wondering if the baby might by some magic look like her 'old friend', as she now named Jabez Smith whenever the thought of him flitted into her head. This memory was not quite so frequent now but when it came it was just as intense.

* * *

They named him Herbert and he continued to feed easily. 'Our Harbie,' they called him. George said she was an ideal little mother, which pleased her. They intended to have him baptized Herbert George in the Methodist chapel down the road as soon as she had finished what they called the lying-in time. She didn't have a very long lying-in, for it was not easy to find someone to cook and clean and look after the rest of the family.

Isabella dropped round and took the girls off her hands after school, which they had begun a day or two after the birth of their half-brother, and Hannah looked in now and again to see how she was, but they couldn't afford any other help so, like most women, after a few days she got up and got on with it.

Even so, the baby was four months by the time they got around to the christening. It was George who was most keen on the baptism. His first wife had been from a family of 'Primitive Methodys' and she had influenced him, though Emma suspected he had never shared her faith completely. After all he had married her, his second wife, in Snetterton parish church.

Now that she had her baby, who took up a lot of her time, she thought she had all she wanted. The baby soothed her when she worried that George had been in her opinion a bit too stern with her brothers, especially with Bob. It was true her younger brother was a handful, but he meant well. He just took life more lightly than George. Many women had told her how lucky she was to have such a good husband who did not drink and was careful with his wages. She knew that. Just sometimes though she wished that he could enjoy himself more. She couldn't help thinking once or twice of Jabez Smith, her Friend, who had always seemed light-hearted and enjoyed his life, even when his own life must have been quite hard. She would have liked to be able to tell him she had had a baby. In a curious way it seemed they were quits!

Having a family made all the difference to a woman. As she cuddled Polly she often thought of Elizabeth Ann and how sad it was that her life had been so brief. She sometimes tried to imagine what her own mother, Eliza's, married life had been like, and felt guilty for speculating. Her mother had been much cleverer than her father, but in her own case she was sure George was a lot cleverer than she was.

Percy it was who put her thoughts into perspective. They were sitting by the fire one Saturday afternoon. George was still at work and Bob was out with his new mates. Polly and Ann were playing in the street with two little sisters they had met at school. Even little Ann now seemed in better spirits.

'I wish George did not have to work so hard,' Emma had just said to her brother.

'He would work even if he was not obliged to,' replied Percy.

'Yes, I know. It is better than being lazy.' She laughed.

'*You* are different now as well, Sis,' he said. 'With the baby and all that. You used to be more light-hearted yourself.'

She stared at him. Had she really changed? Percy loved his little nephew and had never criticized George or anything about their way of life.

'I am a respectable married woman, and I have a little one to look after as well as the girls,' she said half teasingly.

'But you always had a lot of imagination,' said Percy who had begun to come out with such words. She thought he must have heard them at the chapel.

Then she thought, 'imagination' is perhaps what George lacks. Jabez Smith, her 'Baz', whom she had in some ways not known well — she admitted this to herself — was a person whom she had known in another way: instinctively, like a baby knows its mother.

What she knew was that he too had been full of ‘imagination’.

‘Like I remember our mam having,’ Percy added softly.

After a pause, Emma said, ‘I wish Mam could see my baby — he’s having to do without grandparents. But perhaps he’ll be able to sing like Mam could — or like you, Botty.’ The little childish name came out without her thinking.

He smiled. She thought: Percy and Poll are my greatest comforts. And then she wondered why she did not see George as a comfort. He was a hard worker, dealt at home with the coal and the fires, cleaned the boots and dug their patch of ground. Anything to do with the baby was of course woman’s work, but she had once or twice wished he would talk to her about the births of his daughters. Perhaps he had preferred to avoid talk of his first wife, or knew nothing about childbearing. Why should she expect him to be any different from the rest of men?

He trusted her though, and she had made an effort to get on with Ann for his sake. That daughter was like him: not easy to get to know, perhaps not as naturally kind as her father. George, in spite of his overwork and his silences, was a kind man, even if he hadn’t a lot of ‘imagination’.

* * *

Emma had begun to remember some of the ways her mother had looked after them all in Norfolk when she was little. Eliza Saunders had used many country remedies for their childish illnesses, had recited proverbs and sayings and given her daughter many homely tips which Emma had thought she had forgotten. They all came back now she was responsible for her own family. Eliza had been a clever herbalist as had her mother before her, but Emma Eliza had not been sure whether the herbs that were so plentiful at home in Norfolk would grow here up north.

After six months in Yorkshire she knew that some of the ones she remembered were to be found. She would make it her job to discover others. Conkers now, they used to be held in the hand to prevent rheumatism. She remembered Granny Saunders telling her that, and there had always been some shiny new ones in October in her grandmother's pockets. In Yorkshire there were certainly plenty of *them*! As for garlic, one of the most useful remedies of all for digestion and good health, George could grow it. Percy said he had seen plenty of knotgrass here and she knew Mam had said it was useful for the rheumatics. The oats that the Norfolkers said calmed the nerves were certainly in evidence here too: fields and fields of them up at Norwood. Bob had seen them when he went to gather open-cast coal in the late summer. The trouble was, the fields were not close at hand but always in outlying parts away from the centre of Calderbrigg. Not like home where you wandered between village and village, down lanes all bordered by fields or meadows, the Queen Anne's lace creaming over the hedge tops.

George might grow carrots, she speculated, for they were good for bad eyesight. He always grumbled about the dandelions that spread over his soil but they might serve for digestive purposes if she made dandelion-tea. Stinging nettles were plentiful in the nearest woods where their road became a lane and crossed a brook the Yorkshire folk called a beck. Near the beck there'd be celandines for sure that were so good to cure warts, and plenty of hawthorn berries that — according to Hannah Sayer — were good for the heart. Nettles had always been used for purifying the blood and for gout. She would try to be a mistress of remedies, she decided, but of feverfew for headaches, valerian for nerves, St John's wort for shingles, linseed for constipation, and ribwort plantain for ear infections, all of which she had discussed with Mrs Sayer, she had so far seen nothing.

Oh, more than anything she missed the cottage gardens they'd had at home, even the poorest folk. Full of mignonette they'd been, and marigolds, sweet peas, columbine, lilies, roses, like the 'Maiden's blush', and gooseberry bushes and gages. She missed the field-flowers too — cowslips and speedwell. It was too cold up in Yorkshire to grow things so easily and the soil was heavy clay and the smoke made even the soil sour. Bob had reported miles and miles of dry-stone walls he'd seen as he walked around, or went up to Norwood for the open-cast coal. He said there were apple-trees and crabs but none of the good old Norfolk apples, the Biffens and Pearmains. How she longed to sink her teeth into them! There were oak-woods here, and Bob said there were larch plantations, and the woods people sometimes walked in with their children were pretty, but bluebells came a lot later than at home. Late May in Calderbrigg! There weren't so many 'squorls', either, or at least she had never seen any. She pondered such things as she worked, or pushed the baby out in his little cart, a little box on wheels with a long handle that Percy had made for him.

There was a walk not far away which she

sometimes took. At first she had intended to look for herbs in the wood they called Freeman's which was not far from the road where their row of houses was built, but then she discovered on the walk that between the river and the canal there was an island. A scattering of cottages stood nearby but all was peaceful and really quite pretty. She supposed that the town had once been a village before the mills came and all the dirt and 'muck' as the folk round here called it. It might even have been as pretty as the villages at home, though she doubted it. There was certainly nothing as grand as Breckles Hall in Calderbrigg! It was so hilly up here and you couldn't linger in places because of the cold winds that came over the Pennines. But perhaps in the summer she'd walk further with Herbert, and he could look at the river. There was a broad long valley leading to a place where they said there was going to be some sort of park built.

Bob had already been up on the nearest moor Halifax way and reported bilberries growing there. They were the same as blueberries, weren't they, which must also be obviously good for something; just 'good for you' perhaps?

What had Mam said bloodroot was for? And wild pansies? And yarrow? She would have to look for them and consult Yorkshire women. She didn't know many of them yet but she was beginning to be friendly with those whose bairns, as they called them, were at the same school as Polly and Emma.

But when her baby was six months old she found she might be expecting again. Our Harbie was on the whole a healthy baby, though he was nervous of loud noises. He had never cried as much as most nurslings when he was tiny.

She would sometimes completely forget that she might be expecting again, refusing to believe it was possible, but Harbie was only fifteen months old and still taking milk from her when she went into labour with what turned out to be another boy: Ernest. 'Our Arnust', as Emma always called him, joined his brother.

* * *

There had been a local election the year after Harbie was born and George had taken a strong interest in it even though he was not allowed the vote. He had made a new Yorkshire friend, a Mr Marshall, who was an engine fitter at one of the small sheds that had just begun towards the valley bottom. He reported that Jim Marshall had told him how at the last general election the parish church bells had rung to celebrate a Conservative victory! All chapel-folk were Liberals, and so was George.

'They've to meet in the public house at Hipperholme,' George told his wife. 'They've nowhere else, but they're saving to rent a building.'

Emma had never taken much interest in politics. At home she had never heard of any woman knowing anything about the matter. George told her that everyone in Norfolk except the real keen chapel-goers were Conservatives, but it was up to the working man to take an interest. One day they would have the vote! Emma did not really believe this but she was used to George knowing a lot more than she did about most things so she took his word for it. Then she reflected, and remarked:

'But we worked for Mrs Upcraft and I know she was a Conservative. I heard her son going on about it once and how all the servants would back them. You never said you didn't agree with them.'

'Ordinary folk couldn't do anything about it even if they wanted,' he replied. 'They haven't the vote, most of 'em. Not all rich folk up here are Conservatives, you know. They say Sir Titus has lent his omnibus to take folks to the poll, and he's the richest man we're ever likely to hear of in Calderbrigg!'

Emma pondered this. It was true there were a few wealthy folk who lived on the outskirts of the town but that they should take an interest in the Liberals and go against what George said were their own interests was puzzling.

'They're for Gladstone, you see,' he explained.

She recalled how long ago at the chapel she had occasionally attended as a child she had realized that the ministers were always on the side of the poor, so perhaps she had better say now that she too was a Liberal. They were poor, true, but not so poor as some folk. They always held their heads up and acted respectable. More respectable than some of her mother's family might have been, she thought once or twice.

By the time the great Liberal Lord Frederick Cavendish was elected a few years later for the West Riding, and the townsfolk joined in a great procession to celebrate, she was too busy with several more children to bother her head about it. Not until he was murdered in Ireland and the consequent riots against the Irish, whom they called 'Fenians', were to terrify everyone, not just the Irish delvers, did she feel herself involved.

She had expected a hard and busy life and she was not disappointed. After Harbie and Ernest and the two years' breathing-space, she gave birth to her first full daughter, in 1877. Not that she had ever treated the two eldest girls any differently but there *was* a difference. Little Polly was by now ten years old and there would spring up between this stepdaughter and her first daughter a deep affection. They even looked alike, both of them resembling George. Polly's sister Ann, now working at the silk-mill, took less interest in children.

Polly said: 'Only have girls, Mam. They are nicer to play with.'

'You can't choose, lass,' answered Emma Eliza who had taken up the Yorkshire word which she used now as often as she still used the Norfolk 'bor'.

In any case, Polly had always been helpful, even with the two boys. But Polly would have to go to work herself when she was twelve; they had allowed her to stay on at school after she was ten. First of all she'd be a half-timer in the silk-mill where Ann was already working. It was not far away and she could walk there and return to school in the afternoon and eat her bread and cheese on the way. Ann reported that if she were in good time the overlooker would let them stay on and eat sitting on the mill wall.

Emma had been overjoyed when her first daughter was born. It was on Candlemas Day. An old saying from home came into her head:

On Candlemas Day, if the sun shines
clear,
The shepherd had rather see his wife on
the bier.

Whatever *that* meant, she thought! Anyway the day was, as usual, cold and drizzling with rain. She named her daughter Beattie, short for Beatrice, because she liked the name, which was that of the Queen's youngest child. She would have called Beattie Eliza, but Elizabeth being George's first wife's name and his daughter Ann's second name, he had not wanted his daughter by Emma to be another Elizabeth.

By the end of the following year, the children's Uncle Percy, who had once been little Botty but who was now twenty-four years old, married a pleasant young Yorkshire girl he met at Bethel Chapel and moved into a small house not far down the same road as his sister.

The couple called their first child Eliza Jane. Emma Eliza was pleased that he had wanted to remember their mother Eliza in this way.

13

Myra was still writing faithfully to her big sister. She was now almost eighteen, had soon left the rectory kitchens and was working as a housemaid at the hall in Caston, which was not as grand as Breckles Hall, but whose owners were, if not quite so old-established, a little better off, and more adventurous in their tastes. Myra made it plain she did not intend to stay there, was indeed destined for greater things. Emma was surprised she had put up with it so long, but one day she received a long missive from Norfolk that took her all afternoon to decipher, in the intervals of calming down Herbert and Ernest who were as usual fighting in the yard, and cuddling Beattie who had a cold.

If ever she could not understand words, or if she suspected it was the sort of thing she did not especially want to ask George's advice about, she would ask Polly, who was a clever little girl and could be trusted to be discreet. But Polly was now working at the mill in the mornings with school in the afternoons.

'At least the rectory got me away from home,' wrote Myra, 'and here last week a visitor staying with us' (Myra always alluded to the hall family as if it were hers) 'told me I could find work singing and dancing on the stage in London!'

Emma's heart sank. Everyone knew what happened to girls who went to London. Who was this visitor at Caston Hall? A man, she felt sure.

Until now, in her infrequent attempts to write to her sister, she had mentioned Jabez Smith only once. She had asked Myra to tell him, if she ever did see him, that she was happy in Calderbrigg and now had three children of her own. Six months later Myra had replied saying she had met the man quite a few times. One afternoon she had spoken to him at a house in the village, whose chimney he was sweeping, and he had seemed pleased to chat with her. He had now disappeared again. He had sent his kind regards to Emma. 'He said he was right pleased for you that you and George now have what he called a 'brood' of your own'.

Emma knew she must write once more to ask Myra to have a word with him. If he was still sweeping chimneys there must be some easy way of getting hold of him. Perhaps the Caston Hall chimney was smoking. Myra could make enquiries as to his whereabouts — she might say it was for a friend — and then she must ask his advice.

She thought, he will remember his promise. She managed after several days' effort, helped by Polly, to write a short letter to Myra begging her to do this. 'You must speak to Mr Smith and ask his advice,' she wrote. 'Say he promised your sister who has written to you.' Before you do anything silly like running away to London, she thought. Myra had once promised on their mother's memory that she would do as her sister asked, and although she was flighty, Emma thought she would keep her promise to try to see Baz if she did intend to leave Caston.

Baz belonged to such a long ago time! He might easily go away for good. She was sure that if he were still around he would help dissuade Myra from a rash course of action. Oh, if only she could just see him and beg him to keep an eye on the girl. But perhaps he had. He had 'welcomed a chat'.

'He might be working in Rockland or Griston or Thompson,' she went on, ending, 'I send you all my love dear and beg you to do as I ask,' before sealing the letter and asking Polly to run to the post-office, now on Commercial Street, and stamp and post it.

After their marriage George had never once referred to Baz, and she was careful to say nothing about her arrangement with him regarding Myra. She did not think of the young man now with longing so much as with a calm joy. The thought of him did not set her heart beating as it had once done, but it did make her feel happy. He had become a sort of talisman left over from her childhood, though she knew he was not a ghost, only a young man. Not all that young either now — he must be about thirty-eight. However, she trusted him with Myra. If he had been unable to love Emma, though it had been clear he was fond of her, he had still treated her well. He was a man of delicacy. She'd have been a willing girl — and Myra might be even more willing — but she was convinced that it was not what a man like Baz wanted. Perhaps he was religious. She had to wait several weeks before a reply came from her sister.

* * *

In Myra's next letter there was more news of Mr Smith.

> I told him I was going to leave home but that you said I must see him first. He has advised me to write to the manager of the concert party that Mr Henshaw at the hall told me about and to enquire if they have orditions — I am not sure how to spell this

but it is when they listen to you sing. If they offered me a Contrackt for a job then I could leave. I told Mr Smith that I'd very soon be eighteen and he said, Good, and I will accompany you to your ordition. I had a reply from the manager in Lynn! and Mr Smith thinks that they have a concert party in Lynn but also other jobs not in Norfolk, but he does not think in London. Oh, well, Emmie it does not have to be London so long as I can leave here. Dad is badly again and She drives me mad. At the Hall they said they would be sorry to see me go! So wait for my next letter and I will come to see you first if there is a job near you or anywhere. Mr Smith has been a real brick I think he must have been sweet on you he does not try it on with me.

All my love, Myra.

Emma waited for the next letter which arrived not long afterwards and was written from Lynn. Myra had been to her audition in Lynn, and there was a job waiting for her in Manchester in three months. She had told her father and her employer, and Mr Smith had been kind enough to lend her the railway fare to visit Calderbrigg first of all.

Emma could scarcely believe it. Myra must be really good to be offered a job! How she looked forward to seeing her again! Over six years since they had seen each other. Her sister had done well to keep in touch. Emma had known their father was poorly, and it was another cloud of worry in her mind but no longer her responsibility. What would his second wife do if he died and she was left with what was now a family of five small children? They weren't Banhams, so the many members of the Banham tribe would not be of any help to her. She would have stayed on for their father's sake, she supposed, if she had been Myra, but Myra was not like her and would take her chance. Perhaps she could ask Jabez Smith to keep an eye on her father too. No, she could not. It would be hard enough to repay him the money he had lent Myra.

And how on earth was she going to fit Myra into their little house, even with Percy now wed? She'd have to go in with Polly and Ann. Bob now had Percy's room along with the two little boys, much to his disgust. She'd be glad if Bob found another nice girl and got himself wed. George was talking about moving a bit further down the road to a slightly bigger house nearer the town centre as his wage had just gone up a little and both his daughters were now bringing in a few shillings.

Polly was often weary from early rising but insisted on trying to concentrate at school. When she got home she often fell asleep after her tea. The second mill-shift did not finish till even later and if the girls worked then instead of the morning they had no time at all at home to enjoy life, only to sleep. Both girls however had deft fingers and were hard working, willingly so far bringing home their small wages to support their family. But soon Ann was to confide to her sister that she thought she should have the money herself since she had worked for it. Polly said it would not keep them in boots and it was good they could help Mam and Dad. As a little 'thank you' to his two eldest children George had had their photograph taken in the town, in their new boots and working-shawls.

Polly was excited about Myra's pending visit but her sister took little interest. There were now problems at one of the silk-mills and in March there was a strike, but Emma had her hands full with Beattie and the two boys and did not take it all in when George tried to explain to her why they were on strike. There was no import duty on foreign silk products so there was competition from abroad. Emma Eliza did not understand quite what import duty was. All she knew was that the two older girls were pleased not to have to work for a week or two and to stay at school all day. But of course it was worrying if their wages were to be missed much longer. Polly had not been at work there very long, taught by her sister to undertake the easiest tasks, and she was always tired out, so their stepmother was secretly pleased they could have a little break.

Just when she had gained a little time to breathe, and not long after Beattie's second birthday Emma Eliza feared she was pregnant again. Unless it was a false alarm the baby would be born at the end of the year. Even more reason now to move. Thank goodness there were no rumours of any strikes at the huge mill by the canal side where George by this time had charge of many horses.

* * *

The day of Myra's arrival dawned. Emma had resolved to meet her at the station, and George, who had been told only that Myra had found a job in Manchester through someone at Caston Hall said he could manage to come up and wait with a cart on his way back to the mill as he had to deliver some bags of flour that evening up Rastrick way. So long as the train was not late! Emma was in a stew of impatience. Polly and young Ann would be at home by the time she set out for the station, and Polly had offered to look after the three little ones whilst their mother went to meet the train. She accepted the offer with gratitude. It was said the strike at the silk-mill would be over by the following week.

It had been a hard winter but spring seemed to have arrived, for a few days at least. It was a lovely evening, warmer than was usual in March, and the town was looking its best in spite of the smoke that always wreathed the streets and sometimes darkened the sky from the myriad chimneys.

George was waiting in the yard and waved his whip in greeting but did not get down from his perch. She felt odd, detached, as though she herself had just arrived rather than the reality of her being the mother of three children, and with most likely another in her belly, a woman whose children were looking forward to her return home with the auntie they had heard so much about.

She did not have long to wait. She heard the chuff and rattle of the engine in the distance and watched as it appeared, pulling the coaches behind, now slowing down with a declining roar and a long hiss of steam, smoke billowing from its chunky funnel.

Then the noise lessened as it came to rest by the platform and stopped. Doors were opened, people were getting down: a businessman with a walking-stick, three young men laughing and joshing each other, and Mr Rathmell the butcher who had been on a visit with his wife to the nearby city. Where was Myra?

Then she saw in the distance a young woman carrying a large case with a young man walking beside her carrying an even larger one. Emma stood on her toes, peered. Soon the woman came up and the young man, who was not Baz — for a moment Emma had thought it might be — came up with Myra, stopped, put the case down raised his hat and disappeared. He was only a fellow traveller.

'Emma my love!' cried the young lady and Emma found herself enveloped in the arms of her sister. It was undeniably Myra, but how changed! A taller Myra with a hat perched on red hair and a velvet choker round her neck. Goodness, how elegant she looked!

'Myra!' she murmured feebly.

'Such a lot to tell you!' Myra was bubbling over with excitement. 'And the little ones — I'm so looking forward to seeing them.'

She took her sister's arm and, each of them carrying a case, they staggered outside to the station yard where the cart was waiting.

George got down from his perch.

'Welcome to Calderbrigg,' he said quietly to his sister-in-law. Emma noticed that he was observing her carefully whilst taking up her two pieces of luggage.

'Sorry about the cases,' she said. 'It's all I own in the world.'

They set off down the cobbled streets. Emma wondered whatever Myra would think of the dirty little town.

'So this is where you live your new life!' said her sister.

'I'm afraid the town is very smoky,' said Emma apologetically. She could not rid herself of the idea that Myra had come up in the world, but of course she had not.

'Oh, anything is better than that stagnating village,' said Myra. 'They've warned me — Manchester is smoky too.'

It was the same when they reached the house and went in and Emma showed Myra the little room she would have to share with the two elder girls.

'I can sleep anywhere,' said Myra.

She appeared determined to see life through rose-coloured spectacles. She would certainly need them, thought the practical Emma.

'Come down for a cup of tea, will you? It's

a bit cold up there. George has the fire going even in summer.'

'You look well,' said Myra.

'So do you,' replied Emma, and it was true. Myra was bursting with energy and well-being. They must soon talk of Baz but that would have to wait until George was out.

The children were running around the room. Ernest and Herbert interrupted a fight to stare at the new aunt, but said little. Beattie however smiled in Polly's arms and said, 'Hello lady.'

'And this is Polly?' said Myra.

Ann came into the room with the teapot and condescended to greet her aunt. Emma-Eliza cleared a space on the floor for Myra's legs and poked the fire.

'You'll have a lot to talk about,' said George, coming in with a towel with which he was drying his hands. 'I've to take back Dobbin and then I promised to see Harry Brown. Keep my tea for me.'

'You must tell me all your news,' said Emma over the tea.

The boys had been given a piece of bread and cheese and had then disappeared into the yard. George had gone out. Ann was washing cups and piling a plate with more bread. Polly took her aunt's cup and poured more tea out for her.

'It's cosy here,' said Myra. Then to Polly, 'Fancy, your auntie is going to sing on the stage!' Polly looked suitably impressed but Ann, hearing this as she came into the room from the kitchen said, 'Why?'

'Because I like singing and I want to be an actress,' said Myra with a sharp look at the cynical girl. With her red hair and her ready tongue Myra was an exotic creature, the like of whom the children would not have come across before.

Emma refused her sister's offer of help in putting the children to bed and was soon back downstairs. The two girls then went up.

Emma and Myra sat down together at the fireside for an hour or two. Myra toasted some bread and her feet, and Emma continued making the rag rug for the stone floor from old pieces of material she had found. She remade almost every item of child's clothing for the next child along and kept all the scraps to use again.

George stayed out, his tea of meat and dumplings kept warm for him in a dish over a pan on the fire. Emma told her sister how she longed for a kitchen-range that could be black-leaded, and how George had promised her one when they moved to a slightly larger house.

The new range was all the fashion; in the

middle was the fire over which pans could perch for boiling potatoes; on one side there was a boiler that made hot water for washing, on the other an oven for all the baking and roasting. The fire heated everything and hardly ever went out. Her friend Isabella had a range like this and Emma had coveted one ever since she had seen it. Isabella said they were a lot of work, but Isabella was not a woman who enjoyed keeping things sparkling and clean. Her stone flagged floor was not swept as often as Emma's and her donkey-stone did not visit her doorstep as often as Emma's did, which was every morning. Emma felt she was talking to cover embarrassment and perhaps to show she had a life too.

'Isabella says I have a lot of energy,' she said to her sister. 'She's a nice easy-going woman, if rather slammocky.'

Myra giggled and said, 'You haven't changed, bor!'

For a few minutes Emma talked about Isabella and her other friends. 'At least neither I nor Isabella have to go out to work to the mill!' she added.

Myra said looking after a family must be just as hard work as weaving in a mill and not the life *she* would ever like to have.

'*You* haven't changed either,' said Emma

with a smile. Somehow you could forgive Myra her fancies. 'Up here, some of the married women go to work in the mills as well as looking after their families, but it's usually the grandmothers who take the babies when the mothers work. If Mam were here I wouldn't mind earning some money in a mill myself!'

They were both silent for a moment remembering their mother who would have been over sixty now if she had lived.

Then Emma plucked up her courage and finally asked the question she had been wanting to ask all evening:

'What did Mr Smith say?' she asked rather timidly. Myra smiled enigmatically. 'Oh, he was very kind. I couldn't have got up here without the money he lent me. He insisted I took his advice about applying in the proper way for a singing part in the chorus, and I'm glad I did, but now it's up to me.'

'What did you think of him?'

Even if Myra was still the same Myra, she was now grown up, different in superficial ways from her childish self. Myra wanted a new life. If it worked out well, it would be so different from her own that Emma felt a gulf might soon open between them if she did not anticipate it now.

Myra was looking thoughtful.

'He has had a strange life I think, Mr Smith,' she said. 'Nobody seems to know much about him yet they all know *of* him.'

Emma felt strangely reluctant to tell her sister of her conviction that she had known him as a child but said instead:

'Well they all know him for a good windmill-builder.'

'He can do anything in that line, I think,' said Myra, 'but he has educated himself. I don't know how. He's very mysterious, isn't he?'

'Perhaps he is just clever?' offered Emma.

'Oh he is that, I grant you, and he took trouble over me because of you, I'm sure. Was he sweet on you?'

Emma felt herself blushing but said, 'Oh no. We knew each other a little when he was around in the village the time I worked at the hall. We got on well . . . '

'He doesn't appear to have a wife or a sweetheart,' said her sister. 'Maybe he's not a ladies' man. I can usually pick *them* out easily!'

'How you have grown up!' said Emma. 'But you must be careful in Manchester. Young women can easily fall prey to rogues.' Especially women as good looking as you, she thought.

'That's what *he* said! If it were not too

good to be true I would say that he's a sort of guardian angel, wouldn't you? He's so good looking! And he seems to have a bit of money. One thing he did say to me and that was that his father was no gypsy! I'd teased him about it.'

'Did I tell you he was?' asked Emma.

'Well, it must have been you — unless it was someone in the village. They know him but he doesn't mix with them much. I had the feeling the Starlings kept their distance from him, and that he wasn't over fond of that family. I shouldn't mention him to your George!'

Emma's reaction to these words was not expressed for at that moment they heard George at the door. She got up and gave him his meal and Myra yawned and said she must go to bed. She was given a candle and the couple stayed downstairs for half an hour chatting till they too went up. George was incurious about his sister-in-law but seemed to regard her with an amused indulgence.

'She can stay with us for a few days before she goes to Manchester,' Emma told her husband. 'She told me she didn't have to make a fuss about leaving home, and I expect Dad didn't mind, but I think she's sorry for him with all those new mouths to feed. Five children he and my stepmother have now.'

She wondered whether this was the moment to tell George she might be expecting again, but decided against it. Oh, she did hope she was not.

'How is your father?' George was asking her now.

'Poorly, Myra says, but at least he has work.'

In bed she could not sleep. In spite of having got over her feelings for Jabez Smith, her old Baz, that Myra had been recently so close to him made her feel a bit jealous. But it — whatever 'it' had been between her and him — was over long ago, she told herself. Even if her sister was young and pretty, she was still sure Baz would not have taken advantage of her. He was just a very kind man, as Myra had said. As for Myra herself, who knew what she had really thought of him? She had said he was handsome and she had taken his help with gratitude, but Emma Eliza knew her sister well enough to know she would have most likely flirted with him. She was a puzzle, for Emma also felt that Myra was not the kind of young woman to risk anything that might turn out to be to her own disadvantage. As the Yorkshire folk up here might say, 'She has her head screwed on right.'

Emma managed next morning to conceal

these feelings from Myra. They were getting on quite well together, for she was used to her sister's attitudes. Myra had always been worldly. Her employers at Caston Hall appeared to have treated her well for she had been able to save a little from her wages over the six years she had worked there.

'Didn't you give Dad some of it?' enquired Emma, remembering how her own meagre shillings had been mostly handed over to her father.

'A little, but only at first,' confessed Myra. 'I had to save, Emmie, it was the only way to prepare myself to leave the place. I did buy the little girls a few ribbons and helped Stepmother with the cooking when I went home. Anyway, Dad and his wife would be glad they weren't to have me around any longer. I expect I could have got a lot more money. If I'd done what Mr Davey wanted me to do!'

'Who was he?' enquired Emma.

'A visitor to the hall. Quite an old man! He was sweet on me but I was very firm and as he was frightened of Mrs Hoy, his aunt, who is a very religious woman, he daren't try anything on. I believe he'd have married me if it wasn't that I was a servant!'

'Was he the man who told you about getting work on the stage?'

‘Oh no, that was Christopher Stevens, another of her nephews — a lot younger. She kept her eye on him too! At Christmas last year — didn’t I tell you in my letter? I sang some sacred music for their house-party!’

Emma was amazed at all these men who had seemingly interested themselves in her sister, and buzzed around her. That a servant should be asked to sing! Even if Myra was exaggerating it was clear that she knew these people quite well, that they thought highly of her and that she did not appear to have come to any harm. This Mr Stevens had actually given her good advice, she supposed.

‘I don’t remember your telling me you sang for them!’

‘Well, I didn’t have time to write very often — I did work quite hard as well, you know.’

Myra was to stay till the Friday afternoon when she would take the train direct to Manchester. Her lodging was being fixed up for her, she said, by the agent who had given her the work. It was to be until the autumn and he promised they would need girls to start rehearsing then for the Christmas pantomime season. She was a little vague about this and Emma did not like to pursue the matter. Myra would go her own way and was, she thought, pretty tough if not quite as tough as she thought.

Emma was shown the letter from the agent who had been in Lynn and who worked with the Manchester manager to produce shows in seaside places.

'But I didn't want to work in Yarmouth,' said Myra, with a toss of her head. 'Manchester is a bigger place and almost as good as working in London!'

'You must promise to let me know you are all right and then I can tell Dad,' said Emma.

Myra copied out the address of the agent in Manchester and the address she had been given for lodgings.

'You know if you are in any difficulty you can always come back here,' said Emma.

'Oh, I shall fall on my feet!' said Myra. Her sister did not doubt that.

'But if Dad gets worse you can let me know,' said Myra placatingly, '*He* won't write and Stepma hasn't the time even if she could.'

Emma had the impression Myra would not be making long journeys back to Norfolk at any time in future.

* * *

On the Friday morning Emma took the boys to the station to see off their Aunt Myra, along with Beattie in a push cart, since her legs were too short to walk as quickly as the others and she was heavy to carry. The presence of the children made their mother less tearful than she might have been. When on earth would she see her sister again? Myra had promised to send her a telegram of her safe arrival with her new address if it was different from where she had told Emma she would be. George had paid for it since his wife was so determined Myra should let them know.

'Don't worry about me, I'll be all right, and if any of your friends in Calderbrigg intend coming to Manchester, tell them to enquire at the Empire,' said Myra.

'You're not sure they'll have you on yet though!'

'Well, if I'm not in the chorus there they will know where I am! They might even send me on to Leeds if they think I'd be any good for their panto. Thank you anyway, old girl, for the rest and the stay.'

'Well, look after yourself, mind — and don't forget that telegram.'

'You look after yourself too, Emmie.'

Emma had confided her suspicions about a new baby to Myra the previous night. Myra had said, 'Well, I scarcely feel like congratulating you, poor girl, but all will be for the best, I'm sure.'

Myra, though kind to the little ones, did not disguise her continuing dislike of screaming babies. Beattie was beyond this stage now but her toddler temperament occasionally evinced itself in tears.

Thus, half admonishing, half attempting cheerfulness, the two sisters parted.

'Well, goodbye, bor.' Emma kissed Myra as the train doors began to be slammed, and held up Beattie to be kissed too. The boys looked on, more interested in the engine than in their aunt.

'I'll write to Dad,' shouted Emma as the train began to move.

'Bye-bye,' shouted Beattie.

Emma had tears in her eyes as they walked slowly back home. She felt sure that the next time she saw Myra she herself would have a new baby in her arms.

Myra did send a telegram. George said she might as well have sent a letter for sixpence but did not say he grudged the shilling.

> Mr Ashworth met me. Lodging at 66b Piccadilly Row for the present. Repetition Monday. All fine. Love to all. Myra.

Well that seemed to be that. Emma wondered what a repetition was. Percy opined Myra meant a rehearsal. So she must have got a part, however small. They would have to wait for a letter.

Myra did write a week or two later. She was to stay in the chorus of *Dolabella* for the time being. By the December of 1879, when she was given a larger part, though not yet in the Leeds pantomime, Emma had given birth to another baby daughter, this time with red hair and very bright blue eyes, as different from Beattie as it was possible to be.

She was named Ada Myra and turned out to be a terrible screamer. Emma feared she was going to be another actress.

14

Baby Ada was six months old and still yelling her head off when Emma Eliza received a letter from her stepmother, Hannah Saunders.

Bob Saunders had just died of broncho-pneumonia. The funeral would already have taken place.

'She didn't even try to tell us in time, but what will she do now, George, what will she do? Five children without a father! Can we do anything to help?'

George said there was nothing they could do. They had just enough money to keep themselves and their children afloat with only a tiny amount over for emergencies. This, though greatly to be deplored, was not their emergency.

'If we were rich, Em, we'd send 'em money, I dare say. But she'll have to go on the parish. Parson has a fund too — he'll advise. And the children are old enough to be working, if there is any work. How old are the twins now?'

'Benjamin and Elizabeth will be twelve and John ten. Eliza's eight, I believe, and then there's the youngest, about four, as well as Hannah's son who must bring in something — if he hasn't got wed.'

'If we sent so much as a pound — which we couldn't — we'd have to wait more months to move up the road,' said George. Emma knew it was true. Each penny mattered and her first duty now was to her own family. George had set his heart on that slightly larger house which they would need an extra two shillings a week to rent. There was continuing unrest at the silk-mill where Polly and her sister worked, so their contribution might not be able to be counted upon for ever.

A depression of trade in general had begun and was to continue throughout the year. George knew about these things but said the corn-mill would be all right for the time being.

With their two older girls and their four children and themselves there were now eight souls crowded into the little terrace house. Bob had taken himself off at the New Year to lodge in Southowram where he had found temporary work on a farm, and then in a 'delf', a quarry. He was rumoured to be courting but nothing had been said to his sister about this.

Worry over the plight of the family took

over from any feelings of grief for her father Emma might have. He had been a weak man, she saw now, but not a bad man, and she remembered how she had loved him as a child. But he had gone and saddled himself with a new family! George had once done the same of course, but George had a good job, even if it was in a strange place. If her father hadn't married again, would he have come North with them?

She'd have to tell Myra. She wrote a short note to her sister straight away. Then she went out to the stationer on Commercial Street and bought two sheets of paper with black borders, and two envelopes, costing tuppence in all, and some ink for George's inkwell for a penny. The old pen would have to do.

'Uncle Jonathan would be the best person for Hannah to approach,' she said to George the next morning before he left for work. 'I'm surprised I didn't think of it before. He has a bit of money and no children. I wonder why we haven't heard from him.'

Jonathan Saunders and his wife did keep in touch sporadically but they had not had a letter from them since Christmas.

'I shall write to him as well,' she said. 'But I expect he knows by now.'

That afternoon, sitting at the window

rocking Ada's cradle with one foot and with Beattie playing with a wooden tub by the fire, she laboured over a letter to her uncle, using up one of the black-bordered sheets, and then wrote a letter of sympathy to Hannah and the children on the other sheet. These children's father had been hers, after all, though it seemed a long time ago that he had been hers.

Ever since George had begun to help her improve her reading and writing — and that too seemed long ago now — she had been less reluctant to write a letter, though it was still an unusual occurrence. Her letters to Baz and her replies to Myra had been different, for she did not really mind if they saw her misspellings. But she was more reluctant to reveal herself to Uncle Jonathan who wrote a good hand, far better than her father's had been.

The girls came in for their tea when the shift finished. The boys usually made themselves scarce in what she had learned to call the 'garth'.

'Polly, read this,' she said when she had finished the letter to Hannah, in which she said how sorry she was to hear the news.

'It's *your* dad who's died then?' asked Ann, looking over Polly's shoulder.

'Aunt Myra's father too,' said Polly. 'It's a

very kind letter, Ma. Will you send Dad's sympathy too?'

'Oh, I'd forgot!' said her stepmother and was about to add 'George sends his sympathy', but was unsure how to spell the word. Polly said, 'They told us another word for that at school . . . '

'Yes, you could say *condolences*,' said her sister.

'What clever girls you are,' said Emma, 'But you must spell the word for me.'

It was true that both Polly and Ann were clever girls. Ever since she had found out that their mother had at one time set up that little dame school in her cottage, even if it had come to naught, she had admired George's first wife. Emma suspected that she had improved her husband's reading and writing. How ignorant she herself must have appeared to George after the clever Elizabeth Ann!

She accepted the girls' suggestions and finished off the letter when they had gone to bed. On her own way to bed she heard muffled sobs from their room. It was Polly crying under the bedclothes. Ann was asleep.

'Why, Polly what is it?' she asked and sat on their bed.

'It's my mother,' said the thirteen-year-old girl. 'Your Dad's dying reminded me.'

Emma hugged her stepdaughter. She was

such a tender-hearted girl.

The next day there arrived a reply from Myra who did not seem put out that nobody from Caston had written to *her*. Even more excuse for her never to go to Norfolk again, thought Emma. As for herself, if only she could just have dropped by Caston for a few days, to see they were all right, not starving, not completely swamped by the waters of fate . . . How she'd love to be able to do that. She did still miss the country and the villages and her friends at the farm and the hall. One day they would go home, one day when the children were a bit older and George had saved their fare. She often used to think how everything at home had been so old whilst here there didn't seem to be many really old houses, even of the last century.

They waited for over a week to hear from Hannah Saunders and the letter when it came was not written by her but by a neighbour, Hannah having told him what to write. The funeral had been simple; the girls had been upset but the boys had gone back to their work scaring crows off the barley. Robert Saunders had been ill a long time. His wife hoped this letter found Emma and family well, and was 'their faithful servant, H. Saunders'. It sounded odd: it must have been Hannah's neighbour's idea of the way to end a letter. Not a word about herself though.

Jonathan Saunders took longer to reply but stated his great grief over his brother's demise. He had already taken round some eggs and butter to his sister-in-law.

Well, that was that. She could do no more. But would she ever see her half-brothers and sisters again?

Because she had not gone to her father's funeral Emma felt that her relationship with him was unfinished. This made her uneasy. She grieved, but could not quite believe he was dead. The Sunday after receiving Uncle Joe's letter she asked George if he would stay at home with Ada and Beattie for an hour or two so that she might accompany Bob to Bethel Chapel. George agreed. He did not have much to do with his youngest children, being most of the time at work. Herbert and Ernest, now seven and five, could more or less look after themselves and employed their time when not fighting in the garth, 'playing out' with other boys, Yorkshire boys. They were fast acquiring Yorkshire accents.

This morning they had gone down to the wood in the valley to gather firewood. Herbert was a strong determined boy; Ernest was more delicate but always willing to help. They both adored their father, took less notice of their mother. Beattie was her mother's favourite, though Emma tried not to show it. Beattie and Polly were inseparable; Ann liked to talk to her father as an adult. She was less sociable than her sister, preferred grown-ups.

In the chapel they sang tuneful hymns which Emma loved to hear since they reminded her of her mother's singing, and it was pleasant and peaceful to shut your eyes and pray. She prayed for her father and hoped he was in heaven, and for her mother, who she felt sure *was*. The sermon was rather long, about them all being brothers and sisters, all over the world, especially brothers and sisters 'in righteousness'. Emma amused herself looking at Percy in the choir and then letting her thoughts drift away. The congregation sang the rousing 'We've a story to tell to the nations' very heartily indeed, and then 'Sun of my Soul', her favourite. It was a real treat to go to chapel and she felt better for it.

Soon though she was back home with the usual tasks awaiting her. She now had four children of her own, two girls and two boys and it would be as well if she could stop there. Ada was unlike the other three, who were neither noisy nor especially demanding. Herbert it was true was an independent type but so long as he was left to his own devices he was equable. George was especially fond of his first-born son and of his first-born daughter, Beattie, who looked rather like him, but he could make neither head nor tail of Ada. As she grew into a toddler she became subject to violent tantrums. He would shake his head and say, 'It's the red hair, I expect.' Emma felt he was pointing out that not only did the Starlings have no red hair in the family, neither did they have temper-prone individuals.

'You've got your Myra, so I suppose Ada takes after her,' he would add. But Ada was not really all that like Myra. Myra had always had a sense of humour and charmed grown-ups, but even before she was two Ada was much more grumpy than Myra had been and if she did not get her own way would shriek and kick.

Poor Ada was destined not to be able to hold centre stage for long, as she would obviously have wished, for eighteen months later another girl was born whom they named Florence. Baby Flo was all Ada was not: quiet and plump and easy-going. Beattie was deputed to look after Ada so that Emma could concentrate on the new arrival, and even Beattie, who at four and a half was a 'little mother' type, found Ada impossible, though she tried her best.

It was even more imperative now that they

move to a slightly bigger house. George had waited and waited until the one he had fixed his eye on for some time was up for rent. Number 28 was set a little further back from the road, next door but one to an off-licence, not that he wanted to visit *that*, and almost at the top of 'Irish Hill', a turning off their old road, nearer both to Percy's house and to the town centre. The end house of the houses opposite had painted on its stonework an advertisement for biscuits in the shape of a drummer boy. The children loved this; it made them feel distinctive.

They moved there in early 1882. There was one more little room upstairs and the kitchen was much bigger. It incorporated the living-room, and there was a pantry larder on the side. At the back was another smaller room, 'the parlour'. But above all, more than all this luxury, there, at last, in the big living-room was the range in all its gleaming blackness. Emma was overjoyed. They moved all their possessions into the new house one Sunday, but it took some time to afford two little truckle-beds for upstairs and two 'new' chairs to stand in their rightful places on each side of the fire, wearing the antimacassars Emma had sewed and embroidered for them. She was now hoping for an aspidistra to put in the window of the back parlour.

What was happening to Myra while her sister was giving birth to Flo, moving house and sewing antimacassars? An ecstatic letter arrived in March from her. After all this time in the chorus at the Hippodrome she had been offered a part, a real speaking and singing part for the summer in Rhyl. The seaside! A concert party on the pier-head: 'Alfred Sugden's Entertainers', they were called, and there would be pierrots too. Myra exulted. Both the resorts of Rhyl and Llandudno were venues for these entertainments and the money was good. Next winter too there was finally the promise of a pantomime part in Leeds or Woolsford where Mr Sugden and his entertainers migrated for the winter rather than to Manchester. But the work in Manchester had not been in vain, had tided her over and got her this new job. The opportunity was an excellent one. Emma wondered if Myra had a follower among the pierrots and the male actors, but forbore to ask. She would hear soon enough, she thought, if Myra had changed her mind about marriage.

But all the excitements of the move, and Myra's news, paled before what happened in the town two months later in May.

Bob, who was still working and lodging in Southowram, in the small stone-quarry, came over for tea one Sunday at the end of April with the tale of how some of his work-mates were up in arms, angry with the Irish lads, who also worked the quarry, for taking work they felt *they* ought to have. The Irish were paid less too when they first arrived, and the Calderbriggers feared they would undercut their own wages. The English lads called the Irish 'Fenians'.

'I don't know what Fenian means,' said Bob.

George told him and the others, listening as they munched their bread and drank their tea, that in Manchester, some fifteen years before, there had been what was called the 'Fenian Outrage', when an Irish mob had set upon a carriage conveying two top Fenians to gaol. The English were very anti-Fenian.

'I never heard of them,' said Emma.

'Well, there weren't any in Norfolk. Fenians are just Irish who want to govern themselves, but in Norfolk we never knew anything about it.'

'I like the Irish,' said Polly. The girls had loved their school, the Catholic school they had been sent to, which mainly catered for the town's Irish immigrants.

'I like the way they talk,' said Bob, 'they're full of fun — right hard workers too. I don't see why they shouldn't govern themselves!'

Emma said timidly, 'I suppose they've just come here to work, like your Dad and me — and you too!'

'Aye, lass,' said Bob, imitating his Yorkshire pals.

The talk turned to the circus that was coming to the town on Tuesday. Bob said he had seen the lions arrive in big pens carried on carts and parked on waste ground at Lane Head. Polly shivered. How did they know the lions would not escape and eat people up?

But it transpired that human predators were more to be feared than wild animals.

On Saturday, the second day of May, a few days after the circus had gone away, the Liberal MP for their constituency of the North-West Riding: 'Our Lord Fred', the son of the Duke of Devonshire from Chatsworth, who had been given the job of Chief Secretary for Ireland, and who had just arrived in Dublin, was stabbed to death while walking in Phoenix Park.

The news spread like wildfire. The whole of England was horrified, especially the citizens of Calderbrigg, some of whom had just been forced to end a strike at the silk-mill. This was not the same mill where the girls worked, but trade in general, especially in silk, was very sluggish.

The next day, those folk who went to mass

at St Joseph's, the church that also managed the Catholic school attended by Harbie and Ernest and little five-year-old Beattie, were advised to keep off the streets. Responsible people feared repercussions against Catholics, as most of them were Irish. There were, George knew, several Fenians in the district, but they kept their heads down and for some time it seemed that all would pass off quietly. Most ordinary folk, both English and Irish, did as they were told. But as usual it was feared that hothead youths of the town might lead a mob against the Irish now that they had an excuse.

Ernest came home from school on the Monday highly excited.

'There's a big group of bobbies walking up and down, Mam,' he announced breathlessly. 'Our Harbie saw 'em on Commercial Street. Are they going to fight the Irish?'

'No, our Arnust, they are not. If there are any extra policemen it will be to stop people fighting, not to encourage them,' replied Emma severely. But as they ate their tea, and as little Beattie was put to bed, tired as usual from school but proudly reciting her 'Our Father' and 'Hail Mary' in Latin without having any notion of what the words meant, crowds were gathering in different parts of the town, especially near the centre of the

Irish quarter in Taylor's Yard. They knew nothing of this till George came home with the news that up in Southowram one of the delvers had been mobbed by a crowd and then badly beaten. The police had moved in, according to a friend of Bob he'd met on the street.

'I do hope our Bob's kept himself out of all this,' said Emma worriedly.

'Oh, he wouldn't want to hurt anyone, he's not the sort. It's whether the hotheads attack the lads who *don't* want to pick a fight with the Irish,' said her husband.

Polly and Ann came running in from work. 'There's crowds near the Sun Dial inn,' they gasped, 'They say they were in Taylor's Yard fighting but they've gone for the landlord of the inn now.'

'He's Irish, true,' said George who, though spending hardly any time at all in such a place, indeed probably not more than a hour or two a year, knew the names of all the tradesmen and the landlords and was known himself for his good counsel.

'They'll go to that other pub,' said Ann, 'further down the road — that's always full of Irish!'

Their new house was only a street or two away from the Sun Dial inn so George said he would go and investigate and try to see what was happening. In the meantime nobody must go out and that meant *nobody*.

'They'll be drunk, if I guess aright,' he said to his wife.

He was right. As he stood on the opposite side of the road from the pub a swarm of young men burst out of its door brandishing beer bottles or drinking from them and waving cigars. All around were a hundred or two of either onlookers or further rioters.

'They've just beaten up the Irish customers,' said his friend Bill Mitchell who was standing some distance away himself.

'Idiots,' said another older man, a Methodist lay preacher whom George had seen with Bill from time to time.

'It's not our Irishmen's fault, that murder over there. They were all here, the ones they're beating up, just trying to keep body and soul together, not killing statesmen. The behaviour of our mob can only justify worse conduct now from the Irish here — who can blame them? Violence never works.'

The crowd was thick in front of the door of the inn and there were several inert bodies he saw now, drawn up on the pavement, bodies of Irishmen.

'Good God, they haven't killed them?' expostulated George.

'Nay, lad,' said an onlooker, a little bow-legged man with a woolly waistcoat. 'Knocked 'em out, that's what they've gone and done!' And he laughed, 'Teehee.'

George felt sick. There was no knowing what a mob would do when their blood was up. This crowd obviously had no notion what to do next either, except make as much trouble as possible. A policeman was trying to push his way through the crowd to the two men lined up on the pavement. Polly had guessed right, for a youth brandishing a bottle cried, 'On to t' Commercial Inn — there's more on 'em there!' The mob turned and streamed down the road to the town, shouting and swearing. It was not a pretty sight.

Where would they go after that? wondered George. But he was going home. You never knew; the mob might take it into its head to attack any houses where Irish might live and some of those houses were not far from their own home. He'd better make sure the family were protected.

Later that night, Emma said, 'They might want to attack any folk who weren't born here. Norfolkers too! The Irish might just be an excuse. They call us all 'off-comers', don't they?'

For the first time, but only for a few

seconds, George thought it might have been wiser never to have come North, to have starved at home in their peaceful little Norfolk village. But common sense intervened. The mob might be of a few hundred men but that was only a few hundred out of thousands. How many Irish lived here? He had no idea. In the morning the children must be kept away from school until their parents saw how the land lay. The school where Irish children were to be found might be the next place to be attacked.

Down by the canal, before he went into the yard to work next morning, were knots of men talking about the events of the previous evening and night. One man spat on the ground before he said:

'Aye they went on till the early hours.'

'They went to that lodging house on Martin Street but t'landlord refused to turn Irish out. Then they pelted t'place with stones.'

'But they say a delver was coming back late and they beat him up. Then t'constables come up, and with 'em their boss — that man Hey — and *he* got 'em to move on,' said another man.

Was it all over, then?

Apparently not, for rumours were soon going round the yard that further mobs of young men had collected. George's heart sank when he heard there were many delvers among them.

'They say they're marching round all the quarries in the district to make the owners sack their Irish workers,' said Harry Brown, the mate of his in the yard.

Would they have arrived at the little Shaw, Hirst and Hardy quarry where Bob was working up at Southowram? If they had, what would Bob have done? George was certain Bob would never be found among the violent men — he had grown up in the last year or two. But he was perturbed enough to walk home at dinner-time to see if he had sent a message. Beattie came running out when she saw him from the window.

'Daddy, Daddy! Uncle Bob is here and he's got a bandage!' she shouted.

He scooped her up in his arms and went into the kitchen. Bob was sitting near the fire with Emma bathing his forehead where there was a nasty gash. The boys stood around gaping, Harbie holding a grubby bandage. Ada stood on a chair shouting incoherently. Only baby Flo was quiet.

'He wouldn't march with 'em so they turned on him with a stone,' explained Emma. Then to her brother, 'Are you sure it wasn't because you're not a tyke?'

Bob said nothing at first, just lay back in his chair.

'I heard they were on the rampage. I walked up just to see you were all right,' said George. 'Trying to make the bosses lose their Irish, were they?'

Bob roused himself and replied to his brother-in-law. 'Aye George, you heard aright. Mr Hardy made a flat refusal to sack anyone, but they say the boss of another quarry'll turn away the Irish lads.'

'How do you feel?' asked Emma anxiously.

'Nay, nay, sis, I'm all right — 'tis only a bump. I got away didn't I?' replied Bob. 'I wasn't the only one. Dick Johnson ran along back with me. The men that were doing it were drunk, like as not.'

'Have you a headache?' pursued Emma. He was after all her little brother.

'It's nowt,' said her brother, who now sounded almost as Yorkshire as the next man.

Emma went on, 'I'll get you both some dinner then.'

'I brought my fourses with me,' said her husband, taking his bag from his shoulder and unpacking his bread and cheese. 'I knew you wouldn't have had time to shop. Bob had better stay here for the time being. Where are the big girls?'

'They went off to work. There's nothing

going on down there, but no school for the rest of them till all this settles down,' said Emma.

'Mam, I want to go and see if they're fighting in our school,' said Herbert excitedly.

'You'll do nothing of the sort,' said George firmly. 'Keep out of trouble. It's nothing to do with us.'

'But they might have 'brayed' Mr Murray!' said Ernest. He sounded quite hopeful.

'What sort of language is that?' said his father.

The children were all eventually gathered up to sit at the scrubbed deal table with bread and scrape or boiled potato.

'It's the Irish church I'm worried about,' said George quietly to Bob, 'I just hope the bobbies have enough reinforcements if the mob takes it into its head to go there.' Before he left in a hurry to return to work George told them all to stay in after tea. Nobody must go out.

'And tell the girls too,' he added. Not that they had much energy for walking round the town after work, except on a Sunday. Now they were full time they were usually weary from standing round all day at the silk-winding machines.

George's strictures did not of course apply to Bob but he too was reluctant to tempt fate.

His mate called in, knowing where to find him, and then they both went on to Percy's.

It was a dull evening, neither warm nor cold, and the girls were standing at the door after their tea, their hands busy with the knitting which they always took up after work. Suddenly Polly, whose hearing was much better than her sister's, heard a noise like the sea on the sand, a sort of roaring in the distance.

'Listen!' she said to her sister.

'I can't hear anything.'

Their stepmother came to the door. 'Yes, I can hear it — it's the crowd. Where's it coming from?' Emma had Flo in her arms and Ada at her skirts.

Beattie said, 'It'll be coming from our school, Mam!'

They craned their necks to see down the road in the direction of the town. The lane where the Catholic church was to be found was next to the school. They saw in the distance a detachment of bobbies marching along, and held their breath, but the policemen turned down the road. People now began to run out of their houses, first one or two, then in groups running along in the direction of the noise which was growing steadily bigger, more now of a growl than a roar.

'Dad'll get into it if he's not careful,' said Ann who was always pessimistic.

'He told us to stay in, so that's what we'll do. He'll come back by the bottom road,' said her stepmother.

They seemed incapable of movement and stood stock still at the door. The other children crowded round.

Beattie began to cry. 'What are they going to do? Will they hurt Sister Bernadette?'

She was fully aware of what was going on, being a careful listener to grown-up talk and extremely fond of the little nun who was her teacher.

'They'll go round the back,' said Harbie. 'Look Mam! Some of the men have stones.'

It was true; some of the young men who were now running down their road in the direction of the town and the church were carrying stones.

'They're senseless,' said Emma. 'We'll go in. I don't want to see any more, and neither should you!'

'Oh Mam! Let's stay and watch!'

'I'll tell you all a story,' she said and shepherded her reluctant flock indoors and shut the outer door.

It was the night Emma Eliza told her children the tale of the Babes in the Wood, the story her own mother had once told her.

But she softened it and made the sleeping children soon found by their mothers and taken home to bed. Then she took Beattie upstairs, and Ada, and Baby Flo, who was asleep, the only one not to be affected.

George's way home was by the Police Station and as he came up to it about half past nine he saw a great crowd of men coming from the opposite direction, the direction of the church, and then wheeling round towards the police building. Soon stones were being thrown by what seemed to be three or four hundred men. But then behind them surged an enormous crowd: what seemed like thousands of men and women and children. It looked as if the whole town was following on.

Police windows began to shatter; doors were being kicked in and he could see policemen at the windows of a higher storey. They can't get out, he thought, but I'm not staying here. He turned and went down a snicket and into a lane that lay parallel to their street off Elland Road.

What could anyone do? They would just have to wait till people got fed up and went home.

Things however were not to be settled so quickly.

15

Wednesday morning dawned with a little breeze. Down in the woods the bluebells wove a vast azure carpet away from the smoke and grime. George went off to work early to find out what had happened the night before and to see how the land lay for the children. Until he was sure, they would stay at home. Poor Emma had her hands full, he knew.

Rumours were rife in the corn-mill yard that apparently after about ten o'clock the previous night, the police had regained control of the situation and sent most of the mob home. The lads would be working again this morning too, most of them, unless their hangover was too great. Work was what they wanted and needed to keep body and soul together. Not for the first time it occurred to George, whilst his friends at work talked over the events, that so long as the men brought in enough money for their families to eat, it was the women who 'kept body and soul together'. No doubt, once the working day was over, the worst elements of the mob would be besieging the public houses again and trying once more to get to the church and the lodging-house, to find men they could wreak their anger on.

He left for home about seven. He had been too busy that day to check up on Emma and the children. He noticed that a crowd was gathering in the direction of the main Woolsford Road and that a posse of police, armed with staves and cutlasses, was guarding the alley that led to the lodging-house and thereby to the church. He heard catcalls, and he was told later of a few incidents of stone-throwing. The mob was trying to get the police on the raw and provoke them into retaliation.

What happened then, according to Bob's friend, who had not been able to resist watching from his mother's shop, was that the police, riled beyond words, had suddenly charged, thinking the mob was about to do the same and there was a right old shindy with several men set upon and thrown to the ground, where some heads were knocked by police staves. One man had blood pouring from his head. This show of strength from the guardians of law and order had apparently frightened many of the lads, for now most of the mob melted away like snow in summer.

As they ate their bread and scrape and drank their tea the following morning Harriet Bracegirdle, Emma's Yorkshire friend, called.

George was about to leave for work.

'Eh, there's that much damage,' said Harriet. 'Shops looted an' all. Nobody'll be at work today. They say t'crowd's going to turn on t'police again.'

'Have they forgot the Irish then?' asked Emma.

'Good if they have,' said Harriet. 'Police can look after themselves.'

On his way to work George heard many shouts and cries around the streets, men and youths vowing vengeance on the police. But the police kept a low profile during the day and some folk opined the worst was over.

No, there was even worse to come.

Some worthy citizens — trades people and professional men — all signed a petition suggesting that honest citizens should aid the police. So long as the bobbies kept off the streets at night, so would they.

'There's bobbies from Woolsford and Huddersfield and Dewsbury, they say,' said George's friend over their noonday bread and cheese. 'They're roosting in't town hall!'

'It'll be worse this evening,' added another.

It was. As soon as the mills 'loosed' at six, an even larger crowd assembled in the Woolsford Road outside where they thought the police were waiting. The corn-mill owner, one of the town worthies, appealed to them to disperse and go home, but the younger men were in no mood for that. They had been in the woods, not picking bluebells but cutting thick branches down from trees for sticks to beat with. Others had heavy clubs.

'Come out then you buggers!' shouted one hothead to the police in the town hall. He was joined by a myriad others, all intent upon avenging the evening before when they had been forced to slink home with their tails between their legs. Nobody mentioned the Irish, who were sensibly staying indoors. A procession of such youths caught up with George as he walked home in the opposite direction, men brandishing clubs as if *they* were the rightful keepers of the law. George was home before they turned and found some 'foreign' bobbies from Barnsley, whom they then attacked.

Later that evening a neighbour called round with the news that three of these bobbies had been severely injured.

'They'll send for more on 'em,' said Neighbour Hopkins. 'They'll drive 'em down from Spen and come over by Clifton — mob'll know that, and there'll be more stones thrown.'

George was glad he had not been called upon to drive a cart over the moor to fetch the police reinforcements. What Hopkins had said was true, as they heard later from Bob who came upon them all together sitting in the half dark of their living-room kitchen, as every law-abiding family probably was. For an hour the town hall had been bombarded with stones and all its windows broken. But the police then decided to threaten to read the Riot Act and assert their authority.

Bob's friend had heard the same rumour and was out watching with another peaceful delver when suddenly the town hall doors were opened and a double line of police came running out, scores of them charging and re-charging the mob with their staves. Later, folk were to say that this was the turning point of the riots. After a few arrests and their threat to read the Riot Act, a few of the most aggressive rioters still demurred. But this time they did not have their way and most of the rest followed the precept that discretion is the better part of valour.

The next morning one man was charged for stone-throwing as a scapegoat for all the others who had done the same. He was remanded in custody. There was a half-hearted attempt to throw a few more stones the next evening but after four days of rioting mob hysteria had been spent and the majority of peaceful citizens had their way and persuaded the recalcitrant to return to normal ways of carrying on.

But the Irish, who had kept their heads well down, retaliated on the following Monday when four of them caught one of the well-known rioters and belted him, disappearing quickly once their job was done.

George thought the boys had better go to school at the beginning of the following week and took them there himself. Harbie and Arnust might very well prefer to wander round the town and get into trouble, so they'd be better off at school. Beattie wanted to go back, so he took her with them.

'What's it all been about then?' asked Emma on the Monday night when the children had returned from school and things seemed to have gone back to normal.

'Well it was that murder in Ireland, I suppose, that sparked it off,' said George, giving himself the rare pleasure of a pipe. 'But it's the unemployed who have most cause to riot and join the mob. Not that that will do them any good but they have a grievance.'

'Hannah says her husband says things'll get worse,' said Emma. 'The town'll never be as good again for jobs as it was when we arrived.'

'One day they will get the vote,' said George, who still read the papers when he had time. 'Being miserable makes men pick fights, but they've no excuse if they can vote.'

The same sentiments were being voiced in the inns by the 'respectable' working class who understood why authority in the shape of the police was hated.

'But what about the Irish?' Emma asked him again.

'They'll work for less, especially the delvers.'

'Bob says he doesn't hold with violence,' remonstrated Bob's sister.

'But they have a point. All the men should be paid the same. Getting rid of off-comers isn't an answer in the end,' opined George. 'There isn't an easy answer, bor.'

'They were frightening though, weren't they. Were you frightened, George?'

'A bit,' he confessed. 'But more on the children's account.'

The rioters all received sentences, one of the delvers among them. They were charged with damaging the church, and two months later two of them were given sentences of hard labour.

'Ann knows one of the rioters,' said Polly. 'He worked at the mill with her once, but he was acquitted.'

Yet it was not quite over. At the end of May the landlord of the Sun Dial inn and his family were threatened by letter. A crude drawing of a pistol and a coffin accompanied the missive. It was signed 'A Land Leaguer', ostensibly from one of the men who agitated not only for land reform in Ireland but for Home Rule. Prime Minister Gladstone was well known for his advocacy of this, which was opposed by many other Englishmen.

The landlord however was never attacked, though there were rumours rife at Whitsuntide that some Irish from Leeds would arrive to wreak vengeance. But Beattie, dressed in her best, and Herbert and Ernest in their cleanest collars, and Ada, and Flo in the pram wheeled by Emma, all joined the usual Whit procession from the churches and chapels of the town and marched along the streets.

Walking along in the sunshine the children's thoughts were now far away from the events of the previous weeks. The windows had been repaired and the Liberal candidate returned to Parliament with a thumping majority. The church too was under repair and the Sun Dial inn had returned to normal. Afterwards, Emma was to wonder if it had all been a dream. She had seen little of the action herself, being too occupied looking after her children, but her children would always remember that exciting week. Especially little Beattie who continued to attend her Catholic school till she was twelve and ready herself to join the silk-minders or winders or dressers or throwers.

By this time Emma Eliza had many women friends. She had always made friends easily, and now not only did she know women who had come, like herself, from Norfolk but others who were Yorkshire born. Most of them were very neat and clean, in spite of the dirt all around them, and they repaid a deeper acquaintance, for they could tell you about the town and give you hints about Yorkshire ways. The special friend of Emma's, Harriet Bracegirdle, was a powerfully built woman with a long nose but a heart of gold. Norfolkers like Hannah Sayer and Isabella King, and young Martha Flegg — who was good with babies and often helped neighbours out — had found Harriet intimidating at first, but Emma had not. Martha, who had cheered up, was living with her sister and brother-in-law and housekeeping for them. Her sister Mary preferred to work in a mill, and Martha was terrified of machinery. Emma often thought it should have been Martha whom Solomon Flegg had married.

And what was happening to Myra whilst all this excitement was taking place in Calderbrigg? In June they had a postcard from her with a halfpenny stamp which Ernest wanted for his collection. He collected many things — pebbles, teeth, pressed flowers, bits of string and old cotton bobbins, and had a 'shop' he carried with him to school, a box his father had given him from the mill. His attempts to sell such goods did not meet with any success as nobody had any money so instead boys swapped goods between themselves.

'Our Arnust will be a shopkeeper,' his mother often fondly said.

Myra's card informed them all that she was singing and dancing on the pier. 'If only you could all come and see me!' She was working for Adeler's Pierrots now but hoped to find better paid work the following summer on Llandudno Pierhead, for Arthur Sugden's Entertainers.

'You have to keep your ears cocked and your eyes skinned to get on you, know,' she added.

Her sister did not doubt that Myra would do both. In December she was going to do the winter season in Yorkshire in pantomime — *Cinderella* — at the Alhambra Theatre, Woolsford. Perhaps they could go and see her then. Emma somehow doubted it. The move and the growing family had almost exhausted their means, even with her putting the rent, the coal money, and the food money in tins every Friday on the shelf above the range.

She might take in some sewing, she thought. That was something she could do well. The trouble was that nobody she knew could afford to have their dresses sewn or their hats trimmed for cash. She had hopes of finding some rich woman who might.

But Emma had suspected two months before the Fenian riots, when little Flo was still less than a year old, that she might have fallen for another baby. At first she could not believe it, and could not even remember how it had happened.

George was not a demanding husband but she seemed to make babies as easily as a cat has a thrice yearly litter. It had made her feel ashamed, so after Flo was born she had taken her courage in both hands and consulted Hannah Sayer. A few words the woman had let drop once or twice about avoiding too many children had alerted her, and after Flo's birth she had determined to find out more, without saying anything to George. The result had been an attempt to use a sponge soaked in vinegar. But by August of the following year she knew that it had obviously not worked. She was thirty-one and everyone knew that women went on having babies until their late thirties, some of them till their forties, usually producing a baby every eighteen months or so. She loved her babies and all her children but the family was poor, and like to remain so with so many mouths to feed.

The child was a boy, David, born at the end of November, a month too early. None of her other babies had been early and she was terrified lest with the vinegar and the sponge she had somehow poisoned him. He was small and puny and although at first he sucked for a few moments he did not do so for long. She could see he was not putting on weight and the worry made her fear her milk would fail.

'What's the matter, Mam?' Beattie asked her one morning as she was going off to school. She had found her mother crying in the kitchen. The baby had wailed all night and George had departed early for work. He was especially pressed at this time because, surprisingly in the trade recession, the corn-mill had taken on a new contract. It was doubly important that unloading from the canal barges was done quickly or they would lose the work to a mill in the next town, which also shared the river and the canal. The number of deliveries had increased and George, now in charge of all the horses in the yard, and in feeding those who pulled the barges, must start work earlier. He had been given no rise in his wages.

The boys had already left. Ada, who was three, was for once asleep in the bed she shared with her two sisters. Flo, at eighteen months old, was shuffling along the floor on her bottom, not yet quite able to walk. It was usually Beattie's job to clean and dress the two of them before she could escape to her beloved Sister Bernadette at the Martin Street school. She could now read from a real book, read in fact better than Ernest who was two years her senior.

Emma did not want to worry her favourite child so said only, 'Get you off to school — I haven't had any sleep.' Beattie squeezed her hand and skipped away.

The baby woke up now and began to wail again. She tried putting him to the breast but he pulled away. She would try 'pobbies', a mixture of the milk from the can filled daily by the man who came early every morning, his cart piled with churns, and a little cornflour. She made it, put it on her finger and hoped he would suck. The others had liked this. True, they had been a little older, but this baby was different and she was at her wits' end trying to feed him.

This time he did not at first bring it up so she held him on her lap and dozed. His repeated scream jerked her from her semi-sleep. She gave him his comforter which he also spat out and put him in the wooden cradle George had bought from the second-hand shop. Flo now had to be rescued from trying to eat a piece of coal. Usually she was a placid child and did not complain overmuch but this time she was furious her plaything had been taken from her and shouted. Ada arrived downstairs, naked. Wearily, Emma dressed her in her cotton shift that had been warming on the creel above the range and cleaned up Flo who was still not trained, She had to get to the market but how could she take David? There was nothing for it, she would have to put both Ada and Flo in the cart on wheels where Ada would torment her sister, and carry the baby in her shawl, pushing the cart with one hand.

Just then there was a knock at the door. Isabella.

'Oh, thank God!' exclaimed Emma, 'I don't know what to do with this baby and I have to fetch potatoes. George hadn't time to dig any up last night.'

'I came to see if I could get you anything,' said Isabella and sat down in the other chair near the range. She peered at David. She herself had given birth to only one child who was now nine. For no reason she could fathom she had stopped falling pregnant. 'Have you consulted Hannah?' she asked.

'I'll go in a few days if he doesn't pick up. There's something wrong but I don't know what it is.'

She thought, it's my fault, I've poisoned him with vinegar. She gave an involuntary catch of breath.

'Why not go whilst I'm here?'

Isabella could see that Emma, usually competent, was distressed and distracted.

'Mam! Mam!' cried Ada, 'I want my shoes!' Ada liked standing on the wooden chair shouting and waving her hands, so to avoid this Emma found her pair of canvas shoes and told her to put them on.

'No, you do it,' said the imperious Ada. Emma complied. Anything was better than one of Ada's famous temper tantrums. Flo meanwhile was beaming at Isabella who took her on her knee.

'Nurse the babby and I'll take Ada and Flo with me to market,' she suggested.

'Oh, would you, Isa? I'm at the end of my tether.' They finally got off with promises of a 'locust' to suck.

The day passed slowly. David, named after a little brother of George who had died at the age of one, not, Emma felt, a good augury, but George had wanted the name, was not restless but strangely inert. He consented to take a little milk at six o'clock and then at midnight but lay in his crib, his eyes open.

That night, however, Emma had unbroken sleep till past five. When she woke her limbs were heavy. George must not yet have gone out for she heard him raking the ashes in the grate and shortly afterwards he came upstairs with a mug of tea.

'I've put the porridge pan back on — the fire had gone out,' he said.

When she leaned over as usual to David in his little drawer on a chair next to their bed she saw that he was jerking his limbs. She had been terrified he might have died in the night. He had vomited up the pitifully small amount of milk he had taken at midnight. Was he having a fit? Surely not. It was teething infants who had those. Usually David was so still.

She took him up quickly and he felt all hot. He began to wail then, not with a great loud yell as the other children had used to do but like a mewing kitten.

'Oh Davey, what is it? What is it?' she cried. George came up to her straight away. He was dressed for work. 'He's acting strange,' she said. 'But he didn't wake me during the night.'

She tried to put him to the breast but he jerked away and then his legs and arms began to thrash about again. When he had calmed down a bit she unwrapped his clothes and his vest to see if he had a rash. George looked at the child.

'You could consult Hannah Sayer. I s'll have to go off.'

The baby would still not feed so she ran a cool cloth over his forehead and imagined he felt less hot. She made the children their porridge that had been cooking till the fire went out, and Ernest and Herbert got themselves off to school, followed by Beattie who had peered anxiously over her little brother.

Emma made up her mind.

She set out to trudge to Hannah Sayer's, Ada walking or rather pulled along, and Flo in the cart. David she wrapped in her shawl. Wasn't a temperature what they told you to look out for with smallpox? Her blood ran cold. But as far as she knew there was none in the town. They would surely have heard if there had been. And David had not been out yet.

She arrived at Hannah's door and knocked. Mrs Sayer opened it straight away. Emma's distraught face made her exclaim:

'Why, Emma, whatever is the matter?'

'He won't feed and he was that hot when he woke up — and still is. Oh, Hannah, what's to do?'

'Come in and let's have a look.'

Emma was hoping that the wisewoman would say it was nothing but when she had seen and felt the child who was now a curious mauve colour she shook her head.

'He might just have something wrong he was born with. You've never had anything like this before.'

Emma's heart sank. Born wrong?

She could see that Hannah didn't want to alarm her but when Mrs Sayer said, 'I think you should go to Dr Wardrop,' she replied falteringly, 'You think it's serious then?'

'I don't know, but better be sure, my dear. It *could* be something wrong with his stomach that he can't eat.'

'I know. He's so thin!'

'He hasn't been anywhere near measles? I hear it's in town?'

'No, and none of the others have been ill except for colds.' The baby now began that curious jerky movement again. 'It makes him too weak to cry!' said Emma.

'Well it could just be convulsions. I've known several babies with those.'

Emma felt that Hannah was just as much in the dark as she was herself. She must have known many babies, many of whom might have convulsions if they were teething, but this baby was tiny, only four weeks old and scarcely any bigger than when he was born, perhaps even smaller. His birth had taken longer than the others' as well, and she had wondered if his head was not rather too large for his body. But all babies' heads were large. Hannah had delivered her as usual and she had received the impression at the birth that there was something not quite right but that the older woman had been reluctant to suggest it.

She couldn't go to the doctor. It would cost the earth.

David was ill for six days and the fits got worse. He would take only a teaspoonful of water and was often sick. She was terrified. All the Norfolk neighbours from Caston who were living across the street and in nearby streets often helped each other when their children were poorly. If the children had a cough they gave them what their mothers used to give them — tar and water. But this was not such a case. The baby did not cough and all the women she consulted were either puzzled or looked at her in a slightly underhand way as though they knew there was something wrong but would not say what.

'Children are a right mardling lot,' said one, but that was no help.

People always feared smallpox if convulsions came but Emma thought maybe he had just been too hot under the swaddling.

Now even George was urging her to take David to the doctor. Finally, a week later she did. He had been without convulsions for a day till the morning she took him, when he kept turning his head from right to left as if he had a headache. None of her herbs had been of any use. There was something wrong with either his brain or his heart or his stomach, she thought.

Dr Wardrop shook his head as if he knew something he was not going to tell her. Isabella King had said that the doctor was not popular because he often blamed parents in Calderbrigg, said they were dirty, their houses damp and overcrowded, their children suffering from weak chests. As though that were their fault.

But all he said was, 'He's a sickly baby,' and did not blame her. There was nothing he could suggest but gripewater and to let him sleep. If he only would! but the painful little mew went on and on.

On the seventh day the baby stopped crying and on the eighth day in the early morning he died.

She could not believe he was gone.

Where had he gone? The baby she had

been with daily, hourly, for five weeks now was *gone*. The enormity of it surprised her. So often she had heard of neighbours' children at home who had died and whose mothers were left alone to grieve, but who had finally to take up their lives. However had they borne it? But why, why, had David died? Was it really what she had done? Her grief was wild and yet she felt angry too and also somehow ashamed of showing her feelings to her husband.

He grieved, of course he did; it was his son, his little lad, who had gone. Did he blame her? She did not think he did but she wondered in the middle of her sleepless nights whether, apart from the vinegar, the fact that before David's birth she had had a nightmare involving Baz, and because David's hair had been tinged with red like the hair she remembered on the head of Baz, she had not been allowed to keep him. But Ada had red hair too!

She kept all her thoughts to herself. She had five other healthy children to look after. She had tried to love this puny baby but her love and worry had been no good. He was buried in the new town cemetery which was a year younger than Herbert.

They could not afford a headstone so a little grassy plot was bought and a simple stone laid flat over where his tiny coffin had been put.

Only when, a few weeks later, Mrs Sayer said, 'I thought when he was born that his head was too large; he may not have been quite normal, Emmie, it may have been for the best,' did Emma realize that they had all felt the same. Only she, the mother, had not really believed that. If the child had been abnormal, well then she supposed it was for the best, but it did not stop her sorrow. They would have another baby; there seemed no way of stopping them arriving though the thought of another made her feel sick. She would not dare to try the sponge again, and she did not want to hurt George's feelings. Her conviction remained that the vinegar might have made the baby weak and caused his death.

For a time it was not necessary to do anything, for George seemed as disheartened as she was and also weary from the extra work. But in the spring of 1883 his hours of labour were reduced when the recession took hold again.

16

One May morning in 1883 Emma went as usual to the market. For once she did not have the younger children trailing after her for Ada and Flo were being looked after by Polly who was now sixteen. Polly and Ann had been laid off since the previous week as there was further unrest in the silk industry. Both girls were restless and wanted better-paid work more suited to their capacities. Ann was even threatening to go back to Norfolk but knew there was nothing she could do until she was twenty-one, which would not be till 1886.

Their stepmother found Polly still very helpful, a real staff to comfort her in bad times. Polly herself was still a great favourite with Beattie. They were still alike in looks, both taking after their father, though Beattie was smaller built. They had similar tastes for they were both to be found with their heads in a book or a newspaper whenever one was available.

Emma was still feeling both guilty and anxious after baby David's death. She could confide in nobody, felt sure Hannah Sayer would not wish to allude to the advice she had given her about avoiding too many children. Myra, if consulted, would uphold her efforts, and never understand her feelings of guilt, her semi-conviction that David's death had been all her fault even if the minister at his short funeral had gone out of his way to say how well her children were looked after. Myra had often said she regarded motherhood with horror:

'Work, work, work, and for what?' she said. Two or three children might be admitted, but a large family, no, certainly not! She had also pointed out that their mother Eliza had given birth to only four children. But Mam had not had her first child till she was nearly thirty-three, thought Emma, trying to make sense of her mixed feelings.

They said God wanted women to be fruitful, and all babies were blessings. But God was not a woman and did not know what it was to be poor, did he? She shocked herself with such thoughts. The trouble was that in the bottom of her heart Emma agreed with Myra, but since Myra had never had a baby she could not understand a mother's feelings. It would have been better if David had not been born, she suddenly thought. If her attempts with the vinegar had worked, she would have been spared the heartbreak!

Oh how she had been punished! If only she could talk to her husband about it all but they had never discussed such things. George's first wife Elizabeth Ann, had only had Ann and Polly, but she had been married at an older age.

There had however been some talk, she now recalled, of her losing a baby. It was whilst she had been working at the hall and did not know George well and had never met Elizabeth Ann. Perhaps it had been a boy and George had wanted a son. Well, he had two now and would have had three if David had lived.

There seemed no escape for a woman who married young. And she *had* been young. Only twenty-one and glad to be married, looking forward to her own little family. She did not mind hard work, would not have wanted Myra's life, but she would not have minded either being like Mrs Upcraft at the hall with three children and plenty of money and leisure. Mrs Upcraft, though, had not been an especially happy woman.

She did love her live children, oh, she did! but why once David was born had she been repaid for her efforts to keep him alive with this awful misery? The minister at Bethel said God had taken him for a little lamb and that had made her cry, but she would rather have had him back! Perhaps David had never been meant to live. Just because she already had five children did not mean she did not grieve for the last dead one.

In a turmoil of mixed and contradictory emotions she went into the open market for some potted meat. It was sold at a little stall in the middle of the market-place and there was usually a line of women waiting to be served. She stood there with them, her mind far away, and then suddenly when it was almost her turn she saw out of the corner of her eye in a patch of sunlight some man turn towards the stall and for a moment look at her.

It was Baz! She was sure it was Baz!

She stood transfixed, and then the sunlight went away and the man was gone, and the stallholder was saying impatiently, 'Aye then, what will you have, Missis?'

Was he talking to her?

Oh, she must go and find Baz! But she had better buy the meat first. She kept looking up as she fumbled in her purse, could scarcely take out the pennies, so much was her hand trembling. The man was holding out her usual amount. He must have known how much she wanted for she was sure she had not asked him.

She snatched it, thrust the pennies into his

hand and turned to go.

Which way? By the end of the stall, near the post that held the trestles up? She pushed through the crowd of purchasers, a few women looking crossly at her, and stumbled in the direction the man had gone. She ran round the back of the stalls.

Nobody.

She ran towards the exit by the stall with the naphtha flares which were for night-time shoppers, and looked up and down the aisles, and then walked round the market in the opposite direction clutching her canvas sack for shopping. Had she put her purse away? She was so out of breath that she had to stop. Her purse was at the bottom of her bag, so that was all right. Oh, where was he? She was sure he had been there, had seen her. But after another twenty minutes she had to stop. It had been a trick of her imagination.

She paused at the wall by the opening to Commercial Street and tried to think. Was it a vision? Had he been sent to cheer her? To reassure her she was not a bad woman? The tears came to her eyes and she wanted to kneel down and pray.

Slowly, as she walked home, the conviction began to grow in her that God had sent Baz to look after her, to take away her guilt.

She had never had such feelings before and was frightened.

Was she losing her mind?

⋆ ⋆ ⋆

Emma had walked home in a daze but feeling curiously lighter. As time went on, whether it had been a real man who looked like her old Friend, or a hallucination did not seem to matter. It had given her the confidence to carry on. And as she made the dinner for the family that morning she had too the sensation that Mam was telling her she had done her best, and that she was not wrong or wicked, and that God was on her side.

Polly noticed that her stepmother had begun to smile again. She had not smiled since David's death. Her appetite had perked up too. For the past month or two Polly had wondered if Emma lived on air, so little did she eat. Now she drank her broth and did not hold back from serving herself because her children might still be hungry. She liked to give her husband meat for tea every night and became even more expert at stews and 'mate dumplin's'. She and the children had flour-and-water dumplings with a slice or two of onion and some turnip. Norfolkers had rarely used suet as they had never had enough money for it. But they were tasty if she added her herbs to the mixture.

George too noticed that she looked a little less pale and would occasionally put his arm round her. After David's death he had feared for a time that she was going the way of Elizabeth Ann.

From that day Emma realized — and gave thanks — that her impossible early dreams had not disappeared but could sustain her in this busy, often wretched, often miserably hard-worked life. She determined not to feel guilty, and not to try and forget Baz but to incorporate him into her thoughts. George would lose nothing; she was still a dutiful wife and helpmeet to him.

If Myra came at Christmas she must pluck up her courage to ask her if she ever had news of Jabez Smith. Was he still in Norfolk? Had he ever gone to see her sister in North Wales? Was he yet wed? She could not ask her these things in writing; she would have to wait.

In the meantime Bob Saunders got himself wed. Since the riots, the once obstreperous lad had become even calmer, more serious, had left the work at the quarry and tramped for miles around to work on farms in the upper Calder valley, returning to Calderbrigg to look for a job in a weaving-shed. After a few months this became an overlooker's job, but Bob had not yet finished his odyssey. He met a young woman, Jenny Crossley, fell in love with her, contemplated moving to Woolsford to a bigger mill, but settled for marriage and remaining in Calderbrigg.

His wife adored him. She was the daughter of a successful artisan who was well on the way to founding a building firm of his own. Charlie Crossley was to make his name in the town for the building of solid terraces of stone houses.

Although it took some time, he was to become relatively well off, for there was an increasingly steady clientele for such houses. Bob's knowledge of stone from his time as a delver was to stand him in good stead now. He left the mill, and went in with his father-in-law. Eventually he would be joined by his brother Percy who had a growing family.

'I've a feeling our Bob will turn up trumps,' wrote Emma to her sister.

Myra was to come for the next winter pantomime season in Woolsford. She scribbled a letter once a month from Wales, still full of enthusiasm.

'I shall get you all tickets for *Cinderella*,' she wrote, knowing very well they could not possibly afford to buy tickets for the whole family themselves.

Before Christmas she would arrive in Woolsford, and promised to come over to Calderbrigg on her first free day.

She arrived in a cab on a clear bright December afternoon, all the family in the road waiting to greet her. Just fancy, their own aunt coming in a cab from the station!

Emma kissed her and they all crowded her into the living-room.

'My, it's a nice house, Emma!' said Myra who had never seen the new house. Emma knew she was being kind, for she must know grander places, surely. Her voice sounded different too, but she looked tired. At twenty-three she was a striking-looking woman, her hair as red as ever. Emma felt sure it would always be red if she lived to be a hundred.

'You ought to see some of the 'diggings' *I've* been given!' exclaimed Myra, flopping into the best chair, carefully taking her hat off before kissing the children one by one. The children stared, looked overcome.

Herbert said, 'Can we go out to play, Mam?' Ernest accompanied him outside, leaving the three girls.

Beattie looked at her solemnly, and Flo squirmed and giggled. Only Ada, at just four years old, appeared mistress of the situation, declaring, 'I'm going to be an actress like you,

Auntie Myra. Will you be Cinderella?'

Their mother had told the girls the story and Beattie and Ada had told it back to each other. Flo now repeated the word Cinderella in a monotone.

'How the boys and Beattie have grown! — and I've never seen Ada and Flo before — just imagine — such a large family!' said their aunt.

She was given a cup of tea and then she handed over the tickets for Christmas week.

'One for George as well,' she said.

'He's at work, but he'll be back at five,' explained Emma. George had thought it tactful to let his wife greet her sister alone with the children but had expressed an interest in going to the theatre. He read aloud well himself but without any theatricality, had attended readings from Dickens in the Oddfellows Hall but had never once been to a theatre. It was said that the town hall would one day open for occasional theatrical performances and music, but he feared he would never have the money to take Emma there. Before, there had only been the plays in temporary marquees. There had been lectures and debates in the town hall for some time but they were attended on the whole by the better-off.

'I'm Dandini,' said Myra to Ada now. 'It's a

good part — I'm on more than the Prince!'

Emma was dying to ask her the questions about Baz she had formulated earlier in the year but Myra was so surrounded by children, so taken up explaining the part of Dandini in the pantomime, that the conversation had to wait until just before she left. By that time Ann and Polly had come home and she felt constrained by their presence. Myra had smiled at them both and asked them about their work and their health and whether they had any sweethearts yet. Polly blushed but Ann looked mysterious. At twenty and eighteen they still looked very different. Ann was taller and slimmer than her sister but Polly was taller than her stepmother now and had a sweet serious face and a full under-lip. Emma wanted to ask whether Myra had a sweetheart, but possibly she had many men after her. It did not seem the time to introduce the name of Baz after this banter about men, but before Myra left she said, George being out in the yard with his sons, and trying to sound casual,

'Do you ever hear from Mr Smith? Has he come to see you on the stage?'

Myra looked surprised but answered, 'I did hear once or twice but I haven't seen him — he's working hard, I expect.'

'Still in Norfolk?'

'I suppose so, though I believe he does travel a bit, repairing windmills over in Suffolk.'

Emma could not bring herself to go into details to Myra about her experience in the market so confined herself to saying:

'A few months ago I thought I saw him in Calderbrigg but it could not have been him. It was in the market, not long after the baby — after David — died.'

Myra looked at her curiously but said only, 'I was so sorry, dear, about that. But you have a nice little family.'

She meant, don't have any more, thought Emma. She wondered for a moment if Myra had ever 'expected', but then censured herself for disloyalty. Myra was not a 'bad' girl, indeed seemed very much in charge of herself.

'Isn't Ada priceless?' Myra went on. 'Such lovely hair. She'll adore *Cinderella*!'

Shortly after this they said goodbye, and the next time Emma saw her sister she was unrecognizable, dressed in blue and silver with spangles and a plumed hat.

That vision of Baz must have been a trick of the light.

* * *

The children were so excited Emma doubted she would ever quieten them down enough to get them all to Woolsford. Flo was deemed too young and was left to Isabella King who doted on her and had offered to take her for the day. They were to take the train after dinner, from the furthest-away station in the town, which had been opened only a year or two earlier; the train went to Woolsford by a direct route. That meant a walk to the station of over a mile in biting wind, unless George could borrow one of the horses he looked after and hitch it to a cart, getting a mate to take it back and meet them on their return. This he promised to do, and Emma was relieved. She wanted them all to arrive at the theatre looking neat and tidy so as not to shame Myra.

Fortunately it was not raining, or the children's best clothes would have been ruined as they sat together in the cart. Emma prided herself on her children's clothes; she made them all herself unless offered hand-me-downs from some of her women friends who had children a little older than hers. Her girls' dresses had tartan sashes and collars of tatting and their boots were shone and shone. Beattie wore a head band with her hair pulled back from the face, and Alice's red hair had been cut short by Emma herself.

Herbert and Ernest affected indifference to clothes and pantomimes. Theatres were girls' stuff, they said, though how they had reached this conclusion nobody knew.

'But Dad is going!' their mother explained and called upon George to back her up, though she knew he went as much from curiosity about his wife's sister as any interest in the drama of *Cinderella* which was indeed 'women's stuff'.

They did arrive in the right place at the right time just before the curtain went up. The theatre was crowded but Myra had got them all seats in the front row. Emma looked round and hoped they did not stand out as poor relations. The people in the audience all seemed to her well dressed and rich. Herbert was more intrigued by the gas-lighting than by the music that had begun from the pit, but Ernest had to admit he liked the violin-playing. He was a musical boy like his Uncle Percy. Herbert shut his eyes to begin with but opened them when they all heard the swish of the red velvet curtain that went up on a scene in a kitchen with the young Cinderella in rags, sweeping the grate, being shouted at by her father and her two ugly sisters who were, indeed, men, and who were discussing the invitation to the ball at the Prince's palace.

'Mam, where's Cinders?' whispered Beattie, having expected to see an obviously beautiful girl on the stage.

'Where's Auntie Myra?' whispered Ada on Emma's other side.

'Shush,' said their mother, and they were silent for a time. Then Buttons arrived, looking remarkably like Herbert, and there was a conversation they could not make head or tail of. But the nasty characters went out and Buttons told Cinderella he loved her and then went back to his shoe-shining.

Alone on stage in a spotlight the girl let down her golden hair and the audience took in its corporate breath.

'There she is!' whispered Emma to Beattie. Ada was still waiting for the arrival of Dandini, being, at the age of five, a little confused about the order of events.

First of all, though, the Fairy Godmother arrived with a long wand, at the end of which was a silver star. They all sat now on the edges of their seats. It was still quite cold in the theatre so they had kept their coats on, but they forgot their cold feet. Emma intended to show off their best clothes when the lights went up.

'You may have three wishes,' said the Fairy Godmother in a piercing voice.

'I have only one,' replied the girl. 'To go to the ball where my sisters have gone, leaving me here to work my fingers to the bone.'

The fairy touched the large pumpkin in the corner of the room.

If only they could all have a fairy godmother, Emma was thinking — and she wouldn't be asking to go to a ball either. But then the stage went dark and the transformation scene arrived.

Suddenly the lights flared and there on the stage was a coach made from the large pumpkin in the corner of the kitchen and drawn by two real ponies. Great was the children's excitement, this time even the boys were stirred. George was wondering who looked after the ponies and who trained them.

Beattie said, 'Look, she's changed her dress!' and there instead of the rags was a glittering ball-gown of pink and gold. An invisible chorus then sang a song: 'Off to the ball', and the curtain went down to the ponies pulling the heroine offstage with Buttons, now as the coachman.

'Did you see? Did you see?' They were all enthralled.

Ada said, 'I shall act the Fairy Godmother with a wand.'

Where was Myra? When would she appear?

Emma was nervous for her sister but need not have been.

In the next scene Cinders had not yet arrived at the palace in her coach and the Prince was waiting with Dandini at the side of a glittering throng of dancers, among them the two tall Ugly Sisters falling over each other's large feet. The Prince in emerald green, and gold lace, and his companion Dandini in pale-blue velvet, both of them in tights and holding plumed hats, moved to the centre of the stage and began a conversation.

Myra was splendid, graceful, and with a well-modulated clear voice.

'Aunt Myra is the Prince, Mam!' whispered Ada. 'The man in blue!'

'No, the Prince is the other one,' whispered Beattie, who also thought Dandini's suit was of a nicer colour than the Prince's.

'S-sh,' went Emma.

Myra smiled right into the theatre when she moved downstage and said, 'Welcome to the ball,' as if she was welcoming the little party to the theatre. Then before Cinders arrived she sang a duet with the Prince.

'Why is the Prince a lady?' asked Herbert.

George had explained that ladies always played the Prince and Dandini and that men played the Ugly Sisters but Herbert had paid no attention.

'That's silly!' he said. Another 'Shush' and a poke in the ribs from his father.

Suddenly there was a peal of tinkling bells and the coach was seen arriving at the back of the stage, Buttons dismounting from his perch and handing out Cinderella.

'Where's the Fairy Godmother?' asked Ada.

The Prince was immediately transfixed by the beautiful vision of Cinderella and sang to her in a soprano voice. Dandini joined in as a mezzo — with a much better voice. Then the Prince and Cinderella danced together to the strains of *The Blue Danube* and Dandini danced with a another lady and the chorus danced at the back. It was an enormous stage and for the whole of the scene the audience was transported to Fairyland. They all clapped madly when the Prince expressed his love.

Before the curtain went down for the interval and the last act, the Ugly Sisters reappeared and did not recognize their sister. They possessed strong Yorkshire accents and were a good comic duo, hitting each other and fighting — much appreciated by Herbert — and asking silly questions of the audience.

'Clap if you think I am the prettiest girl at the ball,' simpered one. Silence, and a lot of laughter.

Her sister asked a similar question. 'Shout 'hurrah' if you want me to marry the Prince!'

'Boo!' went the audience. Then the Prince came to the front and said, 'This girl' — pointing to Cinderella — 'is the prettiest girl here, isn't she?'

The audience answered, 'Yes, she is!' and all the children looked wise and giggled at each other. They knew this bit.

'I am going to marry her!' he added, 'but I do not know her name.'

Some wags shouted 'Cinderella' but the clock now struck twelve and the girl pulled away from her prince, ran down the stairs at the side, losing one slipper in the process, and disappearing.

'Go and find her tomorrow,' said the Prince to Dandini, 'Bring her back here and I shall marry her.'

'What if she doesn't want to marry him?' asked Ernest.

'Of course she does,' said his mother. The curtain came down to enthusiastic clapping.

They all stretched their legs during the interval before a bag of humbugs was passed round. They were to see their aunt at the end of the afternoon in her dressing-room.

'Are you enjoying it?' George asked his sons.

'Yes, Dad,' said Ernest, 'but I like the music best.'

'It's all right,' said Herbert, 'but I don't understand all they say.'

All too soon the curtain rose on the Baron's kitchen once more with Cinders at the hearth in rags, and barefoot. She half-heartedly swept the floor and the Ugly Sisters arrived fighting and causing much merriment in the audience. A roll of drums announced the Prince's messenger and there was Aunt Myra, this time in a fur doublet and carrying a slipper on a cushion. Most of the children in the audience knew the story and listened carefully to its denouement.

One sister tried on the tiny slipper with much groaning.

'There you are you see, it's a perfect fit!' he gasped, falling over his feet, an action repeated by the other sister. Cinders had disappeared but her father was now asked:

'Have you any other daughters?'

'No!' shouted the sisters.

'Oh yes you have!' shouted the children, getting into the spirit of the thing. This was repeated three times and then Dandini sang again.

He's looking for his princess,
The girl, with the little feet,

and the Baron said, 'Well, er, there's only Cinders, but she doesn't count.'

'Fetch her,' commanded Dandini/Myra, but Cinders had already crept on stage accompanied by her faithful Buttons.

'Try on this slipper,' ordered Dandini, and sat the girl down. She advanced her pretty feet which were indeed tiny and the shoe fitted.

A great 'Ah,' went up from the audience.

'Where are your own shoes?' asked one sister. 'Look, her feet are big!'

'Oh no they're not!' shouted the children, round-eyed.

Cinderella's Fairy Godmother then appeared, this time in a stylish grey costume with her wand tucked under her arm like a whip, bearing with her the other slipper.

'My story's different,' whispered Beattie. 'But this is lovely!'

To great rejoicing the scene changed rapidly to the palace — no curtain this time — and to the arrival of Cinderella with Dandini. The Prince was sitting on a royal velvet chair looking sad but when he saw his faithful friend followed by Cinderella he got up joyfully and shouted:

'There she is! Marry me! Marry me!' he sang, and 'Yes, I will,' was then sung by Cinders in a powerful soprano.

They danced in each other's arms as the rest of the cast came on and took their bows.

'They didn't have the white mice,' whispered Herbert who had been looking forward to the transformation of rodents into ponies. But the ponies did come on again and went round the stage twice with the Prince and his bride.

Dandini waved them goodbye and sang the final song, then the curtain came down, the clapping brought it up again and the cast bowed over and over again.

'I wish she had married Buttons,' Beattie said to Myra after the performance. 'Poor Buttons. He was sad, wasn't he.'

Ada only said monotonously, 'I want a wand! Mam, I want a wand!'

They were all in Myra's dressing-room except for George who stayed in the corridor. Emma admitted later that they behaved beautifully, mostly from shyness. Even Ada was fairly silent.

It was the only pantomime Beattie ever saw as a child, the most beautiful thing she had ever seen, even more exciting than Uncle Bob's wedding at which she was a bridesmaid.

★ ★ ★

On a large plot of farmland at the bottom of the hill where Bob had once delved, and where there had once been talk of a park's being laid out, something even better than a park had come into being. It was at the end of the long pretty valley where a wide beck had wandered from time immemorial, a goodish walk from Calderbrigg. The way to this beautiful valley was where Emma had walked by the wood when she had first come to Calderbrigg. More recently, in summer, they had gone blackberrying there, and there too Emma gathered herbs for her infusions.

Walks over in this direction were favourites of Calderbrigg's courting couples. Enthusiastic explorers of all sorts, including many children, would walk or play by the canal and the river and the little island, and then cross over to walk along this more rural prospect for a mile or two. The new name for this part of the valley was Sunny Vale and what had been built there was given the name of pleasure gardens.

Beattie thought it sounded so 'romantic', a word she had heard from a girl in the top class at school. There were to be swings there one day; a boating-lake had been dug out, flooded with water from damming up the brook in the field, and then extended to another, and recently a tea-room had been established. A maze already existed, and the owner was also going to buy up Woolsford's old Palace of Illusions. Children pestered to go there, Emma's no exception, so on a bank holiday, or occasionally on the nearest Saturday afternoon to a child's birthday, so long as he had a little spare cash, George would take them there. It cost tuppence for each child and threepence for adults.

That winter the lake had frozen over, and a whole town-load of children went to slide on the ice on the boating-lake and, if they were lucky, to skate. Percy owned a pair of skates and lent them to George, who also borrowed a child's pair from his friend at work.

As she watched children slip and slide, Emma remembered how a quarter of a century earlier she had watched village boys skating on the mere at home. Bob and Perce had never forgotten how to keep upright on the ice. Ada could usually keep her balance better than most but she was only seven years old and was cross that she couldn't walk straight on to the ice and didn't know how to skate. Beattie was being taught to skate by her father, much to Ada's annoyance. He skated along, carrying Ada and Flo turn by turn.

'My turn!'

'No, it's mine!' echoed through the valley from countless children. On return, Uncle

Percy's ice-skates were returned to him. He greased them and hung them up in his cellar for the next time.

Uncle Bob urged them all to go for a day-trip in the summer further afield to the upper Calder Valley, where he had done his former walking.

'You must gather some of a plant called pudding dock,' he explained to his sister. 'The Crossleys swear by it. Folk up here make a meal from the leaves. Jenny says you mix it with nettles and onions and oatmeal. They used to eat it at Lent but now they call it Easter pudden.'

George, who was listening, said, 'If it's such a delicacy you'd better go and gather some, bor, for your mam to bake!'

'At home, Mam used to make tansy pudding on Easter Sunday,' said Emma. 'I think it grew on the wayside — you could look for that as well.'

'I remember that,' said George. 'It was very bitter — little yellow flowers they were and my mother made pancakes flavoured with tansy. Said to be good for you after Lent. For the worms too!'

The children looked amazed to hear such a detail from their father. Beattie thought, they both lived a long time before they came here. She had rarely seen her parents in this way, sort of different. She would remember about the tansy.

Emma was thinking, Mam knew a hundred times more about plants than I do. I wish I'd asked her more about 'em when I could. She felt sad. But she got Herbert and Ernest to look out for the 'pudden dock' and the tansy when the two boys went with chapel for a long day's walk starting at Hardcastle Crags.

In triumph, they brought back some pink flowers with long heart-shaped leaves.

'Superintendent says it's called bistort,' said Herbert.

'There weren't no tansy,' said Ernest. 'Our teacher says he's seen it growing by the river though, in the country, not here.'

Emma put the bistort blooms in a jug and did her best with the leaves, some herbs of her own, a few nettles and some onions which she boiled up and fried in bacon fat. It was quite tasty. Her sister-in-law pronounced her a real Yorkshire lass.

It was true, she was beginning to feel more at home now up here, even if not all her culinary attempts were crowned with success, or if sometimes her herbs unaccountably failed to cure.

Her family of children was well known in the town now, her little Yorkshire Starlings.

17

The following year Emma gave birth to another child, a girl, a pretty little lively baby with big eyes and a rosebud mouth whom she named Minnie. As she grew from a baby into a toddler Emma dressed her in embroidered frocks with puffed sleeves, protected by broderie anglaise smocks. The dresses and smocks were confected by Emma herself, for when Minnie was born Emma had been over two years without a small baby and had therefore had a little more time for the sewing and embroidering, which she so much enjoyed. Minnie was too small to inherit four-year-old Flo's only decent early dress for Flo had been larger and fatter. Minnie was very tiny. She wore a pair of narrow-strapped shoes lined with fur, very much coveted by Ada. This ostensible extravagance was deceptive; the little shoes were from Myra who had for once correctly guessed the size of her latest niece's feet. Emma prayed this seventh child of hers, George's ninth, would be their last.

That winter Ernest worried her a good deal, being prey to many coughs and colds and infections. She had hoped that the warmer house would help them all, especially him. 'Our Arnust is a bit too thin,' she would often say to George. The girls appeared more robust than the boys, but all the children, even little Minnie, had gone through the measles, which had left Ernest with earache and Flo with sore tonsils. Just before Minnie was born, mumps had been the lot of all except Herbert, which was puzzling. However hard their mother had tried to make sure they would all get these childhood diseases over and done with at the same time her schemes had never worked. Neither had Ada ever caught chicken-pox, even when she had wiped the child's face with the same flannel Herbert had used! Whooping-cough had so far passed them all by and Emma prayed it would stay away. She had however discounted scarlet fever from which no child in the town had recently suffered.

* * *

It was the week after Minnie's second birthday, a cold January day. During the afternoon a neighbour's child, Edith Robinson, visited them, the very day that Emma suspected she might once more be carrying another baby. A few days later Minnie developed a sudden temperature, vomited up her porridge and screamed:

'It hurts! It hurts!' pointing to her throat.

The child was an early and precocious talker and Emma believed her. She looked in her daughter's throat and saw that her tonsils were filmy white. Dread filled her heart. She had seen that white throat years ago in Caston and knew what it was. That neighbour's child last week must have given Minnie the scarlet fever.

Hannah Sayer was called round and pressed the child's reddened skin. The pressure made the skin whiten and stay white for several minutes.

They looked at each other.

'You'll have to call the doctor,' said Mrs Sayer.

Doctor Brown, the younger partner, who was more friendly than the older man, came round and shook his head.

'Wait till tomorrow, but I'm afraid it's scarlet fever. Your other youngsters may get it, meanwhile you must keep them away from other children.'

George plucked up his courage. 'Have you been called to the Robinson's?' he asked.

'I have,' replied the doctor. 'Their daughter has gone down with it. If only we had an isolation hospital in the town, or that people would take their children's symptoms seriously.'

'I do! I do!' panted Emma, beside herself with fear. George patted her hand.

Uncle Bob came round and insisted that Emma send Ada and Flo to stay with him and his wife. They had as yet no children and the girls might just have the luck not to have been too near Minnie. They were, though, the most likely to get it, for the boys had not played with the Robinson child and had stayed outdoors when the party took place. They took little notice of their small sister in any case. Beattie had played with her sister in the morning and then run some errands for her mother whilst Edith Robinson was on her visit. Since then of course Beattie had been near Minnie, for Beattie was Minnie's favourite sister.

The next day Minnie's face was covered with a red rash which spread down to her body and arms and legs, even as far as her hands. Emma neglected everything to sit with the child, who was delirious, to hold her hot hand, and to try to soothe her with a cool flannel on her forehead. Polly willingly took over the household. She was now nineteen and liked nothing better than being needed. Ann preferred to stay at work.

Next morning Minnie had what Emma

remembered was called ‘white strawberry tongue’, and could not swallow.

They waited for her skin to peel. But before it did, she began visibly to fade, her lips parched and now deadly white. Emma tried to get her mouth open to pour water down her throat but it made the child cough. Polly and she sat up all night and Beattie cried herself to sleep.

Next morning little Minnie of the smart shoes and pretty clothes had died.

Beattie had only a mild sore throat. The doctor could not explain it. If Beattie had died too Emma thought she would not have been able to carry on. She had adored little Minnie, and so had Beattie. She telegraphed Myra, feeling she needed the support of her sister for once and Myra came for the funeral at Bethel Chapel, and cried copiously. The coffin, lined with white satin, with the child’s body on a white cushion, had been placed on a table in the back room the night before and George had got in a photographer, thinking that a picture might one day console his wife. The three older children sang a hymn over the little coffin.

‘She was only two years old,’ sobbed Beattie.

Before the funeral service they all kissed her goodbye and after it George took the coffin in his cart, draped in black, to join David in the cemetery. They had still not been able to afford a gravestone but they paid a few shillings each year for the little plot at the edge of the new cemetery.

'We're not paupers,' thought Emma.

Ada and Flo were kept for the time being at Uncle Bob's. Along with their brothers they were never to catch the germ.

Myra stayed at her sister's for a week. She seemed a little more sober, a little quieter, and Emma wondered, in the midst of the haze of her grief — and even anger at the child's death — if Myra had a lover. On the last afternoon they spent together during her stay, Myra, who was helping to sew black bands on to the boys' jackets, appeared to want to say something.

Finally, 'I wasn't going to say anything about it — you've enough to think about at the moment — but I've been asked for in marriage!'

Emma waited.

'He's a widower — was a pierrot — he's still singing — comes from Cardiff, but he's staying on with the concert-party for the time being.'

'How old is he?'

'Oh, about forty,' said Myra vaguely.

'And will you accept him?'

'Probably. It won't affect my job — it'll help, actually.'

'Then I wish you well, love.'

Emma kissed her sister and saw that Myra had tears in her eyes. Was she mourning little Minnie or was she trying not to weep over some lost hope? She did not seem to be thrilled over this prospective husband, but maybe she was shy of appearing happy in a house of grief. Emma had always imagined that Myra would marry a duke or at least a famous young actor. A widower sounded in fact more sensible but she could not summon up any genuine interest at present for anything, not even for her sister's future.

Myra brightened up. 'Oh, I forgot to tell you! I saw your friend Baz — Jabez Smith!'

Such a swift change of subject made Emma's heart leap, yet what was Baz to her now that her charming little Minnie had gone away for good? She had so loved the child.

'He sends his regards. He came over from Liverpool — he was helping with some church work there, he said.'

She stopped, looked reflective. 'He seemed to hint he had once known George's elder brother quite well. Have you ever asked George about him?'

'Oh no, my husband didn't like him — at least I think he didn't — he was never keen on my even speaking to Baz. I never told you? I always thought I had known Baz Smith as a boy when I was ever so small.'

'No, you never told me that. Perhaps you did know him? Anyway,' Myra went on, 'we'd better sew Beattie's dress for her, hadn't we, though I'm sure she could sew it better than me!'

She put out her hand and stroked Emma's arm. Emma had never known her so subdued and loving.

'I know you'll always be sad, Sis, about the little one, but perhaps she's better off in heaven.'

This was a remark very uncharacteristic of Myra. She must be feeling depressed herself, thought Emma later, during the dreary days after her sister's departure. If she had been given a choice between little Minnie's going definitely to heaven and staying as a sinner on earth she knew which she would have chosen. Dr Williams said the scarlet fever had been followed by what sounded like 'ammonia'. Emma knew that wasn't the right word, and was put right by Hannah Sayer.

Ada was later caught trying to fit her little sister's slippers on.

'She got the idea from *Cinderella*, I expect,' said Herbert.

Emma continued to be inconsolable.

George understood that this death had affected his wife even more than that of the baby David, but hoped that a new baby would settle her.

David had died at four weeks and nobody had ever known why, but little Minnie, the child so dear to Emma's heart, her birth in a way her own resignation to further childbearing, had died.

At the end of 1886 when Emma gave birth to another boy, Walter, Ada caught whooping-cough, but survived.

After Minnie's death, Emma found it hard to love the other children, especially Ada and Flo, and she nursed and tended the new baby like an automaton, constantly dreaming that Walter turned into Minnie.

George too was disturbed and even a little irritable. From what he said, his wife wondered whether he thought David's death and Minnie's might be punishments for his neglect of his first wife. He had very occasionally intimated that he had not looked after Elizabeth Ann well enough.

'You were working to give them all a better life!' she consoled him.

But he had a weight on his heart that she could not budge, and a nasty cough that worried her.

* * *

Myra went on writing to Emma, each time mentioning her widower acquaintance, who was called Tom Evans. Perhaps she had not made her mind up whether to marry him, thought her sister, or wanted to do even better on the stage than she had so far. She was uncertain to what Myra aspired. Myra had once alluded to the 'legitimate stage' but she had not liked to ask what that meant. She had the feeling that Myra had not yet fulfilled all her ambitions although, goodness knows, she had escaped being a servant and was actually being paid a wage for doing what she liked. What was wrong with concert-parties and pantomimes? Maybe there were other, better jobs she still wanted, but found she could advance no further.

Emma tried to remember what the other actors had said when they were introduced to the family outside the tiny dressing-room that afternoon in Woolsford. They had shaken hands with her, and smiled at the children, before George said they had better not stay any longer if they were not going to miss the train.

Myra was obviously popular. A man had said to Emma something like, 'And this is our thespian's sister?' when he shook hands with her, but she had no idea what a thespian was. Did Myra want to be a play-actress in London?

The opportunity to see a 'real' play had come up the year after they arrived in Calderbrigg; she remembered the lads who had gone round handing out notices. The performances were in marquees on land opposite the Co-operative Hall but she could not imagine they would have been as good as the Alhambra! A lot more was going on in the town now; lectures at the Mechanics Institute, which Percy had attended; and the following winter, as well as the usual plays at the Oddfellows Hall and the Co-operative Hall, a company was at last to play in the town hall! There had been a *Messiah* there, but now there would be an opera, as well as a play. Emma would dearly love to see the play, *East Lynne*, that everyone talked about, but the seats were too dear for her and George to go, even if they could have left the children.

Polly and Ann might go. They had recently come into some money from their dead mother's father, and there were plans to be finalized for the rent to come to them from certain cottages in Watton. All this had been a complete surprise to Emma but she knew Ann wanted to go back home, and was now old enough to choose for herself.

Ann was friends with a tall handsome young man who wanted to be a farmer and Emma was sure she was encouraging him. Whether the friendship would blossom into anything else she knew not: Ann had always kept her own counsel. Polly too dreamed of opening her own shop but so far it was just a dream.

Eventually Polly and Ann did go together to a performance of *The Bohemian Girl*, and Emma suspected they were joined — or at least Ann was — by the handsome John. She told her sister Myra all this in a letter and asked her if that was the sort of theatre Myra wanted to play in.

Myra replied, saying such work was very precarious. She would stay where she was, and by the way, Tom Evans sent his best wishes to her family! Well that was real news. She must be engaged.

A month or two later, Myra wrote that they had had a quiet wedding in the Register Office at Rhyl. She had not wanted to make a big thing of it since Tom was a widower and the company was busy, including the newly weds. She apologized for not asking her family but as soon as they could afford it they would come to see them all. She sent her love and her new address.

The children were growing up fast. Once

they were twelve they would be found work in various mills, and their parents hoped their boys might a little later be apprenticed to a better trade. Beattie was a girl, so her fate would be to go in 1889, as her half-sisters had once done, as a half-timer. Ada and Flo were expected to do the same. Meanwhile, Ernest turned out to be gifted at playing the harmonium. It was Percy who had encouraged him to practise on it at chapel where there was a Young Persons' Society that met as an offshoot of the Sunday school every Wednesday.

All the children except for Herbert were musical. Ada was less so but she could talk like an actor, just like Myra. Beattie had a lovely singing voice and Flo at eight was fascinated by an old banjo her brothers had found and brought home.

After the child's death, Emma used to imagine that little Minnie would have been an opera singer. She put flowers on her grave every year on the day she died.

Emma was thirty-eight and George fifty-four when their last child was born three years after Walter in 1889. It was another boy and they named him Alfred, Alfie for short.

* * *

Walter was only four but he was perhaps the most naturally musical of all the children. He astonished Emma one day when they were visiting Isabella King. She had an old piano in her parlour that her own child had never bothered to play, but little Walter went up to it and picked out the hymn tune he had heard in Sunday school a few days before. After this, he was invited to go round whenever he wanted and his diminutive figure could be glimpsed through the window, seated on the piano stool. The organ grinder's tune, or the music he had heard the organist play in chapel, or a song Polly was humming — all were grist to his mill, with all the changes of key. His mother thought him quite remarkable and felt guilty that she had not truly welcomed his birth so soon after little Minnie's death.

'Where does he get it from?' she wondered to George. 'It's called playing by ear,' he said. 'You're born with it, I suppose.'

Ada was deeply offended by her small brother's expertise at the piano and asked for lessons for herself. Of course no money was forthcoming for such a thing, so instead Ada was encouraged to learn long passages of verse to recite at Sunday-school concerts. Emma wished Myra could hear her but Ada was not a child she really wanted to show off since she showed off enough as it was. Emma sometimes called her 'snaisty', not a compliment, but a word nobody but George and the older girls could understand. Ada took it as a compliment however and went round saying, 'I'm very snaisty like my Auntie Myra.' Beattie found Ada hard to take.

Ernest continued on the harmonium though he could not play by ear like his little brother. He was also good at 'figuring', like his father. What would Baby Alfred do? wondered Emma. Already he could sing little songs when he could not or would not talk. Of the family, George, and his elder daughters and Herbert, had missed out on these musical gifts, so Emma concluded it must have come from the Saunders or Banham side of the family. George's ability to read aloud so wonderfully well might have been inherited by Ada.

George was not getting any younger and he was often tired when he came home. Almost twenty years of hard physical labour at the corn-mill with the horses, as a carter and later as warehouseman had bent his frame. His cough came and went but was worse in the chill Calderbrigg winters.

Emma was working as hard as ever, now no longer regarded as a 'young woman'. She was known for always dressing her children beautifully. The girls' 'best' dresses had even fancier tartan sashes and lace collars, and Ernest and Herbert had celluloid collars for church or for 'best'. The five eldest of her children had their photographs taken one winter in the new studio in town and the result pleased her immensely. She and George had already tested the water by having theirs done — separately — and she had been determined to have a picture of her family. She'd have the two little boys done in a year or two.

The washing of all these clothes and all the underwear and sheets was never-ending, helped by the two big girls, now young women themselves. They toiled and moiled with the dirty clothes, banging them in the deep dolly-tub, pressing and pushing them through the soapy water with the three-pronged 'posser' that needed so much energy to use. Physical work was hard and unremitting.

Then there was the shopping and cooking and baking. The man from the farm came every day with his cart with the churn and measured out the milk with his tin gill-measure, but they could not afford milk every day so Emma bought buttermilk from him, which was cheaper. Once a week the fishmonger came round to deliver cod or hake and the children waited for their favourite meal with impatience. Once a week, the big tin bath was brought up from the cellar and filled with water from the side of the range, when one by one the children were cleaned and scrubbed. If it was a very cold night and they were not warm from a Friday bath they were given stone hot-water bottles wrapped in flannel to share between them all. The adults washed at night when the children were in bed, except for Ann and Polly who had discovered the slipper baths in the town.

Ann had now left the mill and was working in a hardware shop. She did not intend to stay there for long, for she was encouraging the young man, John, who was sweet on her, to save, so that when they got married, which she was determined they would, they could both go to live in Norfolk where John could become a pig-farmer. They would live in one of the cottages Elizabeth Ann's father had left her and Polly in his will. George was surprised at how this was turning out, for both girls were also left the rent money from other cottages near Watton.

George had been earning a steady wage now for three years and Emma had been able to save up enough money to start to pay regularly for a Singer treadle sewing-machine on the new hire system. When the day came that she had paid off the hire and could call it hers she was never so happy. Now she could make more clothes for everyone, all the girls' dresses, and what she still called their aprons and they called pinafores. Life had never looked so hopeful, she thought, in the spring of 1891. The machine was her most 'wallable' — valuable — possession. As well as sewing on the machine she also tatted, and crocheted more collars for herself and for the girls' clothes and lovely patterns on the edges of tablecloths and runners and mats.

Emma still put aside the coins in their tins on the 'chimbley' piece. If the younger children ran errands for their mother they got a halfpenny if their mother could spare it. George still wasn't a man for much baccy and beer, and she still thanked God he had never been a violent man, and always treated her well. Many men in the town were not like him. He was a mite strict with his sons, but more indulgent with his daughters.

Her nightmare had been not having enough clothes and boots for the children. Eventually there were seven children to be shod, as well as Polly and Emma. Boots had to be handed down from two boys to three girls and then to two more boys. If little Minnie and little David had lived, how would they have managed?

She and George managed a few family treats, though they had not yet saved enough to go to the coast along with some neighbours who now went for day trips to Blackpool, or even stayed a week in boarding-houses. The Starlings went instead to the pleasure gardens in the valley, now enlarged with more swings and roundabouts; and went on the Whit Walk, dressed to show off their new clothes. Then, all the Methodist scholars from the town Sunday schools marched along to end up in a field where they were given buns and 'pop' and the adults cups of tea. The children enjoyed the day, once they had forgotten their mother's injunctions:

'Now mind you look after your new clothes!'

But they probably enjoyed the swings in the new recreation ground just as much. The 'rec' had been created a mile up the road in 1889. Here the boys could play cricket or watch the amateur Rugby League teams try their paces.

* * *

Emma had always taught her children to be polite, to say 'Ef you please,' and 'Thank 'ee,' the way she'd been taught by her own mother. Even when the little ones were still crawling — 'craping', as she called it, they knew what was right and what was wrong. She already had a reputation in the little town for keeping a beady eye on the behaviour of children. But she never interfered with her own brood's 'playing out' as long as they came home at the time she had stipulated.

All the children except for Ada and Flo loved walking in their home patch, playing for hours in the woods, sometimes going as far as the wood called Freeman's, a mile or so away, where Uncle Percy found earth-nuts and Beattie and Polly gathered bluebells. From an early age, they all loved walking along the tow-paths on the canal banks, avoiding the horses that pulled the heavy barges, and staring at the working of the locks. Ada and Flo preferred hopscotch on the pavement outside the house, which kept them busy for hours. But Beattie had tired of this game and went further afield to the canal banks.

'Everything is so nice and peaceful down there,' she said to her father, whom she adored. 'No hurry and no mills!'

When they were little, Polly had been deputed to keep an eye on the younger ones in case they were too small to understand that water was dangerous. But gradually they learned, and later Beattie used to wheel out her two youngest brothers on their favourite walk to 'Ganny Lock'. This was one of the many locks on the clean, pretty, canal and only ten minutes walk from their old grey terrace house, down a 'snicket' between some cottages and then on to the canal bank.

Beattie loved watching the gypsy-like life on the barges whose owners and workers wore colourful clothes and where there was always a baby in some woman's arms and, on one barge, a parrot in a cage. 'I wish I were a gypsy,' she said to Emma when she was about nine. She would look out for barges she had got to know well and was once even invited aboard one of them, but decided she'd better ask her mother.

Emma had been a little worried, and decided against Beattie's going on to the barge. The idea of 'gypsy' brought back all her old ideas about Baz. But Beattie was such a sensible girl, even if she might like to dream about a free open-air life. No wonder, with the mill work she had done from the age of twelve. From six o'clock in the morning till noon, she toiled in the silk-mill at Brookfoot, along with other children who couldn't keep their eyes open in class in the afternoon. Beattie, though, always kept her eyes open, and was a bookworm. Harriet Bracegirdle used to bring round a newspaper that was printed over the Pennines in Bolton called the *Weekly Journal* in which there were stories that went on from week to week. It was Polly and Beattie rather than Emma who read them avidly.

'What a pity,' said George to his wife, 'that Beattie has had to work so hard and won't get educated for much longer.'

He was not a man who thought all girls were good only for marriage and babies. The trouble was, you had to earn enough to live on, and girls could not earn as much as men, so needed husbands to keep them fed. Then, along would come the children, as he well knew. Beattie, who loved her brothers and sisters, had however decided that if she got married she would have only two children. Isabella King's sister over in Huddersfield had just died in childbirth and it had scared Beattie, who had an imagination.

'Beattie's ever so like Polly,' Emma would say to her husband. Beattie was also quite good at 'book-learning' like George and his elder daughters, but Polly and her sister had had the advantage of a mother who taught them to read when they were four. Ernest and Herbert and Flo were not so keen on learning, but folk were all different and needed different treatments. Had George found her wanting in such things? He might have improved her own reading and writing but she had no time to read for pleasure as Beattie and Polly did. Yet she did not really believe he blamed her for her early lack of polish. She was a good housekeeper as well as a good mother, and he had needed above all a mother for his girls. She had done her best by them, and by her own children.

They would have to wait to see how the two youngest boys turned out. At least Walter had his music.

18

It was just about the time of her twenty-second birthday that Polly met an ambitious young man at chapel called Henry John Walker. Most of the town's businessmen were Methodists and voted Liberal, and this young man, four years older than Polly, though not yet a businessman, intended to become one. This may have been one of the reasons he was an assiduous attender at Bethel. He could catch sight there of — one day might even speak to — the elders, older successful men, men 'in the know'.

Henry John was also a man much attracted to women and it must be said that at this time Polly was a handsome young woman. Not exactly pretty but full featured, and well spoken, which Henry John admired. They had got talking in the first instance at a decorous Young People's Bazaar and the young man made up his mind then and there to find out more about her.

She was obviously a very capable girl; you could see that from her demeanour and her speech, and she was also a very kind young woman for she nearly always had with her one of her many half-sisters or brothers. Her half-brother Ernest was known at Bethel, since he filled in if the regular harmonium player was unavoidably absent. Plans were afoot for building a grand new chapel one day, though the worshippers knew it would be years before they had enough funds to make the building a reality rather than a pipe dream. Not long after the new century began it was to be the pride of most of the townsfolk including Henry John but at this time of his life he was a poor man who certainly had no spare cash to add to the appeal. He knew that Polly's family was poor but respectable, but he kept his own family background fairly quiet for he liked to appear mysterious. He came in fact from a neighbouring town where he had worked as jack-of-all-trades.

After eighteen months of greeting her, and six months of chat, he spoke to Polly of his plans which were both practical and ambitious. He wanted to own a shop, and this appealed to her. What the shop would sell he had as yet no idea. Matters were at this stage between them: a weekly meeting, but not yet 'walking out', much conversation but no hand-holding, when Polly's father, who had suffered from his chest for years, had a worse attack than usual.

On the surface everything had been going

on well for George until one day he came home from work with a nasty wheeze and a cough worse than his usual one. He would not stay warm in bed the next morning, saying he could not afford to miss work, so he struggled on. After a few days he said he felt a little better, well enough to recover completely when the spring weather came. But the smoky atmosphere in the town and the work he was now doing in the mill warehouse to earn more than his from previous work with the horses were not good for a man with a bad chest who was already weakened by years of overwork. He was now responsible not only for keeping some of the accounts, itemizing all that came in and went out, but also had to lug around sacks of grain, and get them ready to be picked up by younger men for transportation to the station.

Emma begged him to ask the bosses if he could now work only at the books and not have to carry heavy sacks. It was true that if his employers had realized earlier that their 'Norfolker' could add up and write and was capable of getting on with the work without supervision he could have had an easier time. But he was a modest man, grateful to have had continuous employment since his arrival in the town eighteen years before, even though the hard labour had debilitated him.

He had never blown his own trumpet or expected the mill could offer him better employment now he was older.

He struggled on but eight months later, one November morning, he was found by a carter, gasping for breath in the yard. George was leaning against the flank of his favourite horse, a chestnut mare, feeling the warmth of the animal, which he had always said 'did his chest good'. But this morning he was clutching his chest. He had suffered pains there before but when he had got up for work an hour or two earlier, a sudden pain had attacked him. He had gone to work hoping exercise would banish it but now it had come on worse, and he was both sweating and shivering. He could not get enough breath into his lungs and was breathing rapidly and shallowly. He had suffered with the same cough for years but this morning it had felt as if a large rusty key was being turned behind his heart.

For once, in his eagerness not to frighten Emma, who had been up in the night with their youngest boy who had a stomach-ache, he had forgotten his 'fourses'. When his daughter Polly arrived with his box she found him in the yard with the carter who was looking concerned.

Polly took it all in immediately and was so

agitated that though her father begged her through gasps not to say anything to the foreman of the warehouse, she plucked up her courage and went into the mill to find him.

'My father — he can't breathe!' she said, adding, as she might as well be hanged for a sheep as a lamb, 'Is it not possible to let him work only with the books so that he doesn't have to carry heavy sacks?'

Her own words surprised her but she had heard Emma's own opinion on the subject. As she spoke, she was thinking, but it's all musty in here too! The grain was in clouds all over the loading bays.

The foreman promised he would speak to the manager. Their master, the mill-owner, was not a cruel master. He was not unconcerned about his workers.

The overall manager came up then to see what all this was about. One look at George, who had now staggered back into the warehouse, as pale as death, made him decide to send him home for the day. He couldn't have a man dying on him! At the end of the shift he went up to the master's office to explain the situation.

'We could use him in the office,' he said. 'Starling's a good worker and has a good hand.'

His boss agreed that George might in future confine himself at the same wage to checking the books.

The warehouse foreman did tell the manager and the manager spoke to the owner, to intercede on George's behalf, but it was really too late.

This time, after a day in bed, he seemed to make a slight recovery in spite of a hacking cough and went back the next day in spite of Emma's begging him not to. He was to work at checking ledgers in the warehouse, but a month later he caught a cold which went straight back on to his chest. Chronic bronchitis had dogged him for years but this time it had taken a hold and once again become acute. Emma feared it would turn into what she now knew was its proper name 'broncho-pneumonia'.

On the twenty-first of the month her husband was too ill even to attempt to get up. A cough tore at his lungs; even trying to expel the copious phlegm exhausted him. His temperature went up again and his breathing became more laboured. He clutched at his chest where the pain was. Emma sent Polly to fetch the doctor. By the time he arrived George was in and out of delirium.

'He will recover for Christmas, won't he?' asked Beattie.

'Why must we be quiet?' asked Ada.

Flo cried and Herbie and Ernest were subdued.

Polly and Ann took over the running of the household whilst Emma stayed at her husband's bedside, willing him to turn the corner to recovery. There would be what they called a 'crisis', said the doctor, who had listened to George's chest, and taken his pulse and his temperature. Doctor Brown looked inscrutable, but Polly and Emma both knew that this 'crisis' would mean either that the patient would make a sudden recovery, or slide into death.

Harriet Bracegirdle and Isabella King both called round the following day, bringing pies for the family and offers of help.

The cough stopped and for a time Emma was hopeful, but she noticed his breath was now rapid and shallow and his body seemed to be on fire.

On the morning of Friday the twenty-third he was no better and she sent word to his younger brother Henry to visit. He who had followed his older brother to Yorkshire, now worked in a nearby town, having married a Huddersfield woman.

'Can he swallow?' whispered Henry, seeing Emma wiping his lips with a sponge.

'Not very well.'

She felt strangely light-headed from lack of sleep.

Henry patted his brother on the hand and George opened his eyes, and looked at him.

When he had gone — he did not stay long — Emma kissed her husband on the forehead.

In the evening George rallied a little, filling her with new hope.

'Henry called,' she said trying to sound normal.

George whispered in a hoarse voice that she had to bend to hear:

'Minnie.' Then, 'David.'

Did he mean he was going to see them again, that he knew he was dying? But he went on, fixing his eyes on her and then he said, 'Sorry.'

She wanted to say, it was not your fault they died, but he held up his hand that looked now almost transparent and said after a long pause:

'I was punished for . . . for thinking . . . '

He lapsed again into silence but continued to look at her searchingly. Emma squeezed his hand.

'You have never done anything wrong, George, I am sure.' He took as deep a breath as his lungs would allow him.

'I fancied you still loved that man. He was

related to me . . .'

Was he delirious? Who was he talking about? Could he mean Jabez Smith? There was no one else it could be. But what had little dead Minnie or baby David to do with Baz? And how could he be related to George? He had never mentioned any link between them before.

'You were wrong,' she said, though she knew he had not exactly been wrong. But it had nothing to do with their dead children. She had always been faithful to George.

He shut his eyes and seemed to fall asleep then.

After about ten minutes he opened them again and whispered weakly, his words slurred, 'Minnie looked like my father.' The effort to say this cost him a great gasp and a terrible coughing fit.

His father? He never said that before, but why should Minnie not have looked like his father? He had been her grandfather after all, and had died a few years back.

Should she tell him that she had never seen the man again whose name he had so much difficulty in saying? But she might not exactly be telling the truth, for maybe she really had seen Baz in the market that day after David's death. It was true that the idea of him had sustained her, even after Minnie had died.

George was rambling; her knowing Baz all those years ago must have preyed on his mind. There was nothing to reproach him for, but she said, 'Minnie and David looked like you, dear,' in case he had really imagined she had been unfaithful to him. But how? She had never been away from him for nineteen years!

He smiled then, and said, 'Yes.'

In his weakened state, that she might once have been sweet on Jabez Smith must have freshly upset him. In his right mind he would never have alluded — indeed never had — to that particular part of her past. Her 'past' had in any case been innocent.

She had never realized that he might have been jealous. How much more cause had she had to be jealous of his love for Elizabeth Ann! His eyes were shut again and he said nothing more for a time, but she pulled her shawl protectively round her shoulders and waited. He kept his eyes shut and she thought he was asleep, but he murmured in an urgent voice,

'It could not be! No, no, it could not be!'

Why should his delirium make him keep harking back? Yet his words sounded perfectly rational.

She thought, as she sat there beside her husband, that Baz must now be about fifty. It was true that she had never forgotten him, but other things since the death of her two children had thrust that last memory of him away and made her live in the present. And then she had borne two more of George's children after that time.

'Forgive me,' he muttered again.

The effort to speak had exhausted him, so Emma took his hand and pressed it to her cheek.

'There is nothing to forgive,' she said.

'You are a good wife,' he whispered, and then he shut his eyes and fell asleep.

For a while she thought that this would be a calm sleep and that after ridding himself of this baseless self-reproach he would wake refreshed and on the mend.

'You have been a good husband,' she said but he did not hear her.

He slept on then, tossing and turning and coughing, lying feverish and yet pale. She crept down to the kitchen to have a cup of tea with Polly.

He slept on fitfully and she sat beside him until the dawn of the next day, a Sunday, Christmas Eve, his birthday. He had taken no nourishment but a few sips of water. There was no hope; Emma knew that now.

* * *

She was right. Christmas came and went. For the sake of the children she had baked a plain cake with a few raisins and filled the little ones' stockings with an orange or an apple and a penny.

But George was a strong-willed man and held on all week, until the thirty-first of December. He was very feeble, unconscious now, his breathing either scarcely audible or suddenly raucous. Emma sponged his face and body every hour to cool him down. Occasionally he would murmur, but she could never make out what he said. She would doze a little and then Polly would come in and relieve her for an hour or two.

Two work mates called, and left embarrassed over the family's suffering.

On the twenty-eighth, Beattie, remembering the nuns' teaching, said, 'It's Holy Innocents Day today, Mam!' Still he lay there, just about breathing.

On the Sunday, New Year's Eve, the children were sent off to chapel. Doctor Brown called in the early morning without being asked, and shook his head.

On their return, the children ate the Yorkshire pudding made for them by Harriet Bracegirdle, whose turn it now was to be of help to her friend. She had been sleeping overnight in the kitchen.

Warned by their mother, Herbert and Ernest, Beattie and Ada went in to make their farewells to their father. Ann had looked in to see him every day but never stayed long.

Emma took the three littlest ones in to see him and say 'Goodbye': Flo, Walter, and three-year-old Alfie on tiptoe.

Ann said she had promised to meet her beau, and as there was nothing further she could do she would go out. Emma and Polly stayed with him then, whilst Harriet saw to the two little boys. It all reminded Emma of over a quarter of a century earlier when Mam had died of a similar affliction and she had been taken to kiss her in her bed.

On the stroke of Saturday midnight, just as Sunday and the New Year 1893 was about to begin, George Christmas Starling died.

His death certificate, signed by Doctor Brown, was to state as cause of death only broncho-pneumonia.

After the laying out, accomplished by Hannah Sayer, and once the only coffin Emma could afford had been delivered by the undertakers, his body was taken to lie downstairs.

George had always saved for funerals in a special jar of his own, not thinking his would be the next. It would be on the Wednesday, the service at Bethel. Emma must first let Myra know.

Myra's last letter had spoken of her and her husband working for Adeler's and Sutton's pierrot groups on the piers in both Rhyl and Llandudno. They wouldn't be working there at present in winter, and Myra had mentioned something about not leaving Wales for the Christmas season — perhaps they were doing a panto there? so she would have to send a telegram to one of the Welsh resorts. She'd try Rhyl first.

Would Myra bring her husband with her to the funeral? Her sister was now thirty-two and Emma had wondered how long she could go on acting young girls on the stage. The hoped for break to the London stage had not happened. Would Myra go on trying for fame even now she was married?

In the end it was Beattie who wrote the telegram to her Aunt Myra, and took it to the telegraph office on Commercial Street, for Emma was busy seeing the undertakers and being visited by friends and neighbours and chapel folk. The minister from Bethel called and was given a cup of tea in the kitchen.

There was a reply the next day. Myra had lost no time:

So sorry. Will arrive Tuesday night. M.

No mention of whether her husband would accompany her. Emma suspected he would not. Myra was very independent.

She arrived at midnight, took off her hat, a high black confection, and enveloped Emma in her arms, murmuring, 'Oh how terrible. I'm so grieved.'

It was like a nightmare the next morning, getting all the children into their best clothes, with the new black armbands she and Polly had stayed up to finish, and marshalling them to follow the coffin on its little cart provided by his employers and pulled by one of the mill horses. Several folk had clubbed together to send a wreath of chrysanthemums. Emma could not afford 'weepers' or deep mourning, but the chapel service was a comfort. The minister said things about the family that surprised her, for she had not been aware that George was known so well at the chapel, where he was not a regular worshipper, being too busy. She had always had the impression that his first wife Elizabeth Ann's Primitive Methodism had not truly found favour with him. Neither Ann nor Polly had chosen to continue in that particular sect, and Polly was an ardent 'New Connexioner'. Of course, Mam had been Church; it was only the Saunders who had been Chapel, and George's own family were Church.

She tried to stop this sort of wool-gathering. Today of all days she must concentrate on life and death but she was almost too tired to feel any longer, would be relieved when her husband was buried even if it did not seem possible that his remains were contained in that narrow coffin. She said the Lord's Prayer to herself and listened to the hymns. Myra on one side kept squeezing her hand, which was rather annoying. Polly on the other was staring fixedly ahead. Myra had tears in her eyes, whilst her own were dry. Was it true that if you had loved someone who had died you would weep at their funeral? She had wept enough by herself, but could not summon tears for the public. She had relied on George, could scarcely now imagine life without him, but that was going to be her life in future. This town was home.

The cortège wound its way up the hill to the cemetery built seventeen years before, where Minnie and David had been buried.

After the funeral tea which had been cups of tea and ham sandwiches from a ham Mrs Bracegirdle had brought and insisted upon her accepting, and once the children had gone to bed or into the next room and Ann had gone out with John — Ann's future would now be her responsibility, she thought — Emma sat down with Myra.

Myra appeared subdued and Emma did not think it was just the funeral. She wanted to go to bed herself but knew she was almost too tired to sleep. Myra had promised her husband to return in two days so she must make the most of her sister who was trying very hard to be helpful.

'Talk if you want, but don't bother if you don't want,' said Myra.

'Thank you for coming,' said Emma. She tried to think of all the questions she would normally ask Myra but had to make a big effort.

'I've something to tell you before I go,' said Myra. 'I didn't want to write it.'

'We'll talk tomorrow before you go — but tell me about your husband. He would be welcome here, you know. And your job, how is it going?'

Myra sighed. 'Well, you know, Tom is a real stay-at-home. He loves his work but he's done so much travelling in his life that now he loathes it, so I'm stuck down in Wales as far as I can see. Plenty work there for me — more stage-managing now . . . '

And are you happy? Emma wanted to ask, but she doubted Myra would tell her if she was not. Too proud.

They had changed the sheets and aired the room where George had died and Emma, not being of a squeamish disposition, tried to sleep in the bed he had died in. But it was strange, alone in the night for the first time for nearly twenty years.

The next morning she awoke after troubled sleep to find that the fire had been lit by Herbert before he went off to work. That was a mercy, for it had always been George's job, though during his illness Isabella had seen to it. After more cleaning, and potato-peeling and preparing a meal for Myra before her departure, Isabella called in again, to take charge of Walter for the day. He amused her with his playing of her piano and it was one child fewer for Emma to worry about. Alfie was asleep and the others were either at school like Flo, or at work, after the stresses and strains of the last few days.

Emma sat down with Myra for a cup of tea.

'I don't know whether this is the right time, but as I shan't see you again till Lord knows when — unless you come and stay with us — I'd better tell you now,' said Myra.

Emma waited.

'It's just that I heard again from Jabez Smith.'

Emma started. Why was she suddenly hearing mention of Baz? What with George talking about him, and now her sister . . .

'The thing is — you remember some years ago you said you thought you'd seen him here in the town?'

'Yes, but I don't think I did. It was after little David died. I was in the market.'

She stopped. She suddenly felt so bereft, George gone and nothing ever to be the same again. It was taking time for that to sink in. She'd have to sit down soon and calculate how she was going to manage.

'Oh, now I've upset you. I'm sorry I won't mention him again — '

'No, tell me. It was just that something George said not long ago that brought him back to mind. It was very odd, he said Jabez Smith was related to the Starlings . . . ' Now she could never ask George what he had meant.

'Well, you *did* see him in the market! I'd told him in a letter about your baby dying, and he told me ages afterwards that he *had* been in the North, on some job in Liverpool, and he'd wanted to visit you but didn't want to upset your husband, so he got off the train in Calderbrigg, thought he might just look round and see if you were in the town — and there you were, he said!'

'Why didn't he come up and talk to me then?'

'He didn't want to intrude, just wanted to

make sure you were all right. He felt, I don't know, fatherly, I suppose, towards you. I think with me too — he acted more like a parent.'

Had he thought her husband didn't look after her properly? No, he couldn't have thought that because he had said more than once before she got married that George was a good man.

Emma said nothing though so Myra went on, 'He's always been fond of you, I think, and kind to me because of you.'

'I used to think George didn't like him,' said Emma at last. 'It was before we were married, so I stopped seeing Baz, and of course then I got married.'

She did not mention again her conviction that she had known Baz as a child. She added, 'But how could George have been related to him? Will you ask him?'

There still seemed to be something Myra was not saying, but, 'It'll be some village complication, I expect,' she said loftily as though that sort of thing was beneath her. 'He's married now to a woman called Martha. He wrote to me. I think he wanted me to tell you.'

Strange that George should have left a mystery behind him when she had thought she had known him through and through.

'But it isn't the time to talk about it, I

know. I'm sorry, I did hear some rumour — I'll sort it out and let you know,' Myra said conclusively.

'Send him my regards.'

'Shall I let him know you are widowed?'

Widowed. It sounded so terrible. But what would be the harm if Baz was — at last — married himself?

'Yes, you can tell him.'

Myra changed the subject. 'Now you will be in need of cash — no, don't be cross — but I had a brain-wave in bed last night. I know lots of actors and musicians who play up here — the West Riding is a very musical place, you know — and with a population big enough to give jobs to lots of 'em. So! Why not take in theatricals?' Myra looked pleased with herself.

'You mean lodgers? But there isn't room — not yet, maybe when they're all married, I suppose . . . ' And I shall always need the money, she thought, with visions of the workhouse. 'Thank you. I'll think about it,' she said feebly.

Myra left the next day and Emma was at last left alone to think about George and try to come to terms with his death. It had perhaps been rather tactless of Myra to introduce the subject of Baz at such a time, except that he had come back into her mind after George's muddled words. What with his illness, and the funeral, and the children, and the neighbours and friends, and her sister, it had all been too much of an upheaval.

* * *

Emma Eliza had to confront 1893 responsible for seven children, the youngest only three. Herbert was nineteen, an adventurous youth, now working for the railway, and bringing in some shillings, but not yet the sort of young man you could ask to take on more responsibility. Ernest was more serious, but only seventeen. How could she manage to carry on and clothe and feed them all? The wages of the two eldest boys and Beattie, and now Ada, who had just begun work, much against her inclination, in another silk-mill, would not be hers for ever and it would be nine years before little Alfred would be old enough to earn. Not that she wanted her children to have to start mill work so young, but what else was there for them to do? She must think hard and long about what she could do herself to earn the rent and the food.

Polly would help. Polly would advise. Polly was always a comfort.

One thing she had thought of for herself

was sewing shirts — the Singer would come in even more useful for that.

She'd have to get Herbert or Ernest, perhaps better Ernest, to help her calculate how they were to manage in future with no man's wage. What would they be able to afford? So long as she could go on paying the rent . . . but she'd have to cut down on food. How? She would find out the going rate in the town for shirt-making and mending. As for Myra's idea of theatricals, it might one day be feasible. For the moment there were nine children in the house, three of them adults and Ernest almost one.

And that was another thing, she'd have to find out more about Ann's young man — and ask Polly about that young fellow at chapel she talked to. Polly had been looking thoughtful long before her father died and especially thoughtful whenever Ann mentioned her plans for her John. Well, they'd both have to bring these young men round soon or there'd be talk.

* * *

Polly was twenty-five when her father died and Ann twenty-seven. They were getting on if they were ever to become brides. Polly did not appear to be in any hurry but Ann now announced that she was about to take up her heritage in Norfolk. Their grandfather's will had specified that they must have reached the age of twenty-five before they might come in for all the cottage rents he had left them, and the house where his family had lived since 1800. Emma suspected that this old man must have objected in some way to George as a husband for his daughter Elizabeth Ann, not to have tried to see his granddaughters even once after their removal north. He could have made the journey. He was, if not rich, certainly not a poor man.

George had said little to her about his first wife's family but she knew that a year or two ago he had received a letter from Norfolk asking him to send his elder daughter to see a certain solicitor. Emma had known there was money involved but had not liked to ask more. It was Polly who had told her about a will being proved and about the cottage rents that she and her sister would eventually inherit. Emma had never for a moment thought that she should have any of this money for the family; it belonged to the girls, was their birthright.

'It'll be one less for you to feed, Mother,' said Ann now in her downright way. She had brought John Tasker home to let him announce they were to marry. No permission required. Emma couldn't help thinking that it would also leave half a bed empty. Ann was of age and knew her own mind but, sad to say, Emma had not liked Mr Tasker overmuch, and wondered if Ann had told him before about her inheritance. He had impractical ideas, she thought, and how could Ann be sure the house she was taking him to was habitable?

'Oh don't worry about that. I have written to a cousin — Rose — who has been overseeing the place for us until probate was settled. I saw the solicitor in Halifax and all is arranged,' said Ann airily.

Had she gone behind her father's back? George had never gone into details about the money. She could not ask now. 'Have you ever farmed before, John?' Emma asked him at the tea-table. She had brought out her best four cups and saucers which had been her Grandmother Saunders's, the ones she had brought all the way from home all those years ago, wrapped in paper at the bottom of her clothes bag.

'No, Missis, but I've been helping my uncle out in Rastrick — and pig farming is my chosen trade!'

He was a very tall, excessively good-looking man. No wonder Ann was attracted to him. Polly had voiced her doubts privately to her stepmother. Not that there was anything *wrong* with John but he really had no idea of the hard life of a Norfolk farmer. Emma asked her brothers to enlighten him, begging them to be tactful. But Percy and Bob, first of all conscripted to knock some sense into Ann, had made no headway, and told Emma the girl would have to make her bed and lie on it as there was no more they could do.

It was settled that Ann and her beau would wed down in Norfolk in her mother's village so that the period of mourning for George need not appear to be ignored. They lost no time about the arrangements. Emma, preoccupied with money, had hardly realized what was afoot before they were ready to leave!

'We're promised land behind one of the cottages,' said Ann before they left, 'And by the way, Poll, I think you should come down soon to check your own inheritance!' There was no trace of the girl who had once been a silk spinner.

The rents were to be divided, so Polly could have hers collected on her behalf. Ann was fair-minded towards her sister but she had been saving up for two years, unknown to Emma. Polly determined to do the same but to help her stepmother first, knowing that her overriding worry was financial. But Emma was averse to taking anything from Polly.

Ann never even properly thanked Mother for looking after her all these years, thought Polly. It's the least I can do to help her out, but she's proud and so it will have to be by stealth.

Emma had already set up her sewing-machine and was to be found at night sewing shirt-seams.

George's death had been the end of her marriage, thought Emma, and now Ann's departure would mean another break in the fabric of her life.

What more could life throw at her?

19

The new borough of Calderbrigg was formed in 1893. Polly put her own life on hold for a year so that she could put her stepmother first. She explained this to Henry John Walker who had moved, temporarily he said, to Huddersfield to set up a stall in the market there to sell what were called 'novelties'. Polly wished him well and consented to see him once a month on Sundays after chapel. That would show her whether he was sufficiently interested in her to make the five-mile journey, she thought wryly.

Emma was immeasurably helped by Polly. She took on the family wash, dressed the two little boys in the morning before she left for the confectioner's shop on Commercial Street where she was now working. She baked bread on Thursdays when she got home from work, as Emma now spent as much of the day as possible at her sewing-machine. Walter had started school and was found to chalk beautifully on his slate as well as being allowed to play the school piano. Unlike the others he had been sent to the Board school which was just a little way up the hill and now cost not a penny. Alfie would follow him there when he was four.

None of the other children's jobs brought in much money so Emma worked on steadily and taught Polly too how to use the Singer. Ada had been found work at a milliner's and was so glad to leave the mill that she was quite manageable for a few months. Until such time as Myra should find her a job acting she would be a 'modiste', and did become for a time the milliner's model. It was true that she was a good saleswoman to the wives of the manufacturers in the town when she showed them how to wear the immense felt and buckram and flower constructions.

Herbert worked as porter on the station intending eventually to become a station-master, and Ernest was now apprenticed to a wire-drawing firm, though he found the life tiring and worried his mother with a persistent cough.

The 'baby', Alfred, was spoiled by all, especially by Beattie who was also a great support to her mother. She was now sixteen, still small in stature and serious-looking, her hair tightly scraped back from her broad forehead. It was she who was discovered to be as skilful as Emma on the sewing-machine, certainly better at it than Polly. She could even mend the parts when they went wrong, and kept the machine clean and oiled. She and Polly were very close. Beattie was working as a spinner now in the silk-mill, and on Sundays she sang in the Bethel choir. She had a surprisingly mature contralto, and was very useful singing 'second'. She did not need sheet music and indeed was only just learning to read it. She and Ernest, who sang tenor, would sometimes sing together for their mother and Polly.

A Higher Grade school had just been opened in the town but it was too late for Beattie even if they could have afforded it. Of all Emma's children she was the one who would have gained most from attendance at this new school.

* * *

There came a Sunday the following year when, after chapel one grey November day, Henry John produced what Polly could regard only as an ultimatum. He did not say so in so many words, but said only:

'I think it's about time you introduced me to your stepmother.' And that was it.

Emma did not attend chapel regularly, being more concerned with finishing off work even if it was a Sunday, but Henry John had glimpsed the 'widow woman' once or twice and knew of Polly's determination to help her.

Polly did not want to lose this insistent, ambitious young man, but she was still worried lest Emma would not be able to manage without her help. She knew however that Beattie could now step into her shoes, and Emma was the last person to ask her to sacrifice anything. That was the trouble; she did not want her stepmother, who worked at the Singer like a slave, to have even more work to do. Unless Beattie left the mill — and then the family would lose her wage. Little Walter and little Alfred were still so young and would not earn or be a lesser charge on her for years. There was the faint possibility of Myra's sending them sooner or later that 'theatrical lodger'. For that to happen it would certainly help if she vacated the tiny boxroom she had shared for so long with her sister. Emma would put the younger girls into that room and that could leave a larger room for a lodger. Or she might let this mythical lodger have the front parlour: 'The Room'. Perhaps then her stepmother would not really mind if she did accept a proposal, provided of course that Henry John was about to make her one. She scolded herself: what was she thinking of? — he had not actually *said* anything, had he? But if he did, she knew she'd accept him. She asked Emma if she might invite Mr Walker to tea the following Sunday.

'I was wondering when you'd ask!' replied Emma. 'Of course you may — they do say he's a man who'll go far. That is, if you want him, bor.'

Polly understood that Emma had been making enquiries. She perfectly understood the way things were done up here. It was all in his favour that Henry John attended Bethel Chapel, that he liked their Polly enough to come over on Sundays to see her after the service. *And* he wanted to meet the family. What more could you want?

Henry John acquitted himself well in the humble house, his own origins not being very different. Emma thought as she passed him a cup of tea and a scone on a plate — baked by Polly of course — that George would certainly have approved of him, far more than of Ann's dashing young husband.

Henry John knew what pleased parents. He made a short speech in which he said that he would like to marry Polly if she would accept him, that he knew her sterling virtues and that he had plans that might one day involve the whole family. Polly had already heard of some of these.

'Well, she'll think it over,' said Emma to

Henry John, wanting to spare Polly the trouble of a public reply. 'Come next Sunday,' she added, 'and she'll give you your answer.'

She looked quite fierce, thought Polly.

When he left, promising to return in a week, her stepmother asked Polly outright if she had told Mr Walker of her modest fortune in Norfolk. Polly intimated that the subject had come up.

'I don't want you taken in by a fortune-hunter,' Emma added.

'Oh no, Mother! If I've hesitated it's because of leaving you and the family, and wanting to go on helping you with it all.'

'You're not to worry about that. I shall manage. It's your life now,' answered Emma.

Since George died Emma had curiously found herself capable of much more self-confidence. In spite of the lowly nature of the work she was doing, she was helping to earn all their keep and was proud of it.

Polly met Henry John the following Sunday in chapel. If he asked her, she had decided to tell him straight away, before walking back home.

He walked out of the chapel with her and down the road. They stood for a moment in Commercial Street as a cart passed. Was he not going to say anything? Had he changed his mind? She was very nervous. But he took her arm, piloted her across the road and then said:

'Well, I think you can tell *me* before you say anything to your mother.'

She realized that he was a little nervous himself. She teased him to help him out.

'Well, ask me then!'

'You know what the question is!'

He did not say, 'Will you marry me?' but 'Shall we wed?'

'Yes, Henry John,' she replied and smiled at him. He squeezed her arm. A few people looked at them as they walked along.

'You know there'll be a good deal of hard work. I told you what I want to do. We'll have a partnership!'

He had chosen his words well. He knew what sort of young woman Polly was. Not that he discounted her small capital, but it was her willingness to work towards a better life that he sensed. He knew she was loyal; he did not want to detach her against her will from her step-family, though he had detached himself from his own. For her part, Polly knew very well he was ambitious and that ambitious men were sometimes ruthless, but she approved of a man who wanted to make something of himself. Her own father had tried, but things had been stacked against him. She would aid her husband in every endeavour. She had immense faith in his business ability, and she could indeed help him, help them both, by investing the money inherited from her Norfolk grandfather in whatever business Henry John decided upon.

* * *

Polly married Henry John Walker in 1894. She accompanied him back to Huddersfield, where they started boiling toffee in an outhouse of their first home. The recipe came from Henry John's mother, he said. Polly modified it slightly and they began to sell it on his stall in the covered market and then took another stall in the market in Halifax. The toffee was sold in blocks, broken up by a little silver toffee hammer.

The couple's plans for the sale of this toffee were sensible: make a little name for yourself and then expand. The demand grew. It was Polly who toiled over the actual making of the toffee, her husband who marketed it. Soon they needed larger premises and it was Polly again who had the brain-wave of building a little hut on land they first of all rented, then bought, on the so-called island at Brookfoot in Calderbrigg between the canal and the river. This was where Emma had first explored on her arrival in Calderbrigg, not far from the bluebell wood, and where Beattie had loved to walk.

At first, Polly made the toffee herself in this hut, often visited and helped by Beattie. It sold so well that after a year or two they were making such a profit that they took on an assistant, and then another, and finally moved their premises to a disused mill on the same island, where even more assistants were given work. Still making good profits, Henry John took a business partner and they manufactured great quantities of the toffee, their profits all the time rising.

Henry John's gamble and Polly's little capital were to lead by the next century to a famous toffee-making firm, Walker and Turnwright. Long before this though, Henry John had moved his wife and baby son to a fine house on Calderbrigg high street.

* * *

Emma was managing well but her life was hard and she had not seen Myra since her visit for George's funeral three years earlier. In 1896, two years after Polly's marriage, Myra wrote to her sister:

> I had a letter from our friend Jabez Smith last week. In it he wondered if on his next

visit to Manchester he could call and see you in Calderbrigg. I don't know if you would approve, but I said I thought you would like that. I believe he has some news to impart to you. Let me know and he can then make arrangements.

The rest of the letter was about Myra's husband's ailments, of which he appeared to have plenty, and his decision to retire in a year or two. Emma suspected he must be a good deal older than Myra had ever let on. But she was 'doing fine' and was busy arranging concert parties in Llandudno . . .

But this missive made Emma tremble so much that the thread slipped out of the needle when she was 'mammucking up' shirt collars by hand. First she thought Myra had a cheek to say Jabez would be welcome, then she thought, Oh, how I would like to see him after all these years. Then, but what 'news' could he possibly have for me?

If Baz was to visit it must not be a visit interrupted by children. Flo was now working at the same place as Beattie, and they did not finish till six. Arthur would love to go to Isabella's after school, and he could take Alfie with him. Ada did not finish work until six o'clock either, and Herbert and Ernest came in later, Beattie often buying something for their tea on the way home.

Ada was still a problem; at almost sixteen she had not changed, only intensified her airs and graces. Emma was puzzled by her. She was a little like Myra had been at that age, but more flamboyant. A letter to her mother from her Aunt Myra meant to Ada only that Myra was about to find her a job as an actress. Emma had counselled her daughter to write to her aunt again. In a way it would be a relief if Ada could be found work away. Emma could not see her settling down in Calderbrigg.

Emma therefore asked the ever helpful Isabella to take the boys on after school for the day, and gave them bread and cheese and an apple to eat after morning school, saying that she had some important work to finish. For once she would put herself first. She had an intuition that this visit was to be an important one.

* * *

There was a determined knock at her door. She would easily have recognized the man, middle-aged yet slim, his hair well cut, his shoes shining, who stood on the threshold at eleven o'clock that spring morning.

'Hello, bor,' he said, in a lively and cheerful

voice, as though he had seen her quite recently. 'I had an interesting walk from the station.'

She felt no constraint, that was the odd thing, when he kissed her cheek.

She was eager to talk over old times and led him into her warm kitchen where, on a table covered with her best green cloth, a full teapot and a plate of her drop-scones were awaiting him. The fire was burning brightly and two chairs were drawn up, one on each side of the hearth.

The Singer machine was shrouded today; she always kept it clean and safe from marauding child hands.

He looked round and smiled as he sat down.

'What a cosy place you have,' he said.

She smiled.

He said, 'I'm glad you keep up with Myra. I'd like to see her more often.'

He was here, Baz was here. After years and years and years he was sitting in her kitchen.

Her hand shook slightly as she poured him a cup of tea and took one herself. She went to sit opposite him.

He began by commiserating with her over her husband's death. Just, 'I was so sorry about George.'

She asked after his wife, he rapidly

conveyed the details and then there was a short silence.

Then she said, 'Myra tells me you have some news for me.'

'It will be rather a facer for you,' he said. 'Not news for me though.'

He looked at her over his cup. She was still the same little Elly, he thought. Fatter though.

She cleared her throat. 'George said you were related to him,' she began.

'I'll have another cup, Elly, if I may.'

She looked covertly at him as he seemed to be looking into the fire, and asked quite involuntarily, 'Do you still play your little pipe?'

She didn't know why she had said that but somehow this Baz was nearer to her than the grown-up one she had met in his chimney-sweep days, or later.

'I play the organ pipes when they let me! In the churches I help to rebuild or improve.' After a pause, he said, 'It's true, I am related to George.'

She looked enquiringly at him.

'As I told your sister, I'm not 'gypsy-born' though that's not to say that a bit further back a Starling ancestor may not have been. I don't look like a gypsy, do I?'

A Starling ancestor?

'No,' she replied, 'gypsies are usually dark and you are not. I remember you with red hair, but perhaps I imagined that.'

'It went darker later.'

She remembered his saying that long ago.

He knew she was referring to her earliest memories, as with the little pipe he had played, but for a moment he appeared reluctant to continue speaking. Then he took her hand.

'And who else had — has — red hair, Elly?'

'Well, Myra has, but I suspect she adds a bit of henna now. And my little David who lived only four weeks had a ginger crown — and my daughter Ada of course — she's very proud of it even if the lads call her Ginger.'

'So you'd say there was red hair in your family? But neither of your stepchildren — not Ann nor Polly — have red hair, have they, and neither did your husband.'

'No. But what are you driving at, Baz? Myra is not a Starling but a Saunders like me.'

'I like it when you call me that,' he said simply, 'Baz. Nobody else does now.' Then, 'Ask yourself who else had red hair, Elly! Perhaps you don't remember?'

She pondered and then said looking at him half fearfully, 'Mam once had darkish auburn hair — I suppose by the time I was born it wasn't exactly red, but . . . '

'Aye she had, Elly,' he answered.

'What are you trying to say, Baz?'

'Your mam once had red hair, there's red hair in your family, and I had red hair, so . . . '

'So you belonged to Mam's family as well as George's?' she asked in a puzzled way.

'*That* I did!'

'How so then? You're nearer George's age than Mam's.'

'Oh Elly, little Em,' he said, 'I'm your Mam's first child!'

She stared and stared at him. Shivers went up and down her back. She could hardly get her breath. She put her hand to her throat and said hoarsely:

'But you are ten years older than me! Mam didn't marry till three years before I was born. And your name is Smith!'

'I was born to our mam in 1841 — what they call a love child, though I doubt I was that. Mam called me Smith; it sounded gypsified!'

'That's why you lived with Dad and Mam when I was little? But if it's true what you're telling me, you're my half-brother?' There seemed to be a tight knot of muscle in her throat and she swallowed painfully.

'Aye, your mam kept me with her right from the start and your Dad promised when he married her that he'd keep me around. But he didn't much like to be reminded of your mam's past — her having known another man — and they didn't have much money, though her father helped out a bit. Mam was upset and frightened that he'd really turn against me one day, so when I was thirteen they sent me to one of her sisters in Thompson and after that I was a jack-of-all-trades, as you know.'

Emma tried to take it all in. So it was true, she had known him right from the time she was born. He had been her big brother!

Tears came to her eyes. 'Who was your dad, Baz?'

For answer he said, 'The reason why your husband took against me in a manner of speaking — or leastways didn't want you mixed up with me, even if 'twas only for a chat, like, was that my father was the same as his father, Old James Starling. I was George's half-brother as well, you see — on the wrong side of the blanket again. It was his dad, James Starling, who took advantage of our mam when she was only twenty-two. At the time, James Starling's wife Rebecca was expecting a baby, one of George's brothers, a baby they named David who died as a baby. *I* didn't die and his wife never forgave him.'

Her hand flew to her throat again.

'Like my little David! George insisted on the name and he was so upset when the baby died — more than he was when our Minnie died who was a real child, not a baby.'

'I did come to look for you, Elly,' he said softly. 'In the market. Myra told me your baby had died and he had been called David. I just knew your husband must have chosen that name. Then the infant died, like his own little brother David. I felt I had to come and see if you were all right. I knew it would have shocked him and I was certain he'd never told you who *I* was. But then my nerve failed at the last moment when you looked up. You looked so unhappy. You seemed to look right through me. I felt then that I didn't want to explain. But — that was why George's family didn't make much fuss of you, didn't even go to your wedding, did they?'

'I thought they'd took against me!'

'George knew you knew nothing about who I really was. It must have been a terrible shock to him to see you and me friendly-like, and so I had to be careful. It was my fault talking to you in the first place but I couldn't help myself. You were my little Elly, and I'd never forgotten my baby sister! But I didn't want to spoil the chances of the sweet young woman I used to meet. I couldn't risk any . . . feelings that might spring up on my side or on yours, I *couldn't* tell you the truth, that you were my sister. Before she died, Mam had begged me to keep an eye on you — we saw each other now and then in that little church at the hall gates when she worked there, but she didn't want me to tell you who I really was, she thought your father might not like it.'

But it was you I loved! thought Emma. Mam never thought of that. Did she think I'd forgotten him?

'Whenever I thought of Mam I used to think of you, and when I thought of you, I thought of Mam,' she said.

It all rang true. Poor Mam, but she ought to have told her the truth.

'Still, I was only thirteen,' she said aloud. Then, 'George couldn't bear the idea of *his* father and *my* mother, I suppose. He must have known all along — and in a way perhaps he made it up to Mam, tried to take away his father's fault by marrying me. But he used to insist Mam was a Caston girl and our families had known each other for years . . . '

'I expect he wanted to make it sound all natural-like, but he knew all about your mother. He could have told you later, but he was probably too ashamed of his father.'

She said wonderingly, trying to make it sound real, 'George and I had the same half-brother. You are my children's uncle twice over!'

He looked up, then down again, and went on, 'I didn't know what to do when I saw that . . . I saw that you . . . that you . . . *liked* me, Sis. Oh how I've longed all these years to call you that. You don't mind, do you?'

Her eyes were full of tears as she shook her head.

'When I saw we were still . . . fond of each other, and that you remembered from when you were a tiny scrap . . . *remembered* your old Baz, I knew I'd have to go away. Your husband might have feared I'd inherited his father's, and my father's, nature, I suppose. George hadn't inherited it; he wasn't a bit like his dad, anyone could see that. I was glad you were to be married, you know.'

After a silence she asked him, 'Did you feel as I did, before that, Baz? When we met again when I was growing up, and talked together by the stream and in the market? You came round to my grandma's to see how I was . . . '

'I did. I'd promised Mam to keep an eye on you. I was ten years older than you at the times you mention, so I had to act sensible, but oh, you did bring back Mam! Whenever I thought of you — just like you said — I thought of Mam! I couldn't tell you the reason why I had to go away and invent a sweetheart, 'cos of promising Mam that I'd never tell you till you were grown up who my mam and dad were, and then I couldn't when you were going to marry George. She loved you — and she loved me, Sis, she war a loving woman.'

'And I asked you to do the same for Myra!'

'Yes, I was that glad when you asked me to keep an eye on her; through her I'd be able to know how you were, and hope to glean little scraps about you, after you'd gone away. It was difficult at first when I was working away and your sister was in service. Later, Myra may have thought I was sweet on her, though I made it plain I wasn't. She isn't a bit like you. I've never had any worries about feeling anything for your lovely sister — she's *my* sister too!'

They were both silent then, looking into the fire. Emma was trying to adjust all her ideas and feelings to this momentous news and Baz was thinking of the past and how his mother had really been taken away from him long before she died.

'I always knew there was something to connect you with her or with home,' cried Emma again. 'I thought it was just my being little when you were in the house with us

— and not being able ever to forget you . . .'

'She wanted to forget it all too but sometimes she cuddled me though I was a great lad of twelve. Only when your dad was out, though — maybe you saw us together. She hadn't liked my father at all — she wanted to forget him. After I was born she told me she even got her cousin Harriet to go with her to the Register man and say I was Harriet's babby, not hers. I've got proof. It's all wrong on my birth certificate but it ain't wrong in the Parson's hand in Caston Church! I tackled Harriet Banham about it one day. It was after I'd built 'em the windmill they were so proud of, and she confessed.'

'Oh Baz, what a life for you. If only I'd known . . .'

'Well, as I said, Bob Saunders, your dad, put up with me living with them for two or three years but then he didn't want me there any longer. I was too close to you, he said. That made me so angry! Not that we even needed to have liked each other. But we did, and he knew it, and George guessed you had a partiality for me too, didn't he?'

'Yes, I see it now, though I never strayed from him. You know, Baz, Bob and Percy are your half-brothers. Shall I tell 'em?'

'It's up to you, Elly — it doesn't matter any

more now, I dare say, them all being dead now, your mam and your dad and George, and my father too. I didn't know James Starling was my dad till I was eighteen. It was when we were bell-ringing together, James and his son, George's brother — James the younger, and me and Mam's own brother George. They all knew, but I didn't. Till one day the old man had drunk a bit too much after a practice and he said, 'That there windmill of yours is good. You've got the talent for building — *I* used to be a right good bricklayer myself once, you know. 'We were all sitting in the inn together and suddenly there was a silence, and then I knew.'

'I used to think about you so much,' said Emma after another silence. 'They told me I'd imagined you and that there had been no boy at home when I was a babby. But I *knew*! I was sure I hadn't imagined it. I never forgot you. You made music and you took me on walks — how could I forget you? You were My Friend — that's what I called you, *My Friend*, and then later I was so unhappy when you didn't want to . . . to court me . . . '

She dared not say that she had been in love with him. All that time was now a dream, perhaps a search for an impossible earlier dream.

It was better to have the real Baz here as a *real* friend. She was a widow and a mother now, no longer a lovesick girl, but she still *loved* him. She liked him and admired him and felt affection for him. He would always remind her of her mother and of all the past. She had nothing to reproach herself with. George could surely not have imagined she would ever have been unfaithful to him.

'So it's from Mam's side of the family we get the music?' she asked finally. 'My brother Percy and almost all my children have it — singing, or playing the piano and the organ.'

'Yes. Mam and her dad, William Banham — you remember him? — he was my granddad too! — he used to sing to the sheep when he was a shepherd. Now *he* was always kind to me, *and* he had red hair when he was young!'

* * *

She wanted him to stay and meet the children. A new uncle, she'd say, but he said he had to get back to Martha and there was only one train if he wasn't going to stay over, which he wasn't.

He'd come again though and see them all then and if ever Emma could make the journey, he'd be there waiting for her in Thetford. He said he'd write, and so must she.

He'd tell his wife Martha about her now. She already knew he was James Starling's bastard but now he would explain that he was half-brother to both George Starling and George Starling's wife whom he had known as a child long long ago.

Then he took his little sister in his arms and hugged her and held her hand to his face and they both felt that their mother, the young Eliza, was somehow, somewhere, able to see that her two eldest children were together at last in spirit.

Before he left, he gave her a locket his mother had given him when he'd had to leave her cottage and go to work.

'There, it's yours now,' he said.

And Emma went to her treasure-box and found one of Mam's ribbons and gave it to Baz.

And then Beattie arrived home early because the mill had gone on strike. Just before he left for the station, Emma was able to see her favourite daughter and her favourite brother meet and shake hands. But oh, her throat was tight with tears when he left.

* * *

'What a nice man — I didn't know about this uncle,' Beattie said afterwards.

Emma did not go into details. Baz was her own little secret, but she didn't mind casually referring to him to the children as an 'uncle'. Only Beattie took any interest in him.

Later, she did mention his existence to Percy and Bob, thinking they had a right to know. They were surprised, a little embarrassed, but not truly interested, and referred to him just as a 'Norfolk relation'.

Myra of course had not been embarrassed. Now that she could mention Jabez Smith openly in letters to her sister she found the whole thing quite romantic. She was busy trying to find a job for her niece Ada who had written to say she was pining away. Emma said, yes, Ada did appear to live on a diet of water and air.

Emma did not directly mention her relationship to Baz to any of her children but wrote to him each month till the day he died.

Epilogue

Emma Eliza had preferred to talk to Lily about her childhood, her young womanhood and the circumstances of her marriage, rather than her years of babies and small children. She told her she still dreamed of Norfolk and remembered how beautiful it was.

Folk in Yorkshire would say to her, 'Oh, you lived miles away from anywhere!' but it didn't feel like that to her. 'Home' might now be Calderbrigg but her long ago home still came back in dreams: the Norfolk villages, Breckles Hall, the fields and the horses, the lanes and the trees, and the pretty market towns that lay not too far away.

* * *

It must have been at the end of 1895, the very same year of Jabez Smith's coming to Calderbrigg to see Emma that Herbert Starling decided to emigrate to Canada. There were wonderful jobs on the railways there, he stated. Emma was too proud to beg him not to go, but she made it plain his father would not have approved. He, the eldest son, to desert her! Ernest would henceforth take Herbert's place in her heart. She did not wish to feel like this; she did not blame Harbie but truly she was devastated. Somehow, since his babyhood, she had never been able to get through to her eldest son, though she loved him. She wished him well but afterwards rarely spoke of him. His brother Ernest and sister Beattie would keep in touch with him, though Herbert was no letter-writer. Beattie sustained a slightly guilty correspondence but was careful to acquaint her mother with any good news that came from her brother.

In 1896 Beattie was nineteen and married a young man named Bertie Dyson. Once more, Bethel choir, in which Bertie sang tenor, was to be the agent of matrimony.

Ernest was the same age as Bertie and was acquainted with him. John Dyson, Bertie's father, had owned a small delf but had died of silicosis in 1880. His mother was the successful 'landlord' of an inn in Eastcliff on the outskirts of Calderbrigg. Any woman less like Emma could not be imagined. They might both be widows but Maria Dyson was a hard-headed businesswoman.

Beattie, already unconsciously committed to keeping her own family together, took Bertie in hand. He had never known his father, who had died when he was five, but

Maria had seen to it that he did not go near a quarry, and sent him and his younger brother to the small grammar school nearby, until it became obvious that Bertie was no scholar. He was good with his hands, so she had him apprenticed to an engineer.

Young women were marrying very early, sometimes to escape work in the mills, if they could find a husband who would have enough money to let them stay at home and housekeep. This may have swayed Beattie. She was, however, still determined to have only a small family and succeeded in this. In 1897 her first child, Jack, was born, named for his paternal grandfather.

A year later, the grand new free library was formed in an eighteenth-century house with beautiful gardens. It had been a subscription library since 1784 but now the 'lower classes' could borrow books. Beattie enrolled immediately.

In 1901 Lily Dyson was born, Emma Eliza's first granddaughter. Beattie's mission was now to see that Jack and his sister Lily should have a good education and make something of their lives.

In 1899 the building of the Albert Theatre had been completed. At last a theatre for the town! One Edgar Zenoni arrived as permanent violinist at the Albert. He was an old friend of Myra Evans and her husband, and very soon became Emma Starling's first permanent 'theatrical lodger'. He was followed much later by a succession of young women 'in rep'. Emma enjoyed having such lodgers and found they paid better than shirts. She eventually 'lent' the Singer to Beattie.

When a handsome new terrace was built in 1907 near his old home, from pristine stone as clean at first as that in the Cotswolds, Percy moved there. A year later, with her husband and two children, Beattie followed her uncle a few doors down. Bob went a bit further in the end but only a mile or two away.

Lily was a little girl of eight in 1909 when at last the wonderful new Bethel was opened, with a great procession in the town and picture postcards to commemorate the event. The small Lily was among the crowd and very excited. Her mother had spent days and weeks and months baking cakes and making things to sell at bazaars to raise the funds for this smart building with its many beauties, and the comfortable tip-up seats paid for by Henry John.

Lily was also a constant visitor to 'The Island,' that small area between the river and canal where now stood 'Aunt Polly's mill' or, to give it its true name, Walker and Turnwright's, where the famous toffee was made. On the island were a few houses lived in by the toffee-mill workers, many of them provided from Emma Eliza's family, all Lily's relations: uncles, aunts and cousins. All the relatives of both Walker and Turnwright were given good jobs, mostly as salesmen, in a time of slump and depression. Lily knew them all from chapel since many were ardent Methodists. A cricket field was laid out on the island where employees played against other workers, and Lily was allowed to take her part in the ladies' team one afternoon. She acquitted herself well. Like her mother she loved the place. Now there was a greenhouse on the island too, with magnificent orchids, grown by Henry John's gardener.

By this time Emma Eliza was well known to some of the local naughty boys, for she could call the most recalcitrant to heel and was awesome in her vocal authority, expressed in an accent they were not acquainted with. She was soon, in this new century, to enjoy the luxury of a 'holiday'.

Since time immemorial, Calderbrigg had always had its 'Rushbearing Feast', known as The Rush, held on the first Saturday after the second Thursday in August, whose origin was lost in the mists of antiquity, and its Whit

Walks when it looked as if every inhabitant of the town was processing down its streets, the crowd following its soon to be famous brass band. But soon people would take their enjoyment further away and stay for longer.

Emma had always had many female friends, and once her children had grown, decided she enjoyed moving around to stay with them, or going on holiday with them. In retrospect, perhaps she began to understand Herbert a little better. She took her granddaughter Lily to Leigh in Lancashire where other Norfolkers had settled, and to Holmfirth where the King family had moved to be near relatives, and to Whitby to see the sea. Before she could afford it, before the 'theatrical lodgers' had alleviated her finances, Baz had often asked her to go and stay in Norfolk with him and his wife. They had come to Calderbrigg for Beattie's wedding, and she had promised she would go South in the new century. But Baz died that very year, the year before Lily was born, and was now only a picture in Beattie's album entitled 'Dear old Uncle Jabez'.

How Emma wished, on her first return to Norfolk to see Ann and her new and last baby, that she might also see Baz in the old place. Yet when she did finally 'go home', she realized it would not have been the same to see him there. She might not be able now to revel as she had once wished in her lost paradise, but Baz was there in her heart and possibly she had been in his when he died there.

She saw violets by the mere at Thompson, and bird-cherry and bluebells, and dog's mercury; and when she visited Wayland Wood with Ann she saw wood anemones. She loved her old birthplace, and it was Baz's place of birth too. He had told her once that he had seen purple orchids in that very wood but she never found one. She had come to realize how beautiful their Norfolk had been, but accepted also that 'home' was now a little Yorkshire mill-town.

'I've never regretted coming North,' she said to Beattie once. 'But I do wish I could have gone back earlier to Caston. I was too busy with you all to take a breath, never mind being able to put aside a shilling or two to go back till you were all married or earning.'

Beattie was full of admiration for how her mother had coped with being left a widow, how she had sewn shirts to make ends meet. Beattie had taken over the sewing on the Singer 'lent' to her which was she knew to be properly hers one day. Now Emma could have money from Polly to buy her a few little luxuries if she would accept them, yet Beattie knew that her mother was too proud to accept very much.

By the time Emma visited her elder stepdaughter for the first time she was well over fifty. After this, for many summers when Lily was a child, Beattie and her children would go to stay with Ann and her family near Watton, or in Thetford. Lily remembered that first Norfolk holiday, taken when she was about four, and many later trips with Ann's daughter, who came North in return. Ann's husband had failed as a pig farmer, and she had three children to bring up. Aunt Ann in Norfolk had named her first son George, as were both Polly and Ernest to call their sons.

Lily had learned a lot from her grandmother about Norfolk and the little villages where her family had lived for hundreds of years, yet she found parts of the countryside not far from those home villages rather uncanny. Thetford she liked, but Grandma's village was only a few miles away from that strange sandy land they called Breckland, which she found peculiar. The villages of her grandma's old haunts were, however, still abundantly full of sheep and rabbits — and pheasants for the gentry to shoot down.

No wonder Great-Grandma had specialized in rabbit pie, thought Lily.

Lily also enjoyed visiting her grandmother

and all her uncles and aunts in Calderbrigg, above all her favourite aunt, Aunt Polly, who lived on the high street, in a house where there was a rocking-horse, and a magic lantern, owned by Polly and Henry John's only child, George.

Uncle Ernest had married a few years after Beattie and had six children of whom three died as babies. By the time he died he had become a traveller for his step-brother-in-law but died from tuberculosis when Lily was eleven. His eldest child, another George, the only twentieth century George Starling, was eventually to play the new organ at Bethel before he founded a dance band of his own.

The Walker and Turnwright partnership was successful but not very friendly. Other sweets began to be made; an elaborate scheme of wrapping was started and advertising was used extensively. Henry John, sometimes accompanied by his wife, went on many cruises starting in 1905 when he visited Egypt, Jerusalem, Damascus and Constantinople. He only just missed being on the *Titanic*. He and Polly toured the United States and Canada for three months just before the Great War broke out.

Beattie and Bertie and their children were content to go to Blackpool.

In 1908 Baden-Powell had founded the

Boy Scout movement and Jack Dyson had been an early member. Percy's grandson was even named Baden Powell Saunders. But war came to Europe, and Jack, who was an intensely energetic boy, athletic and keen on camping and the open air, was determined to help the war effort. Both Percy and Bob were enthusiastic Territorials, but in 1914 their sister was glad they were too old to fight.

It was a different matter for little Jack Dyson. Before anyone knew how dreadful this conflict was going to be, the Starling and Dyson families had been proud that seventeen-year-old Jack had lied about his age and enlisted in the Sixth Norfolk's rather than in a Yorkshire regiment, in order to be near his two older cousins, Ann's sons, one of them another George. In spite of her pride, Beattie didn't really want him to go, and when these cousins, trained in Thetford as a draughtsman and an engineer, received commissions, little Jack was left over to fight on the Somme. Jack was gassed and was a shadow of himself when he was invalided out, his health affected for ever by the mustard gas of the Somme.

Lily had been thirteen when the first war started and when she was fourteen a young Canadian soldier came to visit Beattie, and was received with rapture. Lily discovered only then that Emma Eliza's first born, Herbert, who must have been not much more than twenty, had emigrated against her wishes to Canada. He had married a year or two later and it was his son, Keith, the first of Emma's grandchildren, who was here to fight for England. Any family rift was now more or less healed, but even in the 1920s Grandma found it hard to talk about the early years of 'our Harbie', who had gone against what she said his father would have wished. John Dyson was furious that he had been robbed of the title of eldest grandchild, but all that was forgotten when Harbie's son died at Passchendaele.

Polly, who through her own and her husband's business efforts had become a member of the middle classes, continued to be Lily's favourite aunt, for she never changed her nature when wealth came to her. Polly's son, another George, distinguished himself as a captain in the army and received the Military Medal. A year after the end of that terrible war Lily went to college in Cambridge to learn to be a teacher, as did her cousin, Ann's daughter.

Aunt Polly had not used up all her savings on toffee, for she still owned her Norfolk cottages whose rents she collected on Lady Day. She used to arrive with her car and chauffeur to take Lily out to dinner at the University Arms and Lily was always overjoyed to see her.

After the house on the high street Henry John was soon to buy a splendid one in its own grounds: West View, from which Lily was later to be married. It had gardens and a tennis-court where the younger generation were often to be seen disporting themselves.

Mayor of Calderbrigg for many years, Henry John was said to have hoped for a 'Lloyd George' title, which apparently cost £30,000, but he was unlucky in this. Polly was also unlucky, for she died before her stepmother, and the business ended pretty well before the next war began. Henry John outlived her by several years and her sister Ann by sixteen years.

⋆ ⋆ ⋆

What of Ada? What of Flo?

Ada had no success on the stage though she did stay for a year or two with her Aunt Myra who found her parts that required a good deal of strutting about in gorgeous costumes. Ada had then returned to Calderbrigg, married a pleasant Calderbrigg man and had two sons. After the first few years of marriage she never spoke to her husband although they lived under the same roof. The sons were said to be extremely kind and always willing to do things for their mother. Ada, her face well made up by Monsieur Coty, her red hair 'improved' with henna, wafted round the town in a cloud of French scent: *Quelques Fleurs* by Houbigant. She wore extraordinary satin capes and long flowing scarves, and often disappeared on mysterious journeys to neighbouring towns. Where did she get the money for the clothes and the scent? She was secretive about her life, but at the same time believed in telepathy. Later, she became a Spiritualist, and heard voices dictating poetry, which she wrote down. She had announced that once she was no longer attractive to men she would take to her bed. Which she did — and also had a short spell in a discreet mental hospital. She returned to Calderbrigg, and lived on until her mid-seventies. Perhaps if she had made good on the stage, even in a minor way, like her Aunt Myra, she would not have needed to make a play out of her life.

Nobody could have been more different from her sister than Flo, who played the mandolin. She was happily married, indulged by her husband, but led an ordinary life, living the longest of all Emma Eliza's children.

Emma Eliza never saw much of her errant daughter Ada. She was once heard to say that bearing children made some women peculiar. Beattie could never abide Ada though she was fond of Ada's children. Was she ashamed of her or disturbed by her?

Beattie kept up all the old ways, was a wonderful housewife but also a great reader, never without the three library books she took out each week. She was renowned for her wine-making and fruit-bottling, and for the tatting and crochet that she did even better than her mother or her daughter. She continued to sing in her lovely deep voice that went on reminding her mother of her own 'Mam'.

Walter was the most musical of them all. He could still play anything on the piano by ear once he'd heard it, but he too earned his living at first by working for Henry John's business. Alfie, another tenor, sang in the chapel choir until he left England for Australia where his son was a cathedral chorister on the other side of the world from the old Bethel.

The first war had changed some things, in both Norfolk and Yorkshire. By the end of the next decade the town silk industry was slowly dying. When Emma Eliza went back to Norfolk she asked herself why George and she had been obliged to go so far away from home to find work. They wouldn't make the journey now, with the mills gone, or on half-time. But the folk down in Norfolk still hadn't much work either. When she thought back, not only she and George, but all that band of neighbours and relations who had accompanied them, good workers like the Kings and the Murrells and the Sayers, had thought it wiser to leave. She talked about it sometimes to her son Walter.

'They didn't want to leave their little cottages, but they didn't want either to starve or go on parish relief and be called paupers like some of their dads and granddads — and probably their great granddads.'

It had been a blessing that George had known all there was to be known about horses and carriages. Before he was taken on as a groom at the hall he'd learned from a wheelwright, and then from a Caston Osborn who was a saddler. In Calderbrigg they'd taken him on immediately to look after horses, his first love. Most of the Norfolk men and lads who had come to Yorkshire had been obliged to take much worse paid factory work.

Her children and grandchildren often wondered what George Christmas might have done if he had lived a little later, when the internal combustion engine was beginning to displace the horse. Horses had begun to disappear after the Great War, and on the land after World War Two. Not one of his descendants followed him in his trade, though there were one or two who loved riding.

Emma sometimes talked to Lily about the folk who had once lived in the villages. There had been a pargeter and a tanner, a thatcher, a cobbler, a saddler and a farrier, as well as shepherds like her grandfather, and ploughboys and labourers, and those who worked for the gentry like George and herself. There must have been a limit to the number of trades a village could support, thought Lily. There were still no factories there, though there was talk of a canning factory.

It was clear that Emma's favourite children were Polly, Beattie and Walter. She admired Beattie, seeing George in her, as she did in Polly too. Beattie had made a cosy little house with china in the cupboard and a clock on the chimney piece and green velveteen sofa and chairs in her parlour. She still sewed all her own frocks and her daughter's, and she was still a lovely singer, could always harmonize anything, sing along in 'seconds' without music. They had many singsongs around the piano that Beattie bought for her parlour with

Walter playing and, before he emigrated, Alfie, singing along with Beattie. Uncle Percy and Lily sang too and sometimes Flo would arrive with her mandolin.

* * *

When Lily went on holiday to Norfolk with her husband Charlie, to visit Aunt Ann and her eldest son, Thetford Forest and much of Breckland had been planted with thousands of Scots pines. For hundreds of years, all that sandy land had been blown hither and thither, useless for farming. Lily still found some of the place uncanny, but later decided there was nothing pleasanter than a little Norfolk country town. After the second war things would change even more in the small country villages, and eventually they would become became pretty dormitories or retirement homes. Some of the great-grandchildren of the once displaced, returned, not to till the soil of their ancestors, but to live more pleasantly than they could in the colder North. Lily thought it was like the wheel of fortune.

In Calderbrigg everything changed once again when industries faded away, or could no longer keep up with foreign competition, or were not needed when coal became redundant, or when silk was displaced by other fibres, or worsted cost too much to weave. But the canal was cleaned and made pretty.

Emma would never know all that pace of change but she would not have been surprised, for she was a woman who had learned that things always changed whatever you did, however much you didn't want them to.

Lily never knew what happened to red-haired Myra and her Tom. They were said to have moved to South Wales. Emma Eliza must have kept in touch with them but Beattie had never seen Myra again after Ada had returned from Rhyl. Perhaps she had died before her elder sister. Beattie did not make an effort to find out, fearing to meet another but older Ada. All Lily knew of Myra was her stage name, Patty Lee, and all that remained of Myra in Calderbrigg was a tattered programme for the Rhyl Pierrots Summer 1889 — and whatever Ada chose not to tell.

* * *

George Starling had fifteen grandchildren, Emma eleven, all of whom succeeded in life in varying degrees. George has forty-one living direct descendants, Emma twenty-six, down to great-great-great-grandchildren.

Starling descendants are scattered all over this country and in Canada and Australia, but as far as Lily knew not one of the family returned to live in Norfolk during the last fifty years.

* * *

My Great-Grandmother Emma Eliza enjoyed that eightieth birthday of hers on 19th April 1931, at which I myself was a guest, but as I was only a few months old I remember nothing of it. My Grandma Dyson had baked her a big cake and covered it with white icing with '*80*' in curly letters. One of my uncles took a photograph of it, which I now own. Emma enjoyed the lovely iced cake, and almost all her family visited her that afternoon. Polly was still alive then but died the following year to the great sorrow of Emma and Beattie and Lily as well as her own family, and Ann was still back in Norfolk. Ernest's wife and family dropped in, his two unmarried daughters and his musical son George, and even Ada came with her sons, and Flo with her son and daughter. Walter was there of course with his wife and six-year-old daughter, but Alfie had been in

Melbourne now for some seven years with his wife and son. My father, Charlie, came along after work. Naturally, my mother was busy helping her own mother, Beattie, accompanied by myself in the pram. I was Great-Grandma's first *great*-grandchild.

The following August, family photographs were taken at West View. One was of Great-Grandma, with my Great-Aunt Polly, my grandmother Beattie, my mother, and myself: four generations. Great-Aunt Polly, Grandma Beattie, and Great-Uncle Walter were always Great-Grandma's favourites, my mother, Lily, said.

Our mother often used to walk down to Beattie's with me and my sister in the pram. She'd stay there for a chat and a cup of tea with her grandmother and mother. By then Great-Grandma Emma Eliza was less talkative and looked much older than she had a few years earlier when she had talked endlessly about her childhood and the place she came from.

Why did Emma Eliza end the story she told Lily when she did? Could she not bear to relive the birth of the son who had left England, her first-born, little Harbie? Or did she not want to tell Lily — or even Beattie — who her 'Baz' really was?

I was able to find the biblical reference

from Chronicles: *His mother called his name Jabez, because she bare him with sorrow.*

My Great-Grandmother, Emma Eliza Starling died of 'myocardial degeneration and chronic bronchitis, eleven days after her eighty-fourth birthday in 1935. The next day, though I have no recollection of it, my mother Lily must have walked down to Calderbrigg to register the death, along with me and my sister in the pram.

After a widowhood of forty-three years Emma Eliza had joined her husband George Christmas Starling on the 'Non-Con' side of the cemetery of that little Yorkshire town, far from their original home.

Both still sleep there.

* * *

One of my strongest early memories is of the afternoon walk I used to take every Wednesday with my mother, Lily, to change the flowers on her grandmother's grave.

It is a grassy grave with a flat stone, the resting place too of the little children, David and Minnie.

Emma's, and Beattie's, and Lily's lives all seem now to mingle into one, but Lily's descendants have different lives, far away.

Jane Chapman

We do hope that you have enjoyed reading this large print book.

Did you know that all of our titles are available for purchase?

We publish a wide range of high quality large print books including:
Romances, Mysteries, Classics
General Fiction
Non Fiction and Westerns

Special interest titles available in large print are:
The Little Oxford Dictionary
Music Book
Song Book
Hymn Book
Service Book

Also available from us courtesy of Oxford University Press:
Young Readers' Dictionary (large print edition)
Young Readers' Thesaurus (large print edition)

For further information or a free brochure, please contact us at:

Other titles in the
Ulverscroft Large Print Series:

DEAD FISH

Ruth Carrington

Dr Geoffrey Quinn arrives home to find his children missing, the charred remains of his wife's body in the boiler and Chief Superintendent Manning waiting to arrest him for her murder. Alison Hope, attractive and determined, is briefed to defend him. Quinn claims he is innocent, but Alison is not so sure. The background becomes increasingly murky as she penetrates a wealthy and ruthless circle who cannot risk their secrets — sexual perversion, drugs, blackmail, illegal arms dealing and major fraud — coming to light. Can Alison unravel the mystery in time to save Quinn?

MY FATHER'S HOUSE

Kathleen Conlon

'Your father has another woman'. Nine-year-old Anna Blake is only mildly surprised when a schoolfriend lets drop this piece of information. And when her father finally leaves home to live with Olivia in Hampstead, that place becomes, for Anna, the epitome of sinful glamour. But Hampstead, though welcoming, is not home. So Anna, now in her teens, sets out to find a place where she can really belong. At first she thinks love may be the answer, and certainly Jonathon — and Raymond — and Jake, have a devastating effect on her life. But can anyone really supply what she needs?

GHOSTLY MURDERS

P. C. Doherty

When Chaucer's Canterbury pilgrims pass a deserted village, the sight of its decaying church provokes the poor Priest to tears. When they take shelter, he tells a tale of ancient evil, greed, devilish murder and chilling hauntings . . . There was once a young man, Philip Trumpington, who was appointed parish priest of a pleasant village with an old church, built many centuries earlier. However, Philip soon discovers that the church and presbytery are haunted. A great and ancient evil pervades, which must be brought into the light, resolved and reparation made. But the price is great . . .

BLOODTIDE

Bill Knox

When the Fishery Protection cruiser MARLIN was ordered to the Port Ard area off the north-west Scottish coast, Chief Officer Webb Carrick soon discovered that an old shipmate of Captain Shannon had been killed in a strange accident before they arrived. A drowned frogman, a reticent Russian officer and a dare-devil young fisherman were only a few of the ingredients to come together as Carrick tried to discover the truth. The key to it all was as deadly as it was unexpected.

WISE VIRGIN

Manda Mcgrath

Sisters Jean and Ailsa Leslie live on a small farm in the Scottish Grampians. Andrew Esplin, the local blacksmith, keeps a brotherly eye on the girls, loving Ailsa, the younger sister, from afar. Ailsa is in love with Stewart Morrison, who is working in Greenock. Jean is engaged to Alan Drummond, who has gone to Australia, intending to send for her when his prospects are good. But Jean shocks everyone when she elopes with Dunton from the big house . . .

BEYOND THE NURSERY WINDOW

Ruth Plant

Ruth Plant tells of her youth in a country vicarage in Staffordshire, a story she began in her earlier book NANNY AND I. Together with the occasional dip back into childhood memories of a nursery kingdom where Nanny reigned supreme, she ventures forth into a world of schooldays and visits to relatives, the exciting world of London and the theatre, the wonders of Bath and the beauties of the Lake District. She travels to Oberammergau, and sees Hitler on a visit there. On the threshold of life the future seems bright and war far away.